The
WAYWARD GIFTED
Broken Point

Donna K. Childree and Mike L. Hopper

The characters, places, and events in this book are fictitious. Names, characters, places and incidents are the products of the authors' imaginations, or are used fictitiously. Any similarity to events, locales, or real persons, living or dead, is coincidental and not intended by the authors.

MiloNerak Press
The Wayward Gifted—Broken Point
Donna K. Childree and Mike L. Hopper

Copyright © 2013 by Donna K. Childree and Mike L. Hopper
All Rights Reserved

All rights reserved. This book was self-published by the authors Donna K. Childree and Mike L. Hopper under MiloNerak Press. No part of this book may be reproduced in any form by any means without the express permission of the authors. This includes reprints, excerpts, photocopying, recording, or any future means of reproducing text.

If you would like to do any of the above, please seek permission first by contacting us at MiloNerak@gmail.com

Copyeditor: Rex B. Sutherlin

Cover Design: Karen Klesel

Published in the United States by
MiloNerak Press
ISBN 10: 1483947823
ISBN 13: 9781483947822

Version: 1.1

Thank you Steven L. Gotlib, M.D., Cheryl Bray, Bethany Fayard, Sherry Lee, Ann McCullough, Ellen Molony, and Susan Silva. Your help, input and encouragement are sincerely appreciated.

Visit us online at: http://www.TheWaywardGifted.Blogspot.com

In memory of Elizabeth

For Dr. Klesel

ONE

Steuart couldn't sleep. He was angry with his mother. "I don't want to leave Atchison Bay," he whispered. "I want to stay here."

Lying miserably in his antique, hand-carved bed, he took a deep breath, pulled at his covers, and stared up at the ceiling before grabbing hold of his favorite pillow and giving it a tight squeeze. Tugging and wrestling with the thing, Steuart pretended it was a child-sized dinosaur discovered earlier in the day during his exploration along the south side of the house. This was just beyond the Oleander and beneath the hedgerow of blue Hydrangeas. Feeling not only paternal, but also lonely, Steuart chose to keep the unusual specimen and raise him as a pet. "I will name you Leighton Jefferson Allnight O'Dowd," he said. "Your nickname will be *Sparky*." Steuart situated himself, took a deep breath, and put the pillow down.

Gazing across his room, Steuart thought about waking too soon from a newer bed in a house he did not care to see. *I don't want a new room. I don't need a new room.* Burying his head in another pillow, he wondered about his new school. *Will we ride a bus? Can we walk or ride our bikes?* He wondered about his teachers. *Will they be nice? What if they smell?* Steuart coughed. He thought about making new friends and considered how Midwestern children might differ from children in the South. *Do they play kickball? Do they enjoy reading? Are they clever?* Sitting up, he squeezed his pillow again and whispered, "Will you come with me?"

Although he loved his mother, Steuart wished she had more time for him and his sister Sam. He also wished she were nicer, kinder, and more fun like his grandmother, Ida Light. While it wasn't immediately apparent, acquaintances could quickly see that Olivia DuBoise had a way of being difficult with the world. You might say she had an abrasive affect, and you might also say that it wasn't her fault. Olivia was born with a narrow personal perspective allowing little room for the ideas and consideration of others. Steuart shuddered as he turned on his side and thought about his mother's preferred devotion. She read daily from an instructional publication titled *Right, Good, and Appropriate*.

"Good etiquette is everything," she liked to say.

"I feel sick," Steuart mumbled as he sat and reached for the cup of water on his nightstand. Ready to vomit, he rushed into his bathroom, turned on the faucet, and splashed cold water across his face. He grabbed a white washcloth and held it under the running water, gagging as he moved towards the toilet and lifted the seat. Heaving on his knees with his head above the bowl, Steuart pressed the cool, wet cloth against his forehead and waited for the nausea to pass. After a while, and finally feeling some better, he returned to bed, stopping first by the switch plate to increase the speed of his ceiling fan. He climbed onto the mattress, plumped his pillows, and situated himself once more. He reached for his cup and sipped. "That's better."

Steuart couldn't sleep. Wrestling with his pillow, Steuart stood on his bed and pretended he and Sparky were in a match. He held his hands high above his head and rotated slowly, nodding to the spectators as the announcer introduced him to the crowd. Hearing the bell, Steuart turned and flopped, belly first, onto the mattress before jumping up, grabbing Sparky, and throwing him across the bed. Steuart moved from one corner to another tossing the pillow, catching the pillow, tossing, catching, and working up a sweat—increasing his speed and intensity with each throw. Standing in the center, he jumped three more times and lunged forward, this time pinning Sparky under his belly. Up again, he clutched the pillow, jumped, jumped again, and threw Sparky into the air. He watched as the pillow, flying high, was grabbed up and spit out by the whirling blades of the fan, hurled across the room, and dumped onto the floor where it laid silent, crumpled, and defeated behind an overstuffed club chair. "Oh no," Steuart sighed as he jumped from bed and ran to rescue his opponent. "Are you okay pal?"

In bed again, Steuart held Sparky close and gave the pillow a squeeze. "I'm sorry about that. Can we continue?" Together they stood and readied themselves for the next round. "Wait," Steuart looked at the referee. "Don't start yet." He dropped Sparky. Once more Steuart leapt from bed, this time running towards the door. "I need to turn down the fan." He lowered the speed, turned around, raced back, and dove onto the mattress. He jumped, dropped, jumped again, and then lunged a final time, pinning his opponent to the bed. Steuart called the count and pronounced himself the winner. Out of breath, he gasped, flipped onto his back, and lay quietly for several minutes before pulling Sparky close. "You're a good man," he whispered.

Steuart drifted into a dream. His grandmother became a helium balloon attached to a string that was 43,026 feet long. He wrapped the string around his waist four times, or maybe five, tying it to his wrist so he could keep Ida with him always, pull her in extra close if he needed help, or just wanted to say "Hello Grandmother." Everywhere he walked Ida floated in the sky above him. On beautiful days she rode the wind with the rafters causing Steuart to walk at a faster pace. On windy days she moved swiftly, lifting him completely off the ground and carrying him high into the air.

Ida could touch the clouds. She added sugar, baking soda and organic vanilla to cumulus clouds and created fresh, fluffy cloud candy. Quite by accident, Steuart learned that he could stick out his tongue and taste little bits of the delicacy as it gently floated towards the ground. When conditions were perfect, Ida used the same ingredients to create Steuart's favorite candy—divinity. If Steuart chose to skip or run extra fast, his grandmother moved with him, even if he moved as fast as the wind. If rain came, he loosened the string letting Ida rise high above the clouds for protection. And, on cold days, he pulled her in close and wrapped her inside his coat.

Once, while racing through a field, Steuart grew concerned and looked up to make sure his grandmother was there. What he saw was her hand gently leaving her mouth as she blew him a kiss. Like the greatest athlete, Steuart jumped quick, straight, and high making the catch. He put the kiss into his pocket for safekeeping and then created several of his own, sending all of them to Ida at once. He watched as she held the kisses and rubbed them together in her palms. "I love you," she said, opening her hands and releasing thousands of white butterflies into the sky.

"I love you too, Grandmother."

For a short while, before the flutter of butterfly wings gave him a need to rest, Steuart felt that his heart might burst open with love. Lying on the grass, beside a gurgling stream, he made a moment of silence. He thought of other children and their grandparents around the world as he sent a silent prayer of hope into the universe for their good health, long lives, and happiness.

Steuart dozed fitfully before waking clammy and wet with thoughts and worries of arriving too soon at a house he already couldn't stand. After all, what could be good about a new house and a new place without his grandmother? *I'll never feel happy there. This is terrible.* At the age of ten, he couldn't remember feeling sadder. Steuart still couldn't sleep. In times past, when this was a problem, Ida encouraged him to make up stories. Quite often it worked, so he began.

Steuart pretended a pirate ship looking for seamen and carrying a recently discovered hidden treasure, sailed into the bay and docked at the end of his pier. Aware of the Galapagos pirates, he was also sadly aware of the giant island turtles, Chelonoidis nigra and their danger of extinction. He was certain that the pirates, infamously reputed for gorging themselves on turtle soup, were responsible for the crime.

Surprisingly, they seduced Steuart's mother into working a full-time rotation between the southernmost Galapagos pirate turtle farms, Takemoore and Arrrrrrr. The job called for a caretaker/cook responsible for daily soup production using a gourmet secret recipe brought from France two hundred years earlier by a 102-year-old, blue-blooded, Huguenot, chef-turned-pirate, named Jacques Supree. Steuart was thrilled until he overheard the pirates pondering their lack of protein. No more turtles meant no more soup—and no need for Olivia.

Negotiations were delicate until Steuart proposed a plan that included not only his mother, but also a delicious new mock-turtle soup recipe created by his grandmother, an excellent cook. In exchange for both Olivia and the recipe, the pirates presented Steuart, Ida, and Sam with a five-year-old donkey named Quantro, a bottle of two year old rum, and twelve chocolate coins—four for each of them. Having never read that there were donkeys on the islands, Steuart reasoned that the pirates seized the unfortunate animal during a raid on another ship with the knowledge that he could be useful in a trade.

For a while, Steuart enjoyed his stories. He smiled, took a deep breath, closed his eyes, and envisioned the taste of chocolate delights and rogue sounds in the night, as pirates sang songs and a contented donkey played happily beside a crackling beach bonfire. He grew sad again thinking about the move. "I'm wishing for a perfect moment of magic," he whispered. Perhaps a friend would appear in the darkness and give him the power to keep time from moving forward. "I need a power that will allow me to live thankfully and happily in the now, *a nowness* so huge that I can stay suspended permanently in the happiness I love with Grandmother and Sam, here on Atchison Bay." Suddenly, for some inexplicable reason, Steuart wondered about his father. *Where's Daddy? Does he think about me?* Steuart couldn't sleep.

He glanced across his big tall room at the giant, antique world map on the far wall. The map belonged to Ida's father, Matt Prescott when he was a boy. Turning away, Steuart watched the moonlight streaming through the transom above his dark French doors. He was beginning to understand what it meant to take something for granted. *This is unfair.* He reached for the cup of water on his nightstand and put it to his lips. The cup was empty. "Great," he groaned. Steuart took a deep breath and closed his eyes.

He thought about eating breakfast under the oaks. He thought about sitting in the swing at the end of the pier with his favorite books. He wondered how Ida would get along without him. *We're a team.* He thought of how he enjoyed throwing a line of cord far out into the bay with a smelly, rotting chicken neck tied to the end. He did this early in the morning as he crabbed the old-fashioned way with his grandmother who refused to use crab baskets.

"It's not sporting if you trap them," she'd say. Steuart didn't object because Ida's way was the most fun. He loved standing shirtless with his back straight, feeling the warmth of the sun behind him, and the coolness of salt-water lapping softly against his ankles. He loved the morning breeze coming in across the bay as he waited for a little nibble, pulling the cord tight. That's how he knew a hungry crab—maybe two, feasted on a hearty breakfast at the end of his line. This was the signal for Steuart to slowly reel-in the cord, while motioning for Ida who ran quickly and quietly with the long-handled net ready to scoop up the crabs that were too busy feasting to notice either of them. He thought of how his toes squished into the sand as she pulled and lifted the net filled with crabs and how just as quickly, with a huge grin and a laugh, she'd turn the net towards the water and release the crabs into the bay. "Steuart *Dahlin'*, I don't think it's their time yet. Do you?"

"Not yet Grandmother—looks like we'll have to find them another day."

"Maybe tomorrow, maybe next year. Those lucky crabs are safe for now." Steuart and Ida watched as the crabs scurried back into the murky darkness of the water.

Steuart blinked. He took a deep breath, exhaled and rubbed his eyes. He thought about swimming in the bay with his sister and grandmother, each of them floating lazily on a raft or an inner tube, all three held together by a long line of cord. He thought about sitting on the screened porch in the late afternoon, sipping sweet iced tea, and nibbling on leftover homemade buttered biscuits from breakfast as he worked on his favorite pastime—anagrams. Steuart thought of the holiday boating parade and the lights on the boats in the darkness. He thought about watching the sailboats in the distance. "One day I'll sail."

He looked up again and listened to the sound of the old ceiling fan, a soft slow exhaling *fwoh, fwoh, fwoh,* rotating gently above his bed. Again, he looked at the tall doors. His mind continued to wander. After a while, Steuart reached for his glasses, grabbed Sparky, and crawled out of bed. He opened the doors and walked quietly onto the sleeping porch that connected his room to his sister's. Steuart couldn't sleep.

* * *

As early as she could remember, Sam collected colors. "I love colors," she'd eagerly share with anyone who asked, and a few who didn't. "They make me happy and I am certain they hold a special magic that I cannot explain. I don't remember how old I was when I began my collection; maybe I was two or three. I can only say that I've done this for most of my life. I can't tell you why I started, but I can tell you that my grandmother is my biggest supporter. *Sam*, she says, *the colors will lead you where you want to go.* Color collection makes me happy."

Sam had a nightly color ritual. To keep her collection organized she kept an expandable folder, purchased one early Saturday morning while visiting community garage sales with Ida. It was pink with illustrations of large white cabbage roses and slid effortlessly into her backpack. Each night she began by locking her bedroom doors and pulling the pink comforter away from her bed. This allowed Sam to take the colors out and examine them against her crisp white sheets. "It's most important to be careful and cautious arranging the swatches," she'd say. "I arrange them in a variety of different ways while taking time to look at how they interact when mixed with different shades or textures."

After looking at the colors and moving them about, Sam arranged them again and viewed them, this time, as a group. She played with various combinations, selecting three or four at a time and then laid them side-by-side in a straight line before putting them into a box formation. Next, she created a grouping that allowed only the corner points of each color to touch.

She walked around the room and watched the colors from the opposite side of her bed, paying close attention to her newest acquisitions. She stood on her chair and stared down at the colors. She jumped up and down quickly, opening and closing her eyes, blinking fast, and then blinking slowly. She looked for shade changes in her groupings as she turned the lights on, off, then on and off again before standing in the darkness and counting to twelve. Next, she flipped the switch on, off, on, off, and on one more time as she continued to watch for changes. Sam knelt down beside the bed and moved her eyes directly across the colors, one by one, moving closer until her eyes failed to focus.

She tried to smell the colors. She turned her back, bowed her head, counted slowly to four, and then quickly counted to three as she jumped up, turned back and looked, once again watching for developments. She bent down close and low. She whispered to the colors. She hummed. She sang a song. She licked her pinkie and touched one corner of each swatch, stopping to record her observations in a small pink notebook.

She used a magnifying glass and repeated exactly one-half of the ritual. However, the part she repeated was not always the same. Once each week Sam chose five colors to put into retention. It was her belief that *colors need a break*. These colors were tucked away for three or four weeks and given a vacation from all the others. The remaining colors were put into a pile and stacked cautiously, one on top of the other, between alternating squares of tissue before sliding into their home. Sam relaxed. She lay next to the folder. She called the names of each color in silence. She stood up. She stood on her head. She stared at the walls. She sat in her chair with her back to the bed and recited a poem.

> You draw me in closely
> Like crowds all around me
> Your silence says little
> Your voice filled with knowledge
> I listen for clues
> To riddles unknown

With the color ritual complete Sam looked outside and noticed her brother on the sleeping porch.

TWO

Steuart lay on a summer bed and held Sparky against his chest. He watched the crescent moon hanging midway over the bay and listened to the gentle sound of waves lapping against the shore. Sam sat on the opposite bed. "Why are you awake?" she asked.

"I can't sleep."

"Neither can I."

"It's happening too fast."

"I know."

"Everything was fine. Life was perfect, and then all of a sudden we're moving. She decides to change everything and that is that. She didn't even ask how we feel about it. Did she ask for your opinion?"

"No."

"How did this happen?"

Sam shrugged, "She made a choice."

"She didn't care. She didn't ask either of us. I mean it. This is all wrong." Steuart had tears in his voice. "Why didn't she tell us sooner?"

"I don't know." Sam was crying too, but as the older sibling, she tried to hold her feelings inside. "Are you scared?"

"No." Steuart squeezed his pillow and spoke softly, "I want to stay here. *This* is our home."

Sam nodded.

"Don't you want to stay here?"

"We can't."

Steuart stood, turned around and then sat down. "Mother's new house doesn't even have a name. How stupid is that?"

"Not stupid, I don't think they do that in other places, at least they don't do it everywhere."

"I think it's stupid. All I have to do is tell my friends I live at Point Taken. People know how to find me."

"The new house has a number out front. Our friends will find us."

"What friends?"

"We'll make friends."

Steuart huffed, "She's taking us away from everything that matters. What will Frank and Caffey do?"

"Dogs adjust."

"Who'll walk with them?"

"They'll be fine with Grandmother. She'll walk with her friends, or she'll go out by herself."

"Friends are not the same as grandkids. She'll be lonely without us."

"That's true, but she has friends." Sam changed the subject, "You know what?"

"What?"

"I wouldn't be surprised if we get a dog once we're settled."

"I'd be shocked. What made you say something like that? Mother won't even let us have a gold fish."

Sam made a face and pulled on her toes. "Wishful thinking."

"I'm serious. She won't even let us have a fish. She told me I'd kill it unless she took responsibility for the thing."

"That's because she killed hers when she was little."

"What?"

"I got the same response. Mother had a couple of goldfish she really loved. She named them Marti and Ben. Grandmother told me that Mother took good care of them. She fed them everyday. She talked to them. And, she made sure they always had clean water. One day, when it was time to change the water, she put them in the sink and forgot to plug the drain. Marti and Ben went swimming. She never wanted a pet after that."

"And you think she'll let us have a dog?"

"Wishful thinking. Forget what I said."

Steuart held Sparky tightly around the middle and buried his head in another pillow. "Have I told you my new pirate story?"

Sam looked up and shook her head. She giggled, adding her thoughts, as Steuart talked. "I think Mother would take over immediately. She'd become the head pirate, and be in charge by the end of the first day. I'd feel sorry for the poor pirates. Just imagine how it would go for them once Mother pulled out *Right, Good, and Appropriate*. They wouldn't stand a chance. They'd run away crying like little babies."

"*Pig-eye traders!*"

"What's that?"

"Greedy pirates. They'd beg us to take Mother back. They'd offer us five million tons of gold."

"That's a lot," Sam shook her head, "but we couldn't take it."

"Blood money," Steuart nodded. "I'd pull out our super official, signed and binding, contract. I'd stand here on the porch, look down at the crowd on the beach and read it for everyone to hear."

"What would it say?"

Steuart took a deep breath. "It would say: *Hear ye, hear ye, Know ye this day that all signed agreements between the Galapagos Pirates, aka Pig-eye Traders, and the DuBoise children of Atchison Point are final and binding forever. That means our agreement is irrevocable. This document is undeniably signed, dated, and properly notarized by all interested parties. It may never, ever, ever, be undone.*"

"Yes!" Sam shouted.

"The pirates would be stuck with Mother forever."

Sam and Steuart giggled as they continued to embellish the story. Then they became quiet again.

Steuart sat in the darkness and looked at his sister, "I can't imagine living anywhere else. I've always felt like this house is magic." He looked around the porch. "This is my favorite room."

"Mine too."

"With the oaks out there it feels like we're sitting in a big tree house. We're part of this place."

"I love it too." Sam looked at her brother and folded her arms. "I think I'm beginning to understand what Grandmother means when she says, *Steuart, you're an old soul.*"

"Whatever," Steuart shrugged his shoulders. "There won't be a sleeping porch. There won't be a bay in our backyard. And we won't be able to go crabbing every morning. They probably don't even have oysters in the Midwest."

"I hate oysters. You do too."

"I'm talking about the crack of oysters under car wheels when people come to visit. I like the way it sounds."

"I don't like walking on those things barefooted."

"That's why we have flip-flops. Of course we won't need those anymore. The new drive is made of cement. Did you know that?" Steuart put his hands to his face. "I've heard they don't have grits, and they don't drink sweet tea up there. They've probably never eaten seafood. Can you imagine that? They might not know what it is."

"I'm sure they have seafood in Maybell. It might not be as good as what we know, but I'm sure they have it."

"Of course it won't be as good. I don't even like the name of that place. I found it on the map. Have you looked at where it is?"

"No."

"It's land-locked. It's a long way from any ocean or gulf."

"But not far from the Great Lakes."

"Who cares about a silly lake?"

"It won't be like the water in Atchison Bay, but…" Sam shrugged, "we might be pleasantly surprised."

"*Idle gab.*"

"Good one. What's wrong with a lake?"

"Lakes are fresh water. They don't count."

"Who says? What's the problem with fresh water?"

"I say." Steuart glared at his sister. "I don't like it. There's no salt."

"Have you ever been to a lake?"

Steuart didn't respond.

"We need to give the place a chance."

"Says who?"

"We have to go. We might as well make the best of things."

"It's going to be so cold. We'll have to learn to walk around in snow and ice. I'm not sure how I feel about snowshoes."

"We're not moving to the North Pole. I doubt that we'll need snowshoes. Think about the fun we'll have making snowmen and ice forts."

"We'll probably get snowed-in and starve to death."

"Let's see how it goes before we decide to hate the place."

"I'm not ready to do that."

"I think you're right about the shells."

Steuart stared at his sister. "Why are you talking about shells? They won't have shells. They'll have ice."

"I'm talking about the oyster shells. They're definitely better than a doorbell."

Steuart bent down and looked under the bed. He reached for a box of action figures and began playing. "How can grown-ups do these things to kids without thinking about how we feel? It's not right."

"Mother doesn't have to think about us."

"Why not?"

"Because we go with her. That's all."

Steuart threw an action figure onto the bed. "She doesn't want me to take these guys."

"Did she say that? What did she say?"

"*Steuart, you are now ten years old. It is time for you to put your toys and childish ideas away in a box. You need to begin concentrating on the concerns of a growing young man. You will quickly learn that well-adjusted men never play with toys or dolls.* Then she read a passage from her book as a way of proving her point."

"I'm not surprised."

"It's irritating."

"I'm sorry."

"Why are you sorry? You didn't do anything. Mother's the one making our lives miserable. She's clueless about these things. Can you believe she calls these dolls? This is not a doll. This is an action figure." Steuart stood and held the figure high above his head. "Meet my friend and esteemed colleague, Captain Crandall of the Creighton Clones."

"Hello," Sam said.

"He is, undeniably, one of the greatest super heroes of the modern day universe. Captain Crandall is the biggest and the best. He is the strongest and he is the most highly intelligent of all super heroes. This man can do anything. Imagine calling him a doll." Steuart sat down.

"I understand. She won't let you have action figures. She won't let me have paints."

"True."

Sam hugged her knees. "My special day's next. I'm asking for a paint set."

"Are you serious? You've forgotten about the *art incident?*"

"Mother can't hold a grudge forever."

"Yes she can. Of course she can."

"She might buy it. I keep telling her how badly I want to paint."

"What planet did you come from? Are we talking about the same person? Ask the neighbors. Ask her former friends. Ask anyone who knows Mother." Steuart stood, flew his action figure through the air and circled the room twice before pouncing, stomach first, onto the bed. "Our mother holds grudges every second of every minute, of every hour, of every day, of every week, of every month, of every..."

"Okay, okay, okay," Sam put up her hands. "I get it. I understand."

"Mother holds grudges for grudges that she's not even thought of holding grudges for yet. She coined the phrase *burn bridges before blood.*"

"You're exaggerating."

"I'm not. You've heard her."

"I'd rather not think about that. I don't think it's an original phrase."

"Maybe I'm giving her too much credit." Steuart shook his head, "But that doesn't change things. You should give up the idea of asking for art supplies. You'll be disappointed again. She'll never change her mind."

"That was years ago." Sam leaned back, stretched against the headboard and yawned. "I was *little*. Besides, I'm her daughter. Eventually, she'll have to let it go."

"We're not talking about Olivia DuBoise are we? Help me here."

Sam glared at her brother.

"Mother holds grudges. She never lets go. She likes to say that she can forgive but she'll never forget."

"Why are you being insistent about this? Why are you trying to burst my bubble? All I want to do is explore my artistic talents."

"I'm not trying to burst your bubble, or keep you from being artistic. I don't want you being unrealistic and ending up disappointed."

"I'm just hoping."

"Stop for a minute and think about the art incident. Who always brings it up? I don't bring it up. Grandmother never brings it up. You certainly don't bring it up. Only Mother talks about the mess you made. And that happens anytime you ask for art supplies. You don't even have to ask. All you have to do is mention that you like a picture."

Sam yawned again, and sighed loudly, "I don't know. I don't even remember ruining everything in the house. I don't remember ruining anything."

"That's my point."

"Either way, I'm asking for paints and I'll keep asking until she agrees. I'm almost a teenager."

"So?"

"So, there's nothing wrong with asking."

"*Uh, twinkling fish.*"

"What's that one?"

"Wishful thinking." Steuart held Captain Crandall high in the air. His voice went into razor sharp, deep, gravely, action figure mode. *"Ma'am, do you actually believe persistence and wishful thinking can penetrate the iron will of Lady Olivia DuBoise? Maybe we'll all travel through time to another world and back again too."*

Sam half laughed.

Captain Crandall continued. *Maybe Olivia DuBoise is going to be hit over the head. Maybe she will be hit over the head with a bottle which will not only cause her to forget every single thing that makes her swear and complain, but also cause her to make a public proclamation that Samantha Leigh and Steuart James are, without question, the most wonderful children a mother could ever have."*

"Ha."

"Maybe I'm not Captain Crandall, action figure extraordinaire, savior of the universe. Perhaps I am a great deal more. Maybe I am alive. Maybe..." Steuart stood, raced towards his sister, and put the action figure directly in front of her face. *"Young lady, maybe I am—your father."* Steuart backed away and began running as he pretended to fly around the porch before coming back and settling again onto the bed.

"I see," Sam said softly.

"I don't want to hurt your feelings. I think we both know Mother buys things she finds on sale."

"Probably."

"Don't forget her motto: *If it's not a bargain, we don't need it."*

Sam rolled her eyes, "Yeah, yeah, yeah, another one from the handbook."

"Have you ever read that thing?"

"I've looked at it a couple of times."

"You touched it? *Aunty Ed rodeo?"*

Sam shook her head, "What?"

"You're not dead?"

"She didn't see me. I looked when she was out of the room, and I put it down fast. Anyway, it doesn't matter. She tells us what she wants us to know. Between you and me, I'd like to burn the stupid thing and give it a burial at sea."

Steuart spoke through Captain Crandall, *"Abase ritual? Ma'am, don't argue with the handbook. Terrible things will happen."*

"Forget that, maybe just help her misplace it during the move."

"I hasten a tad." Steuart whispered a secret to Captain Crandall and then looked at his sister.

Sam put her hands up. She shook her head, "Don't go there. We can't do anything. Forget it. I wasn't serious."

"Forget what? I have no idea what you're talking about. I was thinking about your special day. Maybe Mother will find the paints marked down."

"We both know she buys what she wants us to have, not what we ask for. The paints could be free and she'd still decide against them."

"True."

"Ideas only work if they're hers. I guess I could save my money and buy them for myself, but unless she agrees..." Sam let out another deep sigh and became silent. For a while, the children sat quietly. Sam got up, walked to the edge of the porch and began looking out at the bay.

Steuart broke the silence. "How often do you think we'll be able to come home?"

"I don't know. If I told you anything other than that, I'd be lying."

Steuart began wrestling with his pillow and pretended it was wrestling back. "Mother never listens to your ideas or mine. She made the decision to move without asking our feelings. I'll never understand..." He stopped tugging at the pillow when he realized Sam was watching.

"What are you doing?"

Steuart held it up for an introduction. "This is my new pal, Leighton Jefferson Allnight O'Dowd. He's my dinosaur. You can call him *Sparky*."

"Why would I want to call your pillow by a name?"

"Because it's important."

"It's a pillow."

"No," Steuart snapped, "You only think you're looking at a pillow. He..." Steuart stopped and looked around the room, making sure that no one was listening. He leaned in close and lowered his voice to a soft, slow and distinctive whisper, "He is only *dressed* as a pillow."

"What?"

"It's a *d-i-s-g-u-i-s-e*."

Sam frowned, "Why is your pillow...?"

Steuart nodded, "Sparky, the dinosaur."

"Why is your pillow...?"

Steuart interrupted again, "Sparky, say it with me Sis. *Sparky, the dinosaur.*"

Sam stared at Steuart and nodded. They said it together, "Sparky, the dinosaur."

"That's right."

Sam began again, "Why is your Sparky the dinosaur disguised as a pillow?"

"*Hamster flout.*"

"I'm too tired for your words tonight. What are you saying?"

"Mother's fault." Steuart hugged Sparky, "It's because Mother says I'm too old to play with dolls. I've already told you about that discussion. You know and I know that dinosaurs are not dolls anymore than action figures are dolls."

Sam nodded.

"Mother lacks perspective. Quite simply, the woman is unable to distinguish between dolls, actions figures, or adopted dinosaurs. She doesn't even know the difference between sports equipment and simple beach toys. Frankly," Steuart paused and looked towards the water, "I find it pathetic."

"I guess they didn't teach those things at her school."

"I can't leave Sparky alone."

"Why not?"

"I haven't told you the entire story."

"There's more?"

"Sparky was outside under the bushes when I found him this morning."

"What was he doing there?"

"He was abandoned. I rescued him."

Sam laughed at her brother. "Steuart, that's really silly. You're not big enough to rescue anything."

"I disagree. I rescued Sparky. He needs me."

Sam made a face. "Let me make sure that I understand this. You found a pillow under the bushes in the dirt and now you want to carry it in the car and pretend it's a dinosaur? That doesn't sound sanitary to me."

"No," Steuart let out a deep breath. "I *discovered* a baby dinosaur in the tall grass on the south side of the house early in the day when I was outside working as an explorer. Come on, play along."

"Why?"

"Why not? Everything you do revolves around using your imagination. Don't tell me that you've never heard of a simple thing called *willing suspension of disbelief.*"

"I've heard." Sam impatiently looked at her brother and waited.

"You're not paying attention. I'm trying to tell you. This is important to me. Get it? I need you to understand what I'm saying."

"I'm trying."

"*Dry her art.*"

"Stop it with the anagrams. I'm getting annoyed."

"You're being difficult on purpose."

"I'm not."

"Pay attention, this is what you need to know."

"What?"

Steuart held Sparky and sat beside his sister. "One *finds* a pillow. One *discovers* a dinosaur. We are discussing two different things. I discovered Sparky. He is merely disguised as a pillow."

"So why is he disguised? Why can't he just show who he is?"

"I already told you. You look awake but I suspect your brain's sleeping. I think you're off somewhere far away. Wake up, Sam. Listen carefully. Sparky is in disguise so that he can make the move to Maybell. Unless he remains in costume he'll have to stay behind with all of my action figures."

Sam yawned and rubbed her eyes. "Why?"

"If he isn't in costume Mother will mistake him for a doll and disapprove. If that happens, she won't allow him to make the trip. This is the only way he can safely travel. Sparky needs to go with us."

Sam nodded.

"Sparky needs me. He has to play the game. We have to play the game too. It's not a big deal. All you have to do is pretend he's a pillow when Mother is in ear shot and be aware that he is really a wonderful baby dinosaur in need of love and attention." Steuart hugged Sparky. "We're this guy's family. I'm responsible for his care and upbringing. Please...."

Sam cocked her head and threw her hands into the air. "You're right! Where did I put my brain? What's wrong with me? Of course you're a dinosaur. I see now. Sparky, your disguise is perfect. I had no idea. I was totally fooled. Mother will never guess your secret—*ever*. I don't think anyone will. I won't tell."

Steuart smiled and hugged his pillow. "Sparky pal, you're doing a great job." He looked at Sam, "Thanks. This is exactly what we were hoping for." Steuart moved to the other bed, relaxed for a few minutes and played with his action figures before becoming upset again. "It's not right. Kids should never have to hide toys or choose between them."

"You're right."

Steuart picked up another action figure and threw it onto the mattress. "This shouldn't be happening."

Ready for bed, Sam felt tired and cranky. She didn't want to leave her brother until he was feeling better. "What about making up a story?"

"I told you, I made up a story already. Remember the pirates and the turtle soup?"

"I'm too tired to remember," Sam yawned. "I've already forgotten. I know you're upset. I am too, but we need to go to sleep. We're moving tomorrow."

"No! We can't give up without a fight. Let's ask Mother to change her mind. Let's ask her to let us stay here with Grandmother. She can go. We'll stay here."

"That'd be great Steuart, but it won't happen. Mother won't allow us to stay here without her."

"Why not?"

"We're her children. Besides, we'd miss her."

"Not really."

"I would."

"We'd be fine. We're not even her children."

"Don't say that. Of course we are."

"You're ignoring the truth. Why pretend?"

"I'm not pretending."

"I'm serious. This is the time for mutiny!"

"Stop it! You're not helping things."

"Why won't you talk about it?" Steuart threw another action figure at the bed. It missed and landed on the floor. He jumped across the mattress, picked up the figure and held it against his chest.

Sam shook her head and yawned, "I'm too sleepy to keep talking. It's not important."

"It is important."

"It's late."

"So?"

"We don't need to talk about these things tonight. I'm tired Steuart. I need to get some sleep."

"Then why won't you just say it? You know I'm right. You know it's true."

"Say what? What do you want me to say?"

"If you don't care, just say it."

"I'm going to bed. I refuse to have this discussion with you tonight."

"You sound like Mother."

"Fighting words, Steuart. Don't go there."

"I'm telling you that no one spends more time with us than Grandmother."

"Mother loves us."

"Grandmother loves us too."

"She's not our mother."

"She's like a mother should be. We love being with her, and we love Atchison Bay. We're happy with Grandmother."

"I know, but it's complicated. We can't just tell Mother to go by herself. She needs us."

"This is the only home that either of us can remember."

"That's true, but it doesn't mean that we won't like the new house."

"Why does Mother have the right to force us to leave our home?"

"Hush, Steuart."

"I refuse to hush. Mother's too busy for us. I doubt she'd miss us. I want to stay here and live with Grandmother."

"Mother's busy, but she would miss both of us. We're her family."

"She never has time for us."

"She's busy working hard to make money to support you and me so that we can go to the best schools, become well educated, and have good futures allowing us to lead happy lives as productive, contributing members of our society."

"Whoa! That's impressive. When did you memorize that one?"

"Stop it." Sam rolled her eyes, "Mother takes care of us. She has an important job. We're not the only people who depend on her."

"I know she's busy. That's exactly my point. Maybe she's *too* busy to be a good mother."

"But, she *is* a good mother."

"A good mother wouldn't make us move."

"She got a better job."

"A good job is not the most important thing in the world. Grandmother has time for us. Grandmother loves us. We should stay here with her."

"Grandmother can do all the things she does because she doesn't have to worry about money."

"Mother doesn't either."

"You don't know that."

"I know Grandmother gives Mother money."

"Steuart, you're being stubborn. It's useless. Children don't make the rules."

"Ladies and gentlemen, *that* is the understatement of my entire young life."

"I'm tired of arguing with you. I'd rather stay here too, but we can't change things. Like it or not, we're moving tomorrow."

"Not if I can help it."

"Let's count our blessings and be thankful for what we have."

"And that is...?"

"We're together. That's something, right?"

"Whatever," Steuart huffed. "I'm going downstairs for a snack."

* * *

Steuart paused at the top of the stairs and looked down. Dim lamplight illuminated the front hall, living room and kitchen. Flickering gaslight streamed in through the transom and sidelights that surrounded the heavy front door. The remainder of the first floor was bathed in quiet shadows as a heated conversation took place between Olivia and Ida. Interested in knowing more, Steuart raised his hand, placed his index finger next to his lips, and rubbed his mouth. He considered his options and thought about what he should do. He also thought about what he wanted to do. He considered turning around and returning to bed. He deciding he would, but only after a bit of investigation. Perhaps his grandmother was going to insist that he and Sam stay with her. *Wouldn't that be wonderful?*

Steuart walked down three steps. Listening hard, he bent down, cupped his hand behind his ear and pulled it in the direction of the living room. From the higher stairs, the voices were muffled. Again, he moved down. Again, he put his finger to his mouth and contemplated turning back. Straining to hear what was being said, he moved further down the stairs and found himself both surprised and curious by the realization that one of the voices was unknown to him. He was not hearing his grandmother. Holding the banister, Steuart pulled himself up so that his feet left the stairs. Leaning across the railing he looked back towards the living room, cupped his ear again, and this time lost his balance. Three steps from the floor, Steuart caught himself on the other side, dropped quietly onto the rug, and continued his spy activities.

The voices grew louder. *Who's she talking with,* he wondered? As his mother's voice rose, Steuart considered running up the stairs. Instead, he ran behind the living room sofa and quickly ducked. Stealthily, he began following his mother and the visitor from room to room. Making out a handful of words, Steuart listened intently to shifting voices; raised one minute, low and muffled the next.

While hearing the argument was difficult, moving about was relatively easy. He was small for his age and made no sound jumping from carpet to carpet across the polished wooden floors. Not only curious, but also determined, Steuart moved forward into the study where he crouched low behind a wing chair and listened. The women continued arguing in hushed, harsh voices. At his mother's insistence, the visitor moved into the foyer and stood near the front door. That's when Steuart heard the intruder say, "You must return them. They do not belong to you."

Olivia turned away and walked into the study where she stood at the front window and watched. Ignoring the woman's request, she began with a soft voice that became only louder and more annoyed as she spoke. "A cab is on the way. We have an agreement."

"Coercion is not an agreement," the woman said.

"I want you out of my house."

Steuart peeked from behind the chair and watched as his mother looked out the window. Standing beside the front door, the stranger wore a red floral scarf around her head. The room was too dark for Steuart to see her features. Thinking he might get a better view of things from the other side of the house, he elected to move. He silently counted to three, popped up, and made a dash for the rear study door. He raced through the living room, and into the hallway where a misstep from carpet onto wood caused him to slide, accidentally pushing a magazine out of a basket and across the floor. Fearful of discovery, he quickly stood, dashed towards the kitchen, and through the butler's pantry, moving towards the dining room which stood on the opposite side of the entryway and, unfortunately, offered no adequate cover.

The women continued arguing. They noticed nothing. Steuart reversed his route. He moved from the dining room, through the butler's pantry, and into the kitchen. He crossed the hallway, picked up the magazine, replaced it, and then ran into and through the living room before successfully moving into the study where he stood silent, straight, and tall, this time hidden by the heavy draperies. He peered through the curtains, calming himself and catching his breath while remaining as still and watchful as the twin Magiscopes guarding the study mantle.

Headlights flickering through the brush, moved along the drive as they made their way towards the house. "Get out of my house," Olivia said opening the front door and ushering the stranger onto the porch. "You need to leave." As she approached the door, Steuart saw the woman drop an envelope onto the carpet. Olivia, too busy watching the stranger, noticed nothing.

With her face in the shadows, the woman turned back and spoke, "Even you know that you're wrong." Turning to leave, she suddenly made eye contact with Steuart.

Fearful, Steuart remained still. He tried not to blink. The woman stared for a moment before looking away. She looked at Olivia, and then got into the cab. Steuart watched the car as it exited the drive. He listened as his mother closed and locked the front door. He continued to hide, but began feeling calmer with his focus now shifted from the stranger to the envelope. Steuart waited curiously for his opportunity.

Olivia turned, watching to make certain the car was gone. "This house needs an alarm." She checked the lock and secured the deadbolt. She looked towards the drive, and then let out a deep sigh. She turned and leaned against the door, not noticing the envelope that laid mere inches from her feet. Closing her eyes, she sighed again. "Why do these things always happen to me?"

Steuart continued watching the envelope. He waited for his mother to walk up the stairs. Instead, humming an unrecognizable melody, she stepped across the thing and moved towards the kitchen. Steuart remained quiet in the study as he waited for just the right moment. He watched and listened until his mother opened the refrigerator. Feeling safe, he dashed silently into the hallway, dove onto the floor and scooped up the envelope. The refrigerator door closed. Quickly, tucking the envelope beneath his shirt, and into the back elastic of his pajama bottoms, Steuart began walking up the stairs—too late.

Olivia rounded the corner, making her way towards the staircase. Thinking fast, Steuart did a one-eighty as his mother approached the bottom step and began her climb. Now midway up, her son was stepping down. "What are you doing up?" she asked. "Come on now. You need to be in bed."

"I'm thirsty."

"I have no desire to spend my day driving with a cranky, difficult child in my car. Come on. Let's go to bed."

Steuart heart raced. "I'm thirsty," he persisted. "I need something to drink."

"You don't *need* anything."

"I *want* something to drink."

Olivia reached down, put one hand on Steuart's head and the other on his bottom. He held his breath as she pivoted him in the opposite direction. "You should be dreaming." She popped his bottom with her palm. "Let's go."

Steuart turned. He backed against the wall and looked up at his mother. "I can't sleep. I heard a noise."

"I don't know what you think you heard, but we're safe."

"I need to check things out."

"There's no reason to be scared. It's too late for a young man your age to be awake."

"I'm going to the kitchen. I'm thirsty." Steuart was sweating.

"You have water in your room."

"I prefer a little glass of milk. Care to join me, Mother dear?"

"No, thank you. Go ahead. Just make it quick."

"I won't take long." Steuart looked down at his feet and silently prayed, *please make her leave—make her go to bed.*

Olivia climbed one step before stopping again. She turned around and looked down at her son. "No funny business. Understand?"

Steuart nodded, "I understand." He cleared his throat and shook his head, "No funny business."

Olivia smiled and extended her arms, "Step up here. Mother needs a hug." Steuart's heart pounded. He nervously stepped up. "Don't stay up long. I'm quite serious. Tomorrow will be an exhausting day for all of us."

"I won't. I promise."

"Alright then, I'll see you in the morning." Olivia released her son and started up the stairs towards her room. Steuart continued walking towards the bottom step until his mother stopped again and called to him in a sharp, insistent voice, "Steuart James."

Steuart froze. He half turned, and looked up. "Ma'am?" he whispered.

"Steuart James, turn around now. I want you to turn around and look at me."

Steuart stopped.

Olivia repeated herself. "Are you listening to me? I want you to turn around and look at me. Come on. Look at me."

Certain that his mother knew about the envelope, Steuart worried that his heart was about to explode. Looking towards the wall he whispered timidly, "Why?" Steuart knew not to question his mother.

"Turn around Steuart James. Look at me now. What in the world is wrong with you? You know better than to ask me *why*."

Steuart slowly turned towards his mother.

"Look at me."

He looked up at Olivia. She stared down at her son. Certain of his mother's parental x-ray abilities, Steuart accepted that she could read clear through his body and into his soul. His heart beat harder. It raced faster and faster. He felt hot. He felt clammy. Stars twinkled in front of his eyes as he briefly thought he blacked out. His breathing quickened. Even with his backside turned away, Steuart knew for certain that his mother could see the envelope through his clothing. Life as he knew it was coming to an end—forever.

Steuart had a brief fantasy and imagined himself on a large gurney being taken out to an ambulance after a massive heart attack. His mother ran behind the paramedics crying and pleading for his forgiveness, *If only I had known how fragile you were, Steuart, Steuart, oh, my little darling Steuart, I would never have been such a terrible, awful, overbearing parent. Steuart! Come back to me. I beg your forgiveness. I love you Steuart. Stay with me. Don't leave me. We don't have to move. Steuart...."*

"Steuart—Steuart James DuBoise," Olivia yanked her son into reality. She had just called him by all three names. No doubt, he was done for.

"Ma'am?" His voice was barely audible.

"Are you listening to me? Steuart James, are you listening—are you?"

"Yes, ma'am, I'm listening." He felt pain in his heart as he prayed for the ability to travel through time and leave this moment forever. He reached behind his back and readied to hand over the envelope. Prepared to accept his fate, Steuart looked up at his mother and stood tall and sharply inhaled.

Olivia stared at Steuart.

"Stay out of the cookies."

"What?"

"Don't you dare *what* me, mister. You know better than that. I don't care how late it is or how tired you are. You know how to behave. And if you can't be appropriate, be quiet—I'll tell you what to do. Your grandmother lets you get away with too much. When I get you to Maybell we're going to have a long discussion about manners and proper behavior."

Steuart looked off in the distance. "I'm sorry, Mother."

"What should you have said?"

"Ma'am, I should have said ma'am."

"That's better. Remember, exhaustion is never an excuse for being rude or disrespectful. Did you hear what I said to you?"

Steuart nodded and whispered softly, "*Same yam.*"

"I said *stay out of the cookies.*"

"Yes ma'am, stay out of the cookies."

Olivia turned and walked up the stairs. Steuart didn't budge. He stood in the same spot and silently counted until he heard his mother's bedroom door open and close. He imagined jumping from the ambulance, running into his mother's arms, and offering forgiveness. *It's okay, Mother. You can't help yourself.*

Relieved, Steuart sighed as he continued leaning against the wall.

Several minutes later, and certain that his mother was not about to return, he left the stairs and walked into the kitchen. He pulled the step stool from the pantry and carefully carried it across the floor. He placed the stool next to the cabinet and shelves before climbing up and putting his knees onto the counter. He took a short, clear glass from the shelf and set it onto the countertop as he stepped down to open the refrigerator. He pulled out a carton of milk, stepped back up and poured his glass—half full. He closed the milk jug, stepped down, and returned it to the refrigerator, moved the stool back into the pantry, closed the door, and walked partially out of the kitchen before turning around and going back.

Quietly, Steuart placed his milk onto the counter, opened the pantry, and, this time carried the stool to the opposite side of the kitchen where he stepped up, reached for the paper towels and tore off a square. He laid it on the counter and gently pressed it flat with both hands before reaching across for the cookie jar and silently helping himself to just one cookie. Using extra caution, Steuart avoided leaving crumbs on the counter. With his glass in one hand, cookie and paper towel in the other, he stepped down and tiptoed up the stairs with the envelope in his pants.

Back in his room, Steuart laid his milk and cookie on the nightstand, and placed the envelope on his pillow. He walked to the door, closed and carefully locked it before climbing back into bed where he reached into the drawer of his nightstand and pulled out a tiny red flashlight. Comfortably munching his cookie and sipping his milk, Steuart paused briefly to consider another story.

This time he became a grown man and a great politician. He had both the power and wealth allowing him to purchase Point Taken—the grand old antebellum house which belonged to his grandmother—the place he called home. Immediately, he appointed his mother as the Right, Good, and Appropriate, Global Ambassador—a lifetime position.

Olivia traveled from town to town as an official representative, knocking on doors and meeting everyone. She had the mundane and arduous task of querying each individual as she compiled a worldwide birthday wish list. This information was entered into a central database that fed back to Steuart's main office where a staff worked diligently processing requests twenty-four hours a day.

Olivia's job kept her busy enough with little time to do anything other than work. She stayed in contact with the family through weekly mail and visited home once or twice each year. Steuart lived out his days with Ida, Sam, Frank, Caffey and their four new Old English Sheepdogs; Bear, Pal, Buddy and Sis. Life was perfect.

The cookie was gone. Steuart took one last sip of milk. "It's time," he said, preparing for the information. He raised and lowered his eyebrows several times. He looked at the envelope, smelled the thing and examined it from both sides using his flashlight. Carefully, he opened the back flap, reached inside and pulled out a card. It was heavy and flat. Printed on the front in black ink was a name: Laurel Ivy Hood. He flipped the card. It was blank. "Blank," he whispered. Disappointed, Steuart wondered, *who is this person? Why was she arguing with my Mother?* He checked the envelope to make sure he hadn't missed something important. He looked at the card once more and then closed his eyes. Steuart sighed, "All this work for nothing." He held the card in his hands, curled up next to Sparky, and yawned. *Justly muck.* Steuart finally slept.

THREE

The following morning Sam, Steuart, Ida, and Olivia watched as workers quickly loaded boxes and a few items into a large moving van. The truck was ready right away. "Why aren't we taking our furniture?" Steuart asked his mother.

"Because we have all new furniture waiting for us at our wonderful new house. Isn't that fabulous?"

"Why do we need new furniture? I want *my* furniture. I want *my* things. Why did we need such a big truck if we're not taking our furniture?"

"It's not our furniture. It belongs to your grandmother."

"I want my furniture."

"I just told you that it's not our furniture."

"You're making us leave our home. You can at least let us take our furniture."

"Our home is waiting for us in Maybell with our new furniture."

"I don't want to go to that stupid place. I want my bed. I want my chair. I want my desk. I want my room."

"Steuart," Olivia shook her head, "That is not possible. We are moving. We are moving into a new house, and we are going to have all new furniture. It will be beautiful."

"Why the giant truck?"

"We're not the only people moving."

"I want my things."

"Do you have any idea how spoiled you're sounding?"

"I'm not spoiled."

"You want to leave your grandmother without furniture. That sounds spoiled and selfish to me. We cannot leave your grandmother without furniture. That would be an awful thing to do."

"That's not what I meant. You know that's not what I meant." Steuart turned to Ida, "I don't want your things Grandmother. I want *my* things. Grandmother, you understand, don't you?"

Ida nodded. "It's okay," she whispered.

"It's not okay." Steuart turned back to his mother. "Not okay. I want my bed. I won't be able to sleep without my bed. I want my action figures too."

"Then it's a good thing," Olivia said, "that your wants won't cause you pain."

"I want to stay here. *Yo ma ye uh tormentor.*"

"Cut the crap Steuart. We don't have time for your games."

"It's *hamster flout!*"

"Save your anagrams for later. We're finished with this discussion. Now take a final look around and do whatever you need to do. I'm giving you both thirty minutes, not a minute more..." Olivia glanced at her watch, "beginning now."

Sam, Steuart, Ida and the pups walked towards the water for a good-bye stroll on the pier.

"I'm going to miss you," Sam said, hugging her grandmother and then bending down to lift Frank. "I'm going to miss you too Frank."

Steuart, carrying Caffey on his back, leaned next to Ida and mumbled something under his breath. He felt tears in his eyes and turned away.

Ida bent down and looked at her grandson, "You can do this," she said. "We both know you are every bit as strong as any super hero."

"I hate this. I hate her," Steuart whispered. "I want to stay with you. This is our home. Make her let us stay with you. Please, please, Grandmother, don't let her take us to that awful place. I hate her."

Ida put her hands on Steuart's shoulders, "Look at me. Listen to me carefully. You do not *hate* anyone or anything. Hate is a strong, ugly word. It destroys people. Every minute you spend in anger is a minute of your life that is forever gone. It's wasted time that you cannot live again. Do not let anger rule your life, Steuart. It's not worth it. Focus on the positive things. Everything will be fine."

"I don't want to go."

"I know that, but you can do this. I know this because you are exactly like my daddy. Now, please look at me. Answer my question. Can you do this?" Ida looked at Steuart and waited for his answer.

Steuart looked down at his feet. "Yes," he whispered.

"Are you *sure-as-Matt*?" Ida asked.

A smile grew wide across Steuart's face. Sam joined the two for a group hug. "Yes, we're both sure-as-Matt," the children agreed.

"That's all I needed to hear."

Sure-as-Matt was the strongest promise made in Ida's family. Matt Prescott, Ida's father, was known throughout the county as a man of his word. "You're both going to be fine," Ida said. "I have faith in you." She looked at her watch, "I hate to say this, but it's time to go. Now, before we walk up to the house, I need to see smiles."

The children frowned.

"Smiles please. We'll talk often," Ida hugged the children as they walked towards the house.

"It's not the same," Steuart said.

"We'll send messages. I write beautiful letters. We'll find time to visit. I'll come see you, and you will come see me. I promise. I've already asked your mother to bring you down in December."

"It's too far," Steuart said.

Ida looked at Steuart and then at Sam. "Let's adjust our attitudes. It's going to be okay."

"It isn't the same as living together," Steuart said softly.

Olivia stood next to the car. She waited with the doors open. She looked at Steuart and frowned, "Put that nasty dog down, now. It's time for us to be on the road. I have no desire to drive my car one thousand miles with you sitting in the back seat smelling like a wet, sweaty dog. Honestly, do you ever think about making use of the brain God gave you? Sometimes I can't help wondering if you took it out one day and left it on a rock. Is that what happened?"

"I'm sorry Mother."

"Steuart, if we were not in a rush, I'd stop right this minute and send you inside for a proper shower."

"No problem, I can take a shower." Steuart took Caffey from his shoulders and handed her to Ida. "I won't be long." He turned and began running towards the house.

"Stop Steuart. You will do no such thing. Turn around now. Come back here. We'll let the windows down so you can air out. Come on now, get in."

"Wait!" Steuart insisted.

"What now?"

"I forgot my valise! I have to go back. Come with me Sam. I left it on the pier. We'll be right back."

"Hurry," Olivia called out. "We need to get on the road."

Running towards the pier Steuart outlined his plan. "This is our chance. Let's run away before it' too late. We'll find a boat. We can sail off to the Galapagos. They won't find us. Let's do it!"

"Oh, would that we could. The wind is perfect."

"I wish the pirates would arrive this very minute," Steuart shouted. "I'd point to Mother and say *she's ready fellows. Take her away.*"

"Where are good pirates when we need them?"

* * *

Ida's voice cracked as she spoke with her daughter. "Olivia, you don't have to do this."

"Yes, I do." She pulled away and nodded. "Some people actually work for a living."

Ida shook her head, "Stop trying to play games with me. I am not a fool. I understand you very well. You're going. You've made up your mind. That is that, and I understand this is going to happen. What I do not understand is why you're determined to continue creating chaos in our lives. I refuse to stand here and listen to you tell me this is a career move. We both know this is about something much bigger than a job."

"We know no such thing. You just want this to be about other things. You are the one who insists on creating chaos in our lives. Listen to me. My career is the only reason for this move. There is no other reason. The time has arrived for me to put myself first."

"Seems to me that looking out for self has never been your problem."

"Mother, I respectfully disagree."

Ida shook her head. "I do not approve of what you're doing, but this isn't my call. I only wish you would consider the children. You've intentionally kept them from their father. This is the only home either of them remembers. They're happy here—happy, safe, and secure. Doesn't that mean anything to you? They need the stability."

Olivia glared at her mother. "It's always about someone else, isn't it?"

"I guess we could ask your late night visitor."

"You have no right to say that to me," Olivia looked for the children and shouted, "Steuart James, Samantha Leigh, we have to go—now."

Ida bit her lip. She watched as Steuart and Sam walked slowly towards the car. Steuart put his arms around Ida. "Grandmother will you be okay?"

"Don't waste your worry on me," Ida said. "I'll be fine as long as I know the two of you are keeping your promises. Make this time count for something great. Follow your words and colors. Whatever you put into this is what you'll get out. Enjoy your adventures. Most of all, sweet babies, be happy."

"*Voile You.*" Steuart hugged Ida.

"And I love you too."

Sam reached out and held her grandmother's hand. "Are you sure Grandmother?"

Ida stood tall, held her tears, and looked at Sam. "Yes sweetheart, I am. I am sure-as-Matt." She gave both children one final hug as they got into the car. "You have no idea how much excitement awaits you. The Midwest is beautiful, especially now. You're going to have incredible adventures. Put your best foot forward every day." She looked at Olivia, "Take care of yourself and take care of our babies."

Olivia nodded. She started the car and pulled out the winding drive as Ida stood in front of the house and waved.

* * *

Olivia drove up the road making her way towards the main highway.

"Nothing's better than living on a road where the houses have names," Steuart said, "and the names have a point." Staring out the window, he watched houses and began reading names aloud, "Beside the Point, Point Lost, What's Your Point, What's the Point, Point of View, Point of it All, The Pointers…"

Sam joined her brother, "Pointless, Pointed, Last Point, Resting Point, Point of Reason, Old Point, Victory Point…"

"Match Point, Final Point, To the Point…" Steuart spoke through his tears. "Mother, you're being unfair. This is not fair."

"Who needs *fair*? Fair is where people wait in long lines to pay outrageous prices for cheap thrills and fried butter."

"You're making my life completely miserable."

"Then I'm doing my job."

"What?"

"I'm doing you a disservice if I make your life easy. I don't want you to become a hopeless emotional cripple."

"We'd like to stay here with Grandmother," Sam said.

"You're a hateful and mean mother," Steuart shouted. "We'll never, ever, forget this not even if we both live to be one thousand and twenty-six years old."

"Cut it out, Steuart. Don't say things you're certain to regret." Olivia looked at her children in the rearview mirror. *Right, Good and Appropriate* encourages growth. It is sensible and healthy to try new things. We're trying something new. You will adjust."

"No, we won't."

"Everything will be fine. You're upset because you're too young to understand these things. You'll get over it and then you'll feel bad for being so cruel to your dear, sweet mother. Straighten up now and behave. We have a long way to go.

"What about your dear, sweet mother? What about her?" Steuart asked.

Olivia snapped back, "I've had enough of this bad behavior. This is going to stop. Your grandmother is sixty-two years old. She has lived her life. Now, it's time for us to live ours."

Sam's jaw dropped.

Steuart slammed his fist against the back seat. "I need my grandmother. Turn this car around right this minute. I want to go home! I want to go home now!"

"That's enough. Don't make me pull over and stop. You won't like what happens."

Steuart frowned. He took a deep breath, "Who's Laurel Ivy Hood? Did you take something that belongs to her?"

Olivia pulled onto the highway, "Steuart, I'm not interested in your games. Settle in now. We're playing the quiet game. I don't want to hear another word."

Sam looked at Steuart and whispered, "We forgot Point Taken."

FOUR

Three miles less than one thousand, veering slightly northeast, driveway-to-driveway, sat the new house. After two days on the road, Steuart, Sam and their mother reached Maybell in time for brunch.

    The late September move was a colorful surprise for two children who had never experienced the wonders of autumn. The city was ablaze with fall color. Maybell was beautiful. Olivia was correct. Sam and Steuart were stunned by the beauty of the season. However, it was Sam who found the colors most captivating. Everywhere she looked there were new colors to add to her collection. "Grandmother knew," she whispered. "This must be what she was talking about."

    Walking inside, the children found a new house that was furniture store perfect; everything matched with a Sunday flier sort of feel. "Isn't it wonderful?" Olivia exclaimed. This was in contrast to Ida's house, which felt more like a long loved, well worn, often read novel. The new house was pretty, but it wasn't Point Taken. It felt cold, impersonal, and lacked character.

    Sam and Steuart were pleased to learn that the city connected itself with a network of parks and bike trails. They experienced a sudden sense of independence and were eager to explore their surroundings. "Let's go for a bike ride," Steuart said to his sister.

"Let's do it," Sam agreed.

Always quick to take advantage of an opportunity, Olivia presented the children with a challenge. "Get your rooms in order. Understand me, everything must be unpacked and in place; boxes must be empty, broken-down, and in the garage. Once that's done, you may go out on your bikes and play."

Sam and Steuart went to work immediately. In less than two hours, they were unpacked, organized and ready to enjoy their new town.

* * *

The back porch stood overlooking the Saugahatchee River, a peaceful body of water that was wider than expected. Sam leaned against the railing. She listened and watched her surroundings. She looked across at a protected area of land known as the Preserve. Almost instantly, Sam found herself drawn to one particular tree. It stood directly on the other side—an indescribably vivid orange like nothing she had seen before that moment. This color was on fire. It was persuasive, and Sam was compelled. She knew immediately what she wanted. Breathing in autumn and letting it go, she shouted for her brother, "Come on, Steuart. We've got to find that tree. Trees like that don't exist down south." The translucent leaves glowed as the sunlight touched them. "Steuart, I want one of those leaves for my collection. That's what I plan to have—today."

"What?" Steuart walked onto the porch.

"That's where I'm heading," Sam pointed in the direction of the tree. "I'm going over there."

"Wait a minute. We just got here. Let's look for something on this side before we start running all over the world. We don't even know how to get there."

"I can find it."

"Why do you want to make things complicated?"

"I don't make things complicated. I go after what I want. What's wrong with that?"

"I'm just suggesting that it might make better sense to explore this side first. We need to get our bearings and learn our way around. Let's go over there tomorrow."

Sam shook her head. "I can't do that. I don't know how long it'll be before the leaves lose their shine. Tomorrow might be too late."

"You realize there are hundreds of trees on this side of the river? I imagine that you can find something over here too."

Sam ignored her brother, and pointed in the distance. "I know what I want," she pointed again. "That is the tree. It has to be that one."

"But we don't even know how to get there."

"I do."

Steuart sighed, "You're not listening, are you?"

"No," Sam smiled, exhaled and continued to point. "I'm not. That's the tree. That's where we have to go."

"Why does it have to be that one?"

"Because! Look at the colors. Look at them. When I saw that tree it did something emotional to my lungs." Sam thrusts her fist into her chest. "I have to see that tree up close."

Steuart rolled his eyes.

"If there were words written all over the thing, you'd already be there."

Sam moved into action and decided not to wait for Steuart. She began putting on her sweater and walking into the garage towards her bicycle. She looked back at her brother, "Are you coming?"

"I have a choice?"

"Of course you do. You can start on this side by yourself. You don't have to come with me, but I'm going to find that tree. I'll tell you about it when I get back."

"Wait up. Let me get my valise," Steuart ran into the house and yelled, "If I'm coming, you can at least wait for me."

Sam jumped on her bicycle. She looked at the trail and a group of tall towers in the distance. She waited briefly before Steuart returned to the garage with his valise in hand, running towards his bike. Sam took off. She rode ahead and heard Steuart call out, "Wait up Sam, wait for me."

Sam rode towards the towers looking for a path that might lead down to the river. "There," she saw it. She looked back at Steuart and pointed down the hill towards a bridge. "I knew it," she yelled and laughed.

She rode down the bike path, along the side of the tall buildings, and then down the back of the property onto the grass. She rode close to the water and beside a volleyball net before coasting onto a pedestrian bridge and crossing the river. Back on the bike path, Sam left the trail, jumped off her bike, and walked it through a patch of dirt, down a small hill, across a tiny brook, and then trudged up a steep gravel path towards the train tracks where she walked her bike to the other side.

Sam heard Steuart yelling in the distance. "What are you doing? Wait for me. Where are you going? What do you think you're doing?"

"I know exactly what I'm doing," she shouted. "Trust me." Sam stood and waited for Steuart to catch up.

"Trust me?" Steuart muttered as he trudged up the gravel path and stopped. Steuart and Sam stood looking at one another on opposite sides of a train track. Steuart continued talking to himself, "Trust her? This could end badly." His heart beat fast. With labored breathing, he repeated himself, "*Trust me,* she says. Why do those words always get me into trouble?"

"What now?"

"We shouldn't be here. Mother'll have a conniption fit if she finds out we were playing on train tracks. We'll be in deep trouble."

"No, she won't. No, we won't."

"Yes, she will. Yes, we will."

"She doesn't have to know." Sam shook her head, threw her hands into the air, paused, and looked away, "I think you're scared to cross."

"I'm not scared. I'm sensible. What if a train comes?"

"What are you talking about now?"

"We'll be dog chow. We'll be squashed little bugs. We won't even know what hit us because our lives will be over—forever." Steuart lifted his index finger and pulled it in a slashing motion across the underside of his chin. "Consider that."

"You're being a drama baby."

"No, I am not." Steuart rolled his eyes and made death gestures. A dragonfly moved in front of his face and distracted him. Steuart began slapping his face and the back of his neck. He slapped his hands together as he tried to get the bug to move along. He looked across at Sam as he slapped at his knees."

Sam stopped laughing. She stood with a straight face and waited for the dragonfly to go away. "Little baby brother, tell me this, when did you become a baby chicken? What's wrong with you today? Did you leave your courage and sense of adventure back at Atchison Point? Is it somewhere on the pier?"

"I am not a baby. I am not a chicken. Do not call me names."

"Then, don't give me a reason." Sam stood firm and folded her arms. "Come on and cross."

"What about trains? This is dangerous. We might get hurt."

"I don't see a train. Do you see a train?" Sam didn't give Steuart an opportunity to respond. "Do you hear a train? There isn't a train anywhere close by."

"We're not supposed to do this."

"I'll help you across."

"No, you won't."

"Did anyone ever tell you specifically not to cross a train track?" Sam asked.

"No."

"There."

"*There?* Not *there*. You know and I know that if we mentioned we were thinking about crossing train tracks, Mother would say *no*. She would say *don't do it.*"

"But she has not specifically told us to stay away. Correct?"

"Correct," Steuart nodded.

"So, it's not a big deal. It can't be. She can't punish us for something unless she has given us the rule. Come on. Let's get going."

Steuart didn't budge. "You're kidding me. Yes, she can. I don't need anyone to tell me not to do something when I know potential danger is involved. *This* is dangerous."

"Where's the danger? There are no trains close by. All we're doing is crossing over one little set of tracks. That is that. Look at me. I've already done it. Nothing happened to me. It is no big deal. I'm alive. No breaks, no cuts, no bruises. I'm absolutely fine. We both could have crossed over and back two dozen times by now. I can help you."

Steuart shook his head, gazed down the tracks in both directions and whispered, "I've never crossed tracks before."

"Today is your lucky day. There's a first time for everything." Sam's voice grew quieter, "I'm not going to stand here forever. If you're going to be a chicken, just go ahead, turn around right now and go home. *Shoo*, go home."

"You're being mean."

"I want to get my color. I don't care if you come or not. It's probably best if you don't come. You're too frightened. Go on. It'll be dark soon. I plan to reach my destination and be home before dark. Go home Steuart. I can't leave you here."

"You don't understand. I feel my heart beating too fast."

"That means you're alive."

"I feel it beating so hard that it might come up through my neck and fly out of my mouth, roll over that way," he pointed, "and fall in the river so the fish can eat it. Sam, I feel sick."

Sam felt guilty and decided to back off. "I'm sorry for giving you a hard time Steuart. It's fine with me if you don't want to come. I think you should go home and play."

"What? What are you talking about?"

"No, it's okay. I shouldn't be pushing you. Just go home. You can join me another time. There'll be lots of opportunities. Go home." Sam got on her bike and began riding towards the tree. She stopped behind a group of bushes and watched to see what her brother would do.

Steuart stood frozen by the tracks. He muttered something to himself. He held onto his bike, took a deep breath and quickly walked the thing across the railroad track without saying a word. On the other side, he stopped, turned around and looked back. He put his hand to his chest and felt his heart beating. Steuart looked dazed.

Sam watched from the bushes and felt ashamed for pushing her little brother. That feeling changed when she saw the look of accomplishment on his face. She watched as he held his bike, looked around, and noticed the gorgeous field of wild flowers, the trail, the trees, and a deer. It stood in the distance and watched Steuart.

Steuart jumped onto his bike and began pedaling along the trail in the direction of the tree. Sam jumped on her bike and rode quickly so that her brother would not know she had been watching him. She rode and twisted along the trail, enveloped by tall grass and wildflowers, pedaling hard to stay ahead. Finally, Sam heard Steuart yell as he caught sight of her, "Sam, wait up."

Sam looked back and waved. Steuart and Sam continued riding along the trail until, once again, they found themselves beside the river. This time they stood together on the opposite side, their hearts filled with wonder and satisfaction looking across at the back porch of their new home. They shifted focus to the side they came to see and the colors they had followed. Looking further down the path, Sam saw what she came for.

*　*　*

"There it is. That's my tree!" Sam yelled. The tree stood high, nestled alongside another straight, tall tree, holding a little tree house. Sam and Steuart stood at the edge of the Preserve in an extraordinary backyard belonging to a beautiful home. Sam broke the silence, "Come on. Let's do this." She headed towards the tree house, threw her bike on the ground and prepared to climb the ladder.

"You can't."

"What now?" Sam, with her left foot on the bottom rung, stopped and looked at her brother.

"Pick a leaf off the ground and let's move on. This is private property."

"Why did I bring you?"

"We shouldn't be here."

"Oh, not again! Please don't tell me that you're going to start up with that."

"Find a leaf on the ground, or let's find a tree somewhere else."

"I can't do that."

Steuart backed away from the tree. "Yes, you can."

"I can't. The leaves on the ground don't have the same shades. They're already decomposing. They don't have the same vibrancy as..." Sam pointed high, "the ones up there. I need to climb the tree or climb into the tree house. I think the tree house is the better option."

Steuart shook his head, "No." He held his bicycle and prepared to make a quick dash for home.

"Look Steuart," Sam pointed towards the tree house. "It has windows. This'll be easy. I can climb the ladder, go in, and reach out the window for the perfect leaf. That's all I need. That's it." The sun glistened through the trees as Sam stood enchanted by the colors. Determined, she knew she would get the leaf. She looked matter-of-factly at Steuart and pleaded, "I'm not going to disturb anything other than the leaf."

"How can you say that?"

"Because, I can."

"You're disturbing something just by climbing the ladder—just by being here. None of this belongs to you."

Sam shook her head and looked away. "Why did I want you here? I hate these conversations."

"What conversations?"

"*These*. I hate these conversations where I'm forced to explain everything to you. You have no idea how difficult it is being the older sibling and having to look after you. You don't understand as much as you think you understand. I understand because I'm older and I'm better educated than you."

Steuart folded his arms and nodded, "Do tell."

This is not the same as going into someone's home. This is a tree house. Tree houses don't count in the world of private property."

"Have you lost your mind?"

"No. Tree houses are the same as park benches—they're here for everyone."

"I'd like to know what book you've been reading. You're confused." Sam didn't care. Steuart worried. "Have you forgotten the definition of *private property?* I don't know why you think a tree house is exempt. You know we've been through this before. Have you forgotten the last time that you went into a tree house that didn't belong to you? Do you remember what happened?

Sam gave Steuart a blank stare.

"You hear me, but you're not listening. Is that what's happening?"

"That was different. That wasn't a real tree house. We're here now. We're not there."

"Different *how?* Why do you think that rules only apply to other people? Why do you think that a tree house is any less private than other private property? If this were your tree house would you want the entire world to feel free to climb the ladder and go inside to play?" Steuart didn't stop to take a breath. "I don't think so."

Sam tried to ignore her brother and answered over his talking. "It wouldn't bother me. If I were lucky enough to have a great place like this, I would be proud to share it with other people." She gazed at the tree house and the leaves. With her backpack on her shoulder, she was ready and began climbing, "The door's open."

"So?"

"So—Grandmother said I should follow the colors. That's what I'm trying to do."

"Oh, that's classic. You want to blame this on Grandmother. Do you actually believe this is what she had in mind?

"It's possible," Sam pursed her lips and squirmed. "I'm taking her advice seriously." Sam continued to climb.

"Stop Sam. Stop right now. I'm going to tell."

Sam looked down at her brother, "Are you serious?" She stepped down.

Steuart shook his head, "This is not what Grandmother had in mind. Do you remember the last time?"

Sam glared at Steuart.

"You're not listening." Sam didn't say a word. "Go ahead, ignore me. I know about a lot of things. I know what I'm talking about. I also know that I don't have to be here with you. I can go home." Steuart turned around. "I'm not going to get into trouble for you on my first day in town."

"Go—see if I care."

Steuart took a deep breath and kept talking, "We're both aware of what happened back home. We both know that we both know you remember everything. You're just pretending to be naive."

Sam stopped. "Why do we have to talk about something that happened so long ago when we're here in this beautiful wooded place? Why can't we just be in the moment? All I want at this exact point in time is one beautiful leaf." Sam shook her head and threw her hands in the air. "You're making a big deal out of nothing. You're so exasperating."

"I am not. You're wrong. I'm talking about this because it is a big deal. I'm talking about this because the last time you did this we ended up having to explain ourselves to Mother, Grandmother *and* the neighbors. Why are you pretending that you don't have a brain? Color collection got you into big trouble."

"Have you been reading those books again? Don't worry, we're not going to be put in front of a firing squad."

Steuart looked off in the distance.

"Steuart, do you always have to put a damper on everything I try to do? Why did I invite you to come with me?"

"Because deep down you know that someone needs to keep you out of trouble."

"I don't think so."

"Yes you do, and you know it. You may be the older sibling, but I'm the one who's more responsible."

"I do a lot of things for you Steuart—all the time. I should have just come over here by myself. I should have let you miss this entire adventure. I should have let you stay on your side of the tracks with your baby chicken behavior and attitude."

"Stop calling me names. Grandmother straightened things out for you last time. She isn't here for this."

"If only you didn't make such a big deal about things. I could be home with my leaf now. I could be sitting down enjoying my newest color. Steuart, you are destroying my happy autumn moment."

"Ruining this? I'm trying to keep both of us from getting into trouble."

"Besides, if you remember what happened, you'll also remember that nobody called the police last time."

"Are you trying to say that makes it okay? Hey, I read every day," Steuart threw his index finger against his chest and puffed up.

"Old novels, yes, I know."

"So what? I know that things happen all around the world. You can learn a lot from a good book. There are always consequences to your actions. That's one of the most important things you'll learn."

Sam sighed, "Are you done yet?"

"No, I'm not. Sam, we could have been hurt. Since you know everything, tell me what either of us could have done about that? Do you remember?" Steuart tried to whisper and raise his voice at the same time. "Sam, look at this place. These people probably have a security guard. They may have an entire security force. I wouldn't be surprised if we're on camera now. Go ahead, wave and smile for the camera." Steuart paused to wave and smile. "The juvenile detention officers are on their way. Let's make it easy for them to identify us." He looked into the trees and waved, "Hi, hello, my sister and I don't want to cause trouble. We're trespassing because she would like to take one of your leaves. Please don't kill us." He put his hand down and turned to look at Sam, "We're just minutes from becoming infamous. We'll be locked up with a steady diet of dirty drinking water, cold beans and white bread."

Sam rolled her eyes. "I doubt the water's dirty."

"What's your point? We won't be able to see each other, or anyone else. Mother will sign a release for money, sell our souls to the media and write a book called *Kids Caught in the Act,* followed by a second one titled, *How My Children Embarrassed Me and Why I Can Never Forgive them.*"

Sam shook her head and laughed.

"You think that's funny? That won't be the end of things. She'll keep going with appearances and speaking engagements until she finishes up with her third blockbuster, *Adoption: I Did, You Shouldn't. Please Let Me Tell You Why.*"

"You've definitely been reading those novels. I can always tell."

Steuart reached down, picked up two yellow leaves and held them over his eyes. "We'll never be able to show our faces in public again. I'll never see my children because I'll never have a relationship outside of prison. I'll never have a family unless I hook up with some crazy woman who falls in love with bad men—a nightmare existence.

"Enough. I'm getting tired. Cut the comedy routine. You're being childish."

Steuart shook his head and dropped the leaves. "Maybe, I am. I'm only ten, but I know about these things. Sam, you may be destroying my entire life and your entire life at the same time—wrong place, right time, who knows what might happen?"

"What?"

"You'll never enter politics."

Sam cringed and then laughed. "What makes you think that I have an interest in politics? You're so silly."

"You could change your mind."

"I don't think so. Maybe *you* should go into politics."

Steuart shrugged, "Things like this can follow a person forever."

"You've got to stop reading those Tad Grey novels." Sam turned her back to the tree and leaned against the ladder. "Steuart, you're acting extra silly. Everyone knows that you're entertaining, but I'm getting bored."

"I'm not trying to be humorous." Steuart picked up two more leaves and created a new mask. "I'm serious," he laughed.

"This is not one of your comedy routines. We're losing time with all of this silliness."

"I'm not teasing. I remember. You do too."

"I think we're safe. We're not going to be arrested."

"You don't know that. All it takes is being in the wrong place at the right time. Maybe there's a dead body up there. We could be framed."

"Stop it!" Sam held up her hand and pointed her finger in the air towards the leaves. "I will concede that we shouldn't have gone into that woman's building back home. And I have no problem telling you that I will never do that again. This, however, is not the same thing. This is different." Sam sighed and shifted her feet. "Steuart, we need to get started."

"How is it different?"

"This is a tree house. That was a shed."

Steuart dropped his leaves, "We shouldn't be doing this."

"Don't you think you're overreacting this time—just an itty bitty bit?"

Steuart stared at his sister.

Sam sighed, "I'm sorry that you're feeling upset. I'm sorry that I've picked on you today. I am sorry that you're uncomfortable." She turned and faced the tree, placed both hands on the ladder and looked up at the leaves. "I have to have one of those leaves. I'll climb up, get one, and then I will leave." She turned and looked at her brother, "I have to know that you'll not say anything to Mother or Grandmother. Can I count on you? You can go home now. I won't be angry."

"I don't know. I don't feel comfortable leaving you here alone."

"I'm staying." Sam began to climb the ladder.

Steuart continued to stare. He said nothing.

Sam stopped and looked down at her brother, "You know how important my colors are to me. Do I ever stop you from getting new words? I always support the things you want to do. I never give you a hard time. I always support you, don't I?" She began to cry.

"Don't start with tears. Please, don't do it. Don't cry. I refuse to fall for that." Steuart picked up his bike. "You're not winning any points with me."

"I'm asking for help from my brother. That's all I'm doing," Sam sniffled.

"I never break and enter to get new words." Steuart straddled his bike, folded his arms and looked at his sister.

Sam turned her head and looked at Steuart who was still staring without any expression. "It's just a color," she looked up at the house, "and I doubt seriously that these people have a guard."

Steuart didn't move.

"Tell you what. I'll make a deal with you. Help me get my leaf and in exchange, I'll make your bed for the next three days."

Steuart shifted from one foot to the other. He got off the bike for a minute, changed his mind, and then got back on. "Three days?" He shifted a tiny bit more, pursed his lips, cocked his head, and looked around for watchers.

"What do you say?" Sam asked.

Steuart knew that Ida would be disappointed in the conversation. She wouldn't agree with making these kinds of bargains and would be quick to tell him so. He looked up at the tree house with a curious sort of expression and muttered something under his breath as he let out a sigh. He smiled, "Maybe we can negotiate."

"What?" Sam stepped down a rung, "I can't hear you. What did you say?"

Steuart got off his bike and lay it on the ground, "Sam, I can't let you do this by yourself. I'm your brother, your only brother. Unfortunately, we have to look at the facts. I've not forgotten what happened last time you asked for my help. I've not forgotten that Mother grounded you for an entire month. I have also not forgotten what she said."

"What was that?"

"She said you wouldn't be the only one grounded next time. She'll ground me as your accomplice. As much as I may want to help you, I also have to look at the facts."

"What facts are you talking about?"

"Quite simply, the potential risk to my freedom." Steuart put his hands in his pockets. He walked closer to the tree and looked up at the tree house. He shook his head, "No, the potential cost is too high to do this for nothing."

"Three days are not *nothing*."

"They are if I end up grounded for a month. We're in a new place. This is a new day. We're in a new city. I'm thinking that my services are worth more than a few days of bed making freedom."

Sam rolled her eyes and sighed.

"I don't want to begin my life in a new city stuck inside of the house for a month with that Nanny Claire woman." Steuart made a face, "She makes me uncomfortable. I don't care for her."

"I don't either."

"I'd vomit daily if that happened. She gives me the creeps. I couldn't stand that, even if you were making my bed. Also, Grandmother isn't here to help talk Mother out of extreme punishment. We both know that Grandmother's the only one who can curb Mother's draconian ways."

"So, you won't do it? Is that what you're saying?"

"Simply this," Steuart continued walking around the tree. "If I'm putting myself at risk, I'm going to have to insist on more than two or three days of compensation. That was fine in the old days but not enough now. I don't think so." Steuart shook his head and walked towards his bike.

"Wait!"

"What am I waiting for?"

"Tell me what you want."

"Okay," Steuart scratched his head and frowned, "tell you what…" He bit his lip and then ran his tongue across his teeth. He took another deep breath. "I'm willing to take the risk and lend a hand…"

"Yes! Thank you. Let's get started."

"Hold on," Steuart put his hands out. "Don't get excited too quickly."

"Great, what now?"

"I know this is important to you and I want to help."

"So, help me already."

"Not so fast. I would appreciate something in return. How about making my bed for the next—three weeks." Steuart nodded, stood firm and repeated his demand, "Three weeks; I think that's appropriate compensation."

"I should have known. I've spent all this time trying to appeal to your empathetic nature when all I needed was a bribe. Thanks little brother." Sam put her hands against the tree and took another look. She breathed in the colors. She felt intoxicated by the luminescence of the sun through the trees. She looked at her brother and frowned, "Three weeks? That's too long. You know that."

"Take it—or leaf it." Steuart chuckled.

"Take it," Sam whispered to herself and touched the tree again. She looked at her brother, "Okay," she nodded, "it will be my pleasure to make your bed for three weeks."

Steuart shook his head. "You need to do better than that."

"What? How can I be nicer than that?"

"I need to hear you say: *It will be my pleasure to make your bed for the next three weeks*. I don't want to spend the next sixty years waiting for payment."

"Fine," Sam nodded. "It will be my pleasure to make your bed for the next three weeks. You've got a deal. You get three weeks of bed making in exchange for helping me in the tree house and also keeping our secret."

"Okay," Steuart stepped forward. He walked towards the ladder and then hesitated. He turned back again and reached for his bike.

"Now what? Stop looking at your bike. We have a deal. I'm getting tired of standing here. Come on. There's no reason to hesitate."

"We didn't shake on it." Steuart picked up his bike and stood firm, "What about a month?"

"You've got to be kidding me. You want a month?"

"Yeah, a month. I didn't take hazard pay into consideration when I extended my offer. This is a tall tree house."

"No," Sam shook her head. "Absolutely not. No. No. No. No. No! You're too late. You asked for three weeks. I said, *yes*. Three weeks, that includes your hazard pay. Come on—let's do this thing. This is simple."

"Are you sure?"

"I'm sure-as-Matt. I don't want the color bad enough to throw in an extra week. I should withdraw my offer. We should go home. I'm done."

"What?"

"I'm serious. We can go home now if you're determined to continue this extortion. Three weeks. I'll do it for three weeks, but not a day over. Take it, or leave it. I don't care at this point."

"Of course, you do."

Sam shook her head, "No, I don't. I don't need your help. I'm seriously ready to withdraw my offer. I'll do this alone." She began climbing.

Steuart followed.

* * *

The ladder was much taller than it appeared from the ground and much taller than anything Sam or Steuart had ever attempted. After a climb of thirty-one rungs, Sam entered the tree house and walked to the window. "Oh, Steuart, look at what we've been missing." She took a deep breath and leaned out. "This is so worth everything."

Steuart looked around, "Yeah, this place is cool."

"It's beautiful," Sam clapped her hands, "beautiful, beautiful, oh, so sweet. Look at these colors, what a treat!"

"Oh, for God's sake. Are we collecting colors or writing poetry? We need to get out of here. *Snip, snip*—I said I would help you. I didn't say I'd attend a tea party."

"Oh, yeah, okay," Sam pulled her scissors from her backpack, stood at the window and looked for her perfect color. She reached to cut her leaf from the tree. Further than she estimated, Sam had to lean far, grab a large branch and pull it in close to get at the leaf she wanted. She leaned, strained, looked down and felt her stomach drop as she lost contact. "I can do this," she whispered. Again, she reached and pulled on the branch. Again, she lost contact. The branch was huge. Sam tugged and pulled. The branch was full of spring. She was about to snip her leaf when the branch suddenly pulled back. Sam strained and held tight, pulling the thing close. The branch pulled back again. Sam reached out, this time pulling harder. That's when the branch won, pulling her feet and lifting her from the floor. She was being pulled out the window. She fought to hold the branch and stay inside. Determined to win, Sam gasped for air and continued the fight.

Steuart jumped across the floor. He grabbed hold of his sister's legs and pulled back with all of his weight, continuing until Sam's feet were safely on the floor. The tree, refusing to cooperate, pulled and lifted Sam's body, this time halfway out the window. Steuart thrust his body upward using his weight against Sam's, pinning her between his body and the wall of the tree house. He wrapped one arm around Sam's waist as he held onto the windowsill with the other. "Let it go!" he screamed. He felt a splinter go into his palm. "Let the branch go! I don't know how long I can hold you!"

Sam refused to give up. She continued pulling at the tree, stretching with her arms and reaching with her scissors for the leaf. "I can do this! Don't worry!" she yelled. She eyed the leaf. She looked down at the ground. Sam's ankles were now on the windowsill. Her knees were skinned, but she didn't know.

Steuart felt his feet leave the floor and his body being pulled out the window with his sister. "Let it go, Sam!"

Crack!

The branch broke and snapped into the window as it pushed Steuart and Sam inside, pinning them against the floor. Steuart with his splintered hand lay underneath his sister, her bleeding knees and the extra large branch. He shoved Sam aside and sat up, "*Hazard pay,*" he groaned, catching his breath, "Hazard pay—above and beyond."

"Yeah," Sam breathed hard. "Okay, hazard pay, no problem."

"You could have been killed! Are you absolutely insane? We both could have been killed."

"I know," Sam whispered. She held her hand against her heart and continued trying to catch her breath. She looked at her brother, "Steuart, you saved my life."

"I could have been killed too. We both could be on the ground now with all of our bones broken—totally dead."

"I'm sorry," Sam bit her lip and began crying.

"Maybe you'll listen to me next time when I'm trying to tell you something." Steuart held his palm open and pulled out the splinter. "That was insane. I can't believe what almost happened here. You almost got us killed." He shook his head slowly, "No color is worth this much trouble—ever. I mean it."

Eventually, Sam, still holding onto her scissors, stopped crying. She sat up, leaned against the tree house wall and snipped her leaf from the branch. She held it in her hands and took several deep breaths. She closed and opened her eyes and looked for changes. Steuart shared his mini flashlight as they gingerly held the leaf, discussing the variation of shades and tones, examining the thing from side to side, top to bottom, and back to front. Sam smiled, "I wish I didn't like it so much."

"It's magnificent," Steuart said, shaking his head, "But it's not worth it."

Sam opened her backpack and pulled out the cabbage rose file. Gently, she slid the leaf inside between two pieces of soft white tissue paper. "You're right. It's not worth what it almost cost us. I'm sorry."

"It's okay."

"What a story."

"Too bad we can't tell anyone."

"It's a true treasure. It is. I think this is one of my all-time favorites."

"It should be. Imagine going to all this trouble and not getting the one you want."

"Don't even think that—please."

"I'm glad that you like it considering what could have happened." Steuart let out a big sigh. "You owe me big on this one."

"I know."

"I mean it. I'm not just talking. You owe me big."

"I know."

"Imagine someone trying to explain this to Mother: *Ms. DuBoise, your children were located below the tree house. We are very sorry ma'am. We're investigating ... it looks as if they both jumped. Have your children been unhappy lately?*"

Sam didn't respond. She put the folder away and stood with Steuart. Calm now, she looked at the ground and felt her heart race. Steuart leaned out the window. They could just barely see the river through the trees.

Sam became lost in the moment. "Wouldn't it be great if this were our tree house?"

"Only if you'd promise not to kill us."

"How stupid do you think I am?"

Steuart shook his head, looked at his sister and laughed. "*Sail your peace.*"

"Thanks," Sam frowned. "I wasn't trying to get us killed."

"I know you weren't. I couldn't resist. I'd like to have a tree house too. What would we name it?"

"Name it?"

"Yeah, like the houses back home."

"I have an idea." Sam sat down, removed a pen and a piece of cardboard from her backpack. "Close your eyes. Don't look."

"Okay."

She worked on a sign. "You can open your eyes now." She showed the cardboard to her brother.

"*Sam-Steuart.* Why did you put your name first?"

"Don't you think it sounds better that way? Sam-Steuart." Sam said it again.

"Not particularly, but it's okay." Steuart smiled. "I like it." He repeated the name, "Sam-Steuart."

They said the name together three times, "Sam-Steuart. Sam-Steuart. Sam-Steuart."

There was a quick chill in the air. They watched as the wind picked up and then settled.

"Right, okay. That's fun. I like the name, but as much as I might wish this tree house could be ours, it's not. We should go home."

Sam ignored her brother. She looked out the window again.

Steuart continued, "Can we go now? It's getting late. Maybe we'll see a deer. I saw a deer just after I crossed the tracks. Maybe we'll see a family of deer. Maybe we'll see a sweet little baby deer and her mother." Steuart stopped talking when he heard the train coming.

Sam watched and listened from the window. "That was the four o'clock..." she said, "to Chicago." She said it as if she had been living in Maybell her entire life. "Sam-Steuart," she said it again. "Too bad it's not ours."

"I wonder," Steuart wrinkled his forehead, "I wonder."

"What?"

"Wait a minute. I just thought about something. Close your eyes. I'll show you in a minute." Steuart took the cardboard from Sam, turned it over and began working with a pen before holding the sign up for his sister to read.

"Open your eyes. Look at this," Steuart showed the sign to Sam.

They read it aloud together, *"Sure-as-Matt."* The wind picked up again. "Sure-as-Matt," they repeated it. Both Sam and Steuart giggled, "Sure-as-Matt."

"I don't believe it," Sam said. "Why didn't we think of that one before?"

Steuart shrugged, "Don't know. I've never thought about anagramming our names together before you made the sign."

"I like both names," Sam leaned out the window.

"Don't go anywhere!"

The weather was rapidly changing. "Don't worry, I've learned my lesson." She turned to her brother, "You're right. It's time to go home." Sam packed up her things and started down the ladder with Steuart close behind. As they began the ride home, another train passed.

"Didn't we just hear the four o'clock to Chicago?"

Steuart made a face. "I don't know. Maybe they have two."

FIVE

Adoptive families will sometimes celebrate a *gotcha day*, marking the adoption anniversary of their child. Some families celebrate with parties. These can be similar to birthdays, including invitations, decorations, family, friends, food, entertainment, and gifts. For Steuart and Sam things were different. Their mother preferred the label, *special day*, and insisted it be treated as a private, solemn occasion.

There were rules. Olivia was strict about celebrating on the exact day of each child's anniversary. It was understood that there would be a celebration even if something happened to create scheduling confusion. There was usually a cake. There was also a gift. The occasion was always restricted to immediate family. Olivia, Sam and Steuart ate dinner alone, however, their mother always set one extra place setting for an unknown, invisible guest. Typically, the day was more odd than special, but this was what the children knew. They knew that they did not know exactly what to expect, and that was okay.

The special day was always unexpected. One year Steuart had banana pudding because Olivia had a deadline at work. Another year Olivia forgot Sam's day until late in the afternoon. She spread a tablecloth on the beach and pretended to take the children on a camping trip, complete with pineapple sandwiches and a can of fruit cocktail. Once there was a pistachio ice cream cake. Another year there was a rainbow cake with red, yellow and purple sprinkles. There was the time they had a robot shaped cake. "I thought it was too cute to pass up," Olivia said, "and the markdown was great." None of these things mattered to either of the children. They always smiled and enjoyed the time together.

Sam and Steuart learned early that although the choice was theirs, Olivia had the final word on everything. The children knew to behave. Privately, they joked that the *special* reference created an atmosphere more similar to education than occasion.

Sam looked forward to this particular special day because it was hers. She asked for a watercolor set, one with a pan of paints, a couple of brushes and a pad of watercolor paper. Although this was her third time to ask for art supplies, the possibility looked promising.

Peeping into her mother's bedroom Sam saw a box that looked like it could hold her request. It was perfectly wrapped and waiting quietly with her name written across a soft pink and white dotted gift tag. Sam was delighted and pleased, as her powers of magical thinking felt triumphant. Her dinner choice was vegetarian pizza with pineapple added. Steuart requested extra feta and pepperoni on his portion. Soft drinks were a special day treat. Sam lit the candles as the celebration began. Olivia smiled, "We're fortunate the pizza delivery man made it out tonight. The weatherman says an early winter blizzard is on the way. Are we ready to begin?"

The children nodded.

Each special day was more than a day of celebration. This was the day each year when Olivia set time aside to remind Sam and Steuart that they legally belonged to her. "Make no mistake, pay attention to what I am telling you. Legally, you are my children. You both belong to me." She then confused the issue by explaining that they were not her children. "As much as I wish I had given birth to you, I can only tell you that I did not." At ten and twelve, Sam and Steuart understood the basics, but did not fully understand the concept of adoption. One thing was clear; their family was similar to others in that overlooking daily dysfunction was a choice. This is what they knew.

Beginning with a lecture about blessings, Olivia shared the same story during every special day dinner. The children knew to pay attention, and understood their mother's need to vent. Sam and Steuart were accustomed to hearing how their mother went through many years of interviews and group meetings in preparation for their adoptions. They were also accustomed to hearing how they needed to be thankful for the opportunities she had given them.

First, Olivia talked about her least favorite home inspecting, interviewing, social worker. "To say that I did not care for that woman would be an understatement, but I did what I had to do. And you should think about this because, as *Right, Good, and Appropriate* tells us, *we are each called upon, from time to time, to do things that we find distasteful.* That's daily life, and a lesson best learned sooner than later. We are always stronger than our obstacles. Remember that."

The children nodded.

From there Olivia moved into a mini lecture outlining her personal sacrifices and including how her career suffered throughout the lengthy adoption process. "In those days a woman had to stop working for an entire year because the agency was looking for the complete devotion of a full-time mother. There would be no special day to celebrate had I continued working and taken an available promotion. I'm proud of my sacrifices." Olivia wore them like a thick, heavy overcoat.

She talked at length about the anguish of not being able to have her own biological children and about the embarrassment of having to adopt. "This is not because adoption is a bad thing," she'd explain. "I obviously believe it's quite wonderful. However, we all know that people can be both cruel, and well meaning at the same time. It becomes exhausting trying to explain to everyone that you are unable to have your own babies. I would have preferred not to tell anyone." She shook her head and ate a bite of pizza, "It's no one's business but ours. Unfortunately, you need to know the truth about these things. And, I believe it would be wrong to deceive either of you. So, in my quest to do the right thing, I have responded to, and accepted the prying questions, patronizing opinions, and ridicule of others."

Sam and Steuart listened to stories about the guilt they should feel. "It is not that you are ungrateful. It is quite simply that you do not understand the plight of a single parent. How could you?" She took a sip of iced tea and munched on her pizza. "I do not expect that you will understand. Neither of you is at fault for these things that have happened in our lives. Then again, without these things the three of us wouldn't be a family."

Olivia talked for a long while explaining "the worst humiliation of all…" she looked off in the distance, "when Grady DuBoise, my mistake of a husband, your adoptive father, ran around and left me. I do not know what more I could have done to keep our marriage intact. Truth be known, we're better off without him." She went on to suggest that Grady might not have strayed had Sam and Steuart been his biological children. She took another bite of pizza, frowned and said, "I've done well for myself and I've flourished without that…" She sipped her tea. "I've taken care of things. It's irrelevant now. What is important is for you to know that even though Grady ran from his responsibilities as a parent, a responsibility that he requested and later denied, I have not. I remain ever vigilant and committed to both of your needs as well as my parental duties and obligations."

Sam and Steuart listened to stories about their *unfortunate biological situations*. Olivia explained how she saved them from *a probable trailer-park lifestyle* and then shared the story about Steuart's biological mother, whom she described as "…some sort of odd bookworm who wore glasses all the time; a young woman obviously ignorant about the world even though she and her parents had advanced degrees."

Regarding Sam's background, Olivia had little information. "She was older," but Olivia was unaware of the woman's age. She suggested, "She might have been in trouble with the law but that is merely a hunch." In both situations, there was no mention of a birth father.

Steuart never understood how Olivia made the connection between education and trailer parks. He searched the thesaurus but never found the word *trailer* with *trash* as a synonym. Although he wanted to dispute his mother's words, Steuart understood, as did his sister, that it was unwise to challenge Olivia on this subject. It was best to sit quietly, listen attentively, and participate only when called upon.

Steuart and Sam knew how and when to comfort their mother. They did this frequently, on cue, just as they were taught. They said exactly the things she expected to hear, "Oh, Mother, how lucky we are to have been adopted by you." It was at this moment, convinced that her children were completely aware of their inadequacy as offspring, yet appreciative of her superiority and benevolence that Olivia, now in tears, rose from her chair and left the room in search of her handkerchief. Relieved, Steuart and Sam enjoyed the knowledge that their mother would be away for a while repairing her make-up.

Steuart continued to enjoy pizza while Sam prepared mentally for her new watercolors. Overcome with excitement, she looked at her brother, smiled and softly giggled, "I saw the box," she whispered. Her eyes twinkled in the candlelight.

"Did you get it?"

"Yes! I didn't hold it, but I saw it. It's the right size. I'm almost sure-as-Matt."

"Yay!" Steuart softly, but enthusiastically cheered.

Because they understood the importance of good behavior Sam and Steuart sat straight in their chairs as they patiently waited for their mother to return. Sam tried calming herself by taking deep breaths. She stiffened a bit and closed her eyes. She had a brief daydream about what she planned to do with the paints and then wondered how to mix the colors, keeping them from becoming ugly and brown. Sam hadn't painted in a long while. Before the move, she enjoyed using her grandmother's watercolors. Sam looked forward to calling Ida and discussing art."

The children continued to wait.

Sam thought about painting. She considered what she should wear as she wanted to avoid ruining her good clothes. She thought about the best places to paint. She didn't want to make a mess. She couldn't wait. What would she paint first? Suddenly, she had the perfect idea—a thank you painting for her mother. She would paint a picture of the new house, complete with the big tree in the front yard and the river in the back. "Mother will love it," she whispered softly to herself. She imagined her mother having the gift custom framed before hanging it above the sideboard in the dining room.

Olivia's bedroom door opened and then closed. She spoke with a laugh in her voice, "Here I come." She walked down the hall carrying Sam's gift, stopping first in the kitchen for another box.

One box, wrapped in multi-colored polka dot paper, the one Sam saw in her Mother's bedroom, looked beautiful tied with delicate French ribbon. Olivia placed it to the side. She laid the second, plain white, cardboard box on the table and opened one end. Holding the edges, she pulled out a single layer cake. Frosted in white, the cake delivered a message piped in pink that simply read: *Best Wishes.*

"Pretty, pretty, oh, so pretty," Sam gushed. Steuart finished his pizza and moved his plate aside.

It was time for cake and more of the talk. Olivia began, "Samantha Leigh, we all know you need to watch your calories, so I elected to forgo the ice cream this year. We need to keep temptation out of sight."

"Yes ma'am," Sam nodded. "That's okay."

"Of course it is." Olivia reached for the knife and began cutting slices. She looked at Sam and smiled. "This cake is made with artificial sweetener. Let me cut your slice first." She passed a small slice to Sam before cutting a larger slice for Steuart and an even larger slice for herself. Sam didn't care. She would have been happy with anything.

The little cake looked tasty. It was yellow flavor. Sam took a bite. Her eyes were fixed on the box with the ribbon. Olivia gently tapped on the rim of her dessert plate, "Remember Sam, we must wait until everyone finishes before opening our gift."

"*Hobo rank duels,*" Steuart whispered.

"What was that?" Olivia asked her son.

"This day is cool," Steuart said loudly with a sly smile. "I'm proud to celebrate with my lovely mother and wonderful sister on her special day."

"Steuart James, what a nice thing for you to say."

Sam ate a big bite of cake, chased it with a sip of soft drink, and swallowed quickly, "This is tasty Mother."

Olivia ate her slice slowly. This was partially because of its size, but also because she liked to talk more than eat. It was time to talk about the files. "The files can be opened. You understand what I am telling you?" Olivia repeated herself as she looked at each child.

Bored, they each nodded, but didn't say a word.

"That means the agency will allow you permission to open your files." She took a bite of cake, a sip of iced tea, and continued, "No one other than you has this right. *You* do not even have the right before you turn eighteen and there are many good reasons for that."

"What's that Mother?" Steuart asked.

Sam gave her brother a hard look and kicked him under the table.

"You need to be of sound mind, in other words, you must be old enough to understand and consider what you are seeing. When you are eighteen years of age, you will each have the option of opening your files and finding out about your biological parents, as well as where you came from…" she paused for a bite of cake and continued, "provided the information is included."

Olivia sighed, "You are the only ones who have this authority. Even your biological parents have no way of finding you. That is for your protection. It is entirely up to you…" She grabbed Sam's hand, patted it, let go, and pointed towards heaven in one smooth movement, "Of course, I will never stop you from doing what you want to do. It would be wrong of me to try to influence either one of you in this highly personal matter. Certainly, I have my own ideas, but unless you ask for my opinion, I will keep my thoughts to myself." She took another bite of cake, chewed and swallowed, "I will always love you both. I will always…" she began to tear up, "be your mother, no matter what you should choose to do, and no matter what mistakes you might make along the way. This is a highly personal decision."

Steuart and Sam exchanged glances. Their mother cleared her throat, "Let us hope that I will have taught you well by that time and that you will recognize my contributions as well as my effort. No matter how much pain or discomfort it may bring to me, or to my heart, I will support both of your choices. I realize this is a difficult conversation. I only talk about it on these special days because I am aware of how quickly time will pass. Tomorrow you will both be grown. You must be informed in order to make your best decision. As the only responsible parent in your lives, it's incumbent upon me to help with your preparation."

"Any questions?" Olivia wiped her mouth again before continuing, "There is always excitement regarding things unknown, especially when you are young. Unfortunately, the outcome is not often what we may wish it to be." She shook her head, "If you should choose to look at those files, you will have to live with the consequences of your choices while, at the same time, being mindful that these choices will not only effect you, but will also infect, sorry, I intended to say *effect*, our entire family. For that reason, I recommend that you make your choices thoughtfully and with great care."

Olivia paused, took a breath, looked at her slice of cake, and continued, "Some people feel that it's a good idea to look at the files. I'm not certain how many of those people have actual, practical knowledge or experience. It might be interesting to know. Anyway, some people believe it is a good idea because of medical reasons. I understand that this could be helpful in rare situations. You might receive lifesaving information. However, the information could also create problems for you. Please understand that I am not trying to catastrophize the situation. I just need to make sure that I present you with all sides of the issue."

Olivia paused and took a sip of tea. "We cannot change our genes. Just remember, while you may learn something that you are happy, or even grateful to know, it is also possible that there is some crazy mutant, foreign type of gene lurking around inside of your body. That's why I wonder about these things. Why would either of you want information that you may ultimately regret having." She looked first at Sam, and then at Steuart. "Do you really want to know?"

"No, ma'am," Sam and Steuart replied in unison.

"You understand," Olivia nodded, smiled and looked down at her cake. "I don't know. I am not sure how I would feel in your shoes. My mother wanted me. I am not saying this with the intention of being provocative. I'm telling you this so that you'll understand my difficulty in relating to the two of you regarding this issue. We are looking at things from different angles."

Sam and Steuart exchanged glances. Steuart yawned.

"Regardless of what I say to you or what I understand as truth, you need to consider the facts. I do. We are presented with two large cans of worms. After all, you were both given away. I hate to use a word like *tossed* because it is such an awful, tasteless word; however, the word is accurate. You were tossed away like a pair of beautiful, brand new shoes that did not quite fit."

Olivia looked at Sam. She looked at Steuart. She stopped and took a deep breath. "Please do not get me wrong. You were not unwanted by everyone. No. You were…" Olivia placed her hand across her heart, "…by me. You were wanted by me." She nodded and sniffled, "It has always been important that I have children in my life."

Steuart looked at Sam and rolled his eyes. Olivia showed no signs of stopping. "Facts are facts and I believe in being direct with both of you. There is never a good reason to sugar coat your cookies. You both have good minds and are capable of understanding what I am saying to you. At the same time, I do not want to say anything that will deter you from making a choice that is one-hundred-percent yours to make. After all, this is a decision that is ultimately up to you."

Olivia's speech became rapid, "I will tell you this," the finger went up again, "once you open a can of worms, it is next to impossible to put those slimy things back. You simply cannot do it. Even if you do, you will always know things that you didn't know before—things you may wish you had never learned." Olivia wiggled her fingers and made a sour face. "Sometimes, it's best not knowing, if you know what I mean. In some situations, not knowing is your blessing." She paused, "You're taking chances. Open that can, and you may find those slimy things crawling across your plate." Steuart and Sam rested their forks.

"Just remember that you may open a door and you may choose to close that same door, but once someone knows where you live they may try to come in through your bedroom window." Olivia cut another small slice of cake and laid it on her plate. Steuart and Sam sat quietly as their mother finished eating and then said what Sam had waited to hear the entire evening. "Samantha Leigh, would you like to open your gift now?"

Steuart exhaled.

Sam beamed, "Yes, please."

Olivia reached for the gift and handed it to her daughter. Sam smiled at Steuart. Steuart smiled at Sam. Olivia smiled at both of them.

Sam held the box for a moment. The weight felt right. "Yes," Sam whispered. She looked at her mother and smiled. She looked at Steuart. She laid the box on the table. She pulled the fabric ribbon and untied the bow. She straightened the ribbon between her fingers and laid it beside her plate.

Olivia picked up the ribbon, flattened and rolled it carefully before moving it aside. Sam picked up the scissors and moved the box close to the edge of the table. Carefully, she cut the tape at one end, making certain not to damage the paper. Delighted, almost giddy, she could never remember a time when she was more eager to unwrap a gift.

Olivia, also eager, could not contain her excitement. "I had no idea this was going to mean so much to you. I am pleased beyond expression to be giving this to you now. I only regret that I didn't do it sooner."

Sam was thrilled by her mother's happiness in giving her the paints. Overcome with love and appreciation, Sam continued cutting the tape and carefully dismantling the wrapping. She smiled as she cut. She smiled at Olivia. She smiled at Steuart. Both smiled back. She cut a little more, pulled the tape gently, and put it aside so that it would not accidentally stick to the paper. Sam smiled and continued with great care; pulling paper, smiling, looking over at her mother and softly giggling as she lifted the box from the wrapping paper. "Thank you Mother dear..." Sam opened the box, "I cannot wait to paint!"

Sam saw her mother's face at about the same moment she glimpsed the box's contents. She was not looking at a box of paints. She was looking at tissue paper.

"Paint?" Olivia looked puzzled. She reached for the wrapping paper, folded it slowly, and then placed it under the ribbon. She looked at Sam and shook her head, "No," she said quietly and turned to look at the folded paper and ribbon. "No," she softly repeated.

Sam looked down at the gift, pulled back the tissue, and stared. She was not looking at a set of watercolors and a pad of paper. There were no little brushes. There was no mixing tray. Instead, Sam was looking at white gloves and a book. She was looking at her mother's favorite book. She was looking at a pair of pristine white silk gloves and a book she knew too well—*Right, Good, and Appropriate: The Definitive Guide for All Well Meaning Gentle Beings and Perfectly Behaved People.*

Steuart and Olivia stared at Sam.

Sam felt the blood drain from her face. It was gone. Her skin became bleach white. Her body went cold. Steuart picked up his fork and looked down at the remainder of his cake. He looked over at his partially eaten pizza. The only sound in the room was Steuart swallowing a sip of soda. Olivia looked perplexed. She cleared her throat and began quickly shaking her head. Sam sat frozen in time, wholly speechless. Olivia smiled a weak smile as she pretended everything was normal. She had no idea what she had done. Steuart understood. He sat silently and waited.

Olivia spoke quickly and gently, tapping at the edge of the box with four fingers. Sam heard her mother's fingernails hit the box. Olivia's voice sounded muffled, "Look, look," she said with urgency and excitement. "This is your own personal copy, Samantha Leigh," her voice slowed, "for well-educated ladies of great privilege."

Sam frowned. She watched the room become fuzzy. It started to spin. Everything felt hot. She was sweating now.

Olivia continued talking, "This is more than other presents. There is more. Look here, I autographed this for you." Looking fishlike, Olivia leaned in towards Sam's face. She opened the book to the first page and held it up for her daughter to see. Proudly pointing towards the inscription, she said, "Look, I autographed it with the date and everything. Look, it says *In Celebration of our Special Day, November 19—Love, Your Mother, Olivia Light DuBoise.*" Olivia looked in her daughter's eyes. "You and me sweetheart; this is precious." She closed the book and pointed at the cover. "It has your monogram too—see."

Leaning back, Olivia began talking faster. "Samantha Leigh, you are a lady now. This is your life-guide. This copy is exactly like mine. It's the same edition. I could have waited until you were thirteen, or even sixteen, but I decided you are old enough now. It is time for you to have this and make a committed, daily devotion part of your life. You should begin and end each day with *Right, Good, and Appropriate*, as it will help you find your proper place in this world."

"You obviously do not realize the significance of this moment, but eventually you will reach the proper level of maturity and will rely on this for everything. We live in a world of bad taste, and bad behavior, where the good and bad must be separated. Please understand, this is something made available to those of us who are privileged. Nothing is more important than knowing who you are and how to behave as you walk through this life." Olivia looked at Steuart, "I have a copy for you too."

Sam tilted her head. She looked confused.

Olivia moved into a rant. "Samantha Leigh, it is apparent that you have forgotten something important. This is *my* special day too." She laid her finger on the book. "This is exactly what you need. More than that, this is what I want you to have. Samantha Leigh DuBoise, I am very disappointed in you. Your behavior tonight is shocking. I am only now realizing how badly you are in need of this book." Olivia took a sip of tea, "You are at the age now when you should be buying sweet gifts for your mother, not the other way around. I am the reason you are here. I am also the reason you have this wonderful life. After all, I do everything for you. Do you know how lucky you are?" Olivia paused. She poured another glass of tea, took a sip and returned to her rant. "Do not forget that as you are growing up, your dear sweet mother is growing older."

"The way you remember grandmother?" Sam asked in a whisper.

Olivia stopped. The room was silent. Sam didn't move. Steuart smiled for a moment imagining Olivia with the hungry pirates as they waited for turtle soup. Olivia sipped her tea and looked at Sam. Sam sat quietly and said nothing. Olivia stared at her daughter. Steuart thought about wrestling with Sparky. Olivia leaned in closer, huffed quietly and then spoke. "Well then, I see. I can only say that I am shocked by your incomprehensible behavior. I don't know what to think about this. Samantha Leigh, you have not even thanked me."

Steuart cocked his head. He looked at his mother. He looked at Sam. Sam frowned and clenched her teeth. She felt warm blood trickle down inside her mouth.

"Well?" Olivia waited.

Sam saw her mother's mouth move, but she didn't hear the words. Her life had suddenly ended at the age of twelve. She understood that she would never again have fun. Nothing would be the same. She looked at the book. Her hand moved across the pages as her feelings disconnected from her body. She watched her fingers. She silently mouthed the inscription, closed the book and traced the title with her fingers.

"I'm waiting Samantha Leigh," Olivia took a deep breath.

Still seated, Sam slowly lifted the book from the table and held it high above her head. Using her full range of motion she sent the thing flying across the room. The book barely missed a decorative table holding Olivia's special collection of crystal flowers and angels. It hit the wall, ricocheted across the room, and slid over the table as it raked the crystal pieces, one crashing into the other, pulling them down onto the hardwood floor before landing on top of the newly shattered glass. Sam threw the gloves across the room. She put her hands in the cake, grabbed a fistful and threw it at her mother. She ran out the door crying and shouting, "I wanted the paints!"

Steuart, up from his seat, turned to his mother and began yelling, "*Cherry Matzo!* She wanted the paints. *Cherry Matzo!* My sister wanted the paints! Why don't you care about us? My sister wanted the paints!" He put his hands in the remaining mess of cake and threw it on his mother's dress before running out of the house into the cold November night screaming "*Cherry Matzo!*"

Sam ran down the trail towards the towers, over the bridge, crossed the river, jumped down, and crossed the brook. She jumped up, leapt across the railroad tracks, and continued into the Preserve. She ran to the tree house that she and Steuart discovered on their first day in town, climbed the ladder and sat against the back corner wall. Steuart quickly joined his sister. The two sat together sobbing. The night was cold, snowy and black.

* * *

Sam and Steuart sat huddled together shivering in the darkness. "This is the worst day of my entire life," Sam cried.

Steuart sat close to his sister. "You might have picked a better night to run away. We should have grabbed our coats."

"You think I planned this? I wanted to paint tonight. I feel like such an idiot."

"I wish you hadn't run out of the house."

"You didn't have to follow me."

"Yes, I did."

"I was stupid. I should have known that she wasn't going to give me what I asked for. You tried to tell me."

"You were just hoping."

Sam continued crying, "Why did she give me that stupid book? I don't even believe it. I hate that book."

"She wants us to be grown."

"I know. She said there's one waiting for you too."

"We're in big trouble."

"I don't care. I never want to see or talk to her again."

"You're angry. You aren't serious."

"I am serious. I don't want to see her ever again—as long as I live."

Steuart shivered, "Eventually we'll have to go home."

"Not me. I don't care if I'm homeless, eating out of dumpsters, and living in ditches for the rest of my life. Anything is better than living with her. I'll live under a bridge if I have to. Go back when you get ready. I'm staying here."

A noise came from the ladder, followed by a light. Sam continued crying. She had trouble catching her breath.

"Great," Steuart reached for his sister, "I told you this would happen."

They huddled together in the corner. "You kids must be freezing." A woman carrying a lantern stepped into the tree house.

Sam and Steuart stared.

"Who are you?" the woman asked. "What are you doing out here on a night like this?"

Sam used her most sarcastic voice, "We could ask you the same thing."

"I'm wearing a coat. I'm also wearing a hat, a scarf, and gloves. You will also notice that, unlike you, I have warm fuzzy boots on my feet. The two of you are not even wearing coats. Who are you? Where did you come from?"

"We're not allowed to talk with strangers," Steuart said.

"Excuse me," the woman responded. "This is my tree house. It appears that you're the strangers." She pointed out the door and up the hill. "That's my home. This is my property."

Sam shrugged her shoulders.

"I'm Ceil Nunstern. Now we're acquainted. Are you okay?"

"We're fine." Sam said

"Do you have a bad cold? This is not a good night to be roaming around, especially if you're sick."

"I'm not sick."

"Do you live close by? I've never seen you before."

"We're okay. We just need a place to sit for a while. Is that a problem?"

"Yes, that's a problem."

"Why? We're not bothering anything. We won't be here long."

"That doesn't matter. This is a terrible place to sit during a snowstorm. The temperature is dropping fast and this place is not heated. You could get sick. We're expecting at least a foot of snow tonight. You could get frostbite. If you stay out here long enough, you could freeze to death."

Steuart grabbed his sister and whispered, "We're too young to freeze."

"It doesn't matter where we live. We're fine," Sam tried to back away from the woman, but there was nowhere to go.

"It matters to me."

"Why?" Sam and Steuart asked.

"It matters because you're in my tree house. That makes both of you a liability."

"What's the problem?" Steuart asked. "What's the liability?"

"Let's see. I am an adult and you are not. This is my house. I found you here. That makes me responsible because you're on my property. I can't just leave you here in freezing weather and pretend that I never saw you. It's late and it's not safe."

"Not safe?" Steuart asked.

The woman nodded, "That's what I said. The temperature's dropping and we're going to have a lot of snow."

"Ma'am," Steuart responded, "we don't know you."

"No," Sam repeated and shook her head. "We don't know you."

"I don't know you either. Does that mean I can't help you?"

"Yes it does. My brother told you; we're not allowed to talk with strangers."

"I see. You can't talk to strangers, but you can run into a stranger's yard and climb into a stranger's tree house late at night?"

Steuart looked at Sam and whispered into her ear, "She's got us on that one. I'm cold."

"Maybe you're dangerous," Sam said squinting and shivering.

"Why should we tell you anything?" Steuart asked. "Maybe this isn't even your tree house."

"I see." Ceil pursed her lips and took a deep breath. She shook her head and thought for a moment. "Not my tree house—maybe it's not. Maybe I just came walking out into the snow for a stroll on a freezing night during a snowstorm. Maybe I just decided to climb into a tree house that has no heat or lighting with the hope of finding children to harass me. Yeah, that makes a lot of sense."

"It's possible," Sam said.

"I don't think so."

"Maybe you walk around the Preserve late at night looking for children to murder and put into stew," Steuart said.

"You're obviously very bright and imaginative, but we still have a problem. I can't leave two runaway children alone in weather of this kind. I'm not playing."

"We're not runaways," Sam said.

"Looks like it to me. You have a choice. We can talk about why you're here. You can tell me what this is about." Ceil paused and wrinkled her forehead, "Has someone hurt you?"

"No."

"Do you need to see a doctor? Do I need to contact the police?"
Sam and Steuart shook their heads.

"Are you in danger? Do they need to come to your home?"

"No," Steuart said.

"I need you to work with me."

Sam groaned, "Why can't you just leave us alone?"

"Because I can't. We're going to have to come up with a plan. You can tell me what this is about, or, the alternative is that I can get help from emergency professionals and report that I've found two runaway children. You can work with me, or with them. It's up to you." She leaned against the wall.

"We live on the other side of the river," Sam said. "I'm Sam."

"We're sort of new here," Steuart said. "I'm Steuart."

"I see," she nodded. "It's nice to meet you Sam and Steuart. Now that we're friends let's walk up to my house and continue this discussion where it's warm. I don't know how the two of you are able to sit here without proper clothing."

Sam and Steuart were miserable but refused to go to Ceil's house. Instead, they quickly told her everything. They told her about the day, about the book, about the watercolors, about the tantrum and about visiting the tree house on their first day in town.

"I'm sorry you've had such a bad day," Ceil said. "Your mother must be terribly worried about both of you. The only way to straighten things out is for you to go home and make them right."

"No," Sam shook her head and raised her voice, "I'm never going home again."

"Are you certain? That's a long time."

"You don't understand. You don't know our mother. You have no idea what it'll be like for us at home."

"Do we need to have someone go with you to your home? I've already told you, I can call for help."

"No!" Sam insisted.

Ceil sighed, "You know where you don't want to go. Do you know where you want to be? We need to come up with an answer."

Sam was silent. Steuart was too. Ceil offered to drive them home. "We're not allowed in cars with strangers," Sam said.

"We know our way home," Steuart insisted. "We can walk. It's close."

Sam agreed, "It's very close."

"Okay, I understand. But, It's time for you to go home. Your mother must be worried sick."

"You can't say that," Sam insisted. "You don't know her."

"What do I need to know?"

"She worries about herself, that's all," Steuart said.

"She has rules," Sam said, "According to Mother and her *Right, Good, and Appropriate* handbook, children…"

"Must obediently follow the rules," Steuart said.

"*That's* the book you were given?" Ceil asked. "I know that book."

"That's the book." Sam continued, "Children may participate and talk. They must not talk very often. Children speak when spoken to and they must ask permission if they want to speak in company. Badly behaved children are punished."

Steuart shook his head vigorously, "It's not pretty."

"Rules, rules, rules. Children are allowed to laugh," Sam pretended a weak laugh.

"But not laugh too often, or too loudly," Steuart added.

"Children may occasionally eat sweets," Sam continued as her teeth chattered.

"Infrequently," Steuart finished.

"Children can be creative," Sam.

"Only within boundaries," Steuart.

"Children cannot be pampered, for fear that they will become hopeless emotional cripples."

"Who knows exactly how much is too much in these situations?" Ceil asked.

"That, of course, is the adult who is in charge, the adult who is reading and interpreting the book," Sam looked at her brother as he nodded.

"There are definite restrictions regarding everything," Steuart added. "There are rules for when you get up, when you go to bed, what you say, how you think, where you go, what you wear, what you don't wear, what you eat, what you don't eat, with whom you choose to spend your time, and there are rules for what you ultimately become."

"It sounds as if you've got that down," Ceil looked out the door. "The snow is really coming down."

"There are even rules about when and where you can go to a bathroom," Steuart said.

"We're giving you the tip of the iceberg," Sam looked at Steuart.

"She's right."

"Your mother has rules. I get it. Some of them sound sensible, some others maybe not so much. It's not my place to say, but you're going to find that life is filled with rules. And as you get older you'll learn which rules apply…"

"We're supposed to follow *all* of the rules," Steuart said. "If we don't follow all the rules bad things will happen for eternity."

Ceil shrugged, "We don't have time for that discussion tonight. Right now we have to address your immediate situation. The issue is that you are underage. Unless you are being abused, you must go home."

"I hate this," Sam insisted.

"There's nothing more I can do. We're not talking about a rule. We're talking about the law. All homes have rules. You'll find some are stricter than others. You may not like them, but going home to household rules is better than staying out in the cold and freezing, unless there is something you're not telling me. Are you certain that you're not in danger? If you are, I can get help."

"No," Sam was cold and annoyed.

"Are you sure?" Ceil asked. "Should I come to your house? Would you like for me to talk with your mother? You need to make up your mind. We have to go somewhere. It's getting colder out here. What do you want me to do? Please make a decision."

Sam was embarrassed and began crying again. "I wanted the paints."

"I understand that you're disappointed. Unfortunately, that doesn't change the fact that you're going to have to go home and face your mother."

"When I grow up I'm going to banish the word *unfortunately* from my life, forever."

"In a perfect world that would be a good thing."

"I've asked three times. I think repeatedly refusing my request is abusive."

"Not giving you what you wanted as a gift on a special occasion does not fall under the category of child abuse. If there's a reason that you shouldn't go home, I can get help for you. Otherwise, you need to go home and straighten things out with your mom. I don't know your mother, but my guess is that sooner is probably the better choice in this instance." Ceil looked at the children and waited for a response. Neither of them said a word.

"Come on, it's time to go home. I don't know how you can stand it out here without a proper coat. I'm freezing."

Sam leaned next to her brother, "I hate being twelve."

Ceil shrugged her shoulders and shook her head, "You're allowed to be the age that you are." Neither child moved. "You're welcome to come back and visit my tree house another time. It's been a long time since this place had visitors."

"Thank you," Sam said quietly. Steuart nodded.

"It's a wonderful place for a twelve-year-old and a ten-year-old too, but only in the right weather. This is not a good time."

"How do you know I'm ten?" Steuart asked.

"Lucky guess. Come up to the house and say hello if I'm here. Right now—you have to go. Can I walk with you?" Ceil stood with her lantern, held out her hand and reached down to help.

"We know the way," Sam said. She looked at Steuart and shrugged, "I don't know what else to do."

Steuart looked at Ceil and nodded, "We'll go now."

"Let me share my lantern. Here, let's step down. Be careful. Watch for ice."

Ceil looked at Sam, "I'm sorry that your day was a disappointment. Better days are ahead."

"I don't want to go," Sam said.

"I understand that, but you have to. This tree house is closed for tonight."

Sam and Steuart thanked Ceil for the lantern and began walking home. Ceil followed behind in the distance.

SIX

The following week Sam and Steuart sat on either side of their mother in the office of Harry Klesel, M.D. for an initial consultation and evaluation. "I need you to help repair my children," Olivia explained, "because they—along with ten of my favorite crystal pieces—are broken."

The doctor listened. Steuart and Sam sat quietly; afraid, embarrassed and humiliated as their mother went on about their intolerable actions. Sam looked at her feet and wiggled her toes. She avoided making eye contact. Looking at the doctor's colorful rug she wondered, *Can he read my mind?*

Steuart spent his time counting books and playing word games in his head. He thought of a list of anagrams using the word *psychiatrist*. His favorites were: *this tipsy car, chair typists, thirsty aspic, spits charity, city harpists* and *sir, it's patchy*.

"*Rat physicist*," Steuart said aloud.

"What was that?" Dr. Klesel looked at Steuart.

"Nothing. I'm sorry sir. I was just…." Steuart's voice trailed off to a whisper.

The children tried ignoring the situation. Unfortunately, neither of their activities drowned out the sound of their mother's voice.

Wound up and angry, Olivia cried. Dr. Klesel looked at Steuart and pointed to a box of tissues. Steuart reached for the box and handed it to his mother. She took a tissue, wiped her tears and then handed the box to her son. He placed it on the table.

"Dr. Klesel, my children are badly broken. They are sitting here like two little angels who have never done a single thing wrong in their short lives, but you're not seeing their true personalities."

"Broken is a strong word."

"You're not seeing them."

"What am I seeing?"

"I am a good mother. That's why we're here … because you need to repair the situation. I am hoping and praying that you can do this. I am at a loss…"

"Meaning?"

"I waited a long time for Samantha Leigh and Steuart James to arrive. We were on the waiting list with Family Charities for over five years before Samantha Leigh—two more for Steuart James. The only reason we got him when we did is because the people next in line had a big legal issue and had to drop off. I have made these children the center of my world since before they were mine."

Dr. Klesel held a brown clipboard and made notes. He nodded as Olivia continued. "These children have been given the absolute best of everything. They have been given every advantage."

"Specifically?"

"It would be easier to tell you what they don't have."

"What's that?"

"They don't have a pony. Other than that, they pretty much have everything else. I provided them with the most beautiful nurseries in Atchison Point. Everything matched perfectly. I provided them with the best toys and educational supplies. I've kept them healthy. I've kept them clean. I've kept them safe. I've kept them perfectly groomed at all times." Olivia nodded, "Good grooming is paramount. These advantages, quite simply, have been given to them because I have seen to everything and I have done this as a single parent. Most importantly, I have always made sure that they behave properly."

The doctor nodded.

"Everything was considered carefully. We gave them solid, substantial names. We wanted them to have a good start. Steuart James was named after my great-great-grandfather Congressman James Lewis Steuart. Samantha Leigh was named after my great aunt, the first female bank president in our state."

"Strong names."

"Exactly." Olivia took a deep breath before continuing. "When Samantha Leigh and Steuart James were little, I made all of their clothing by hand. If a single stitch was not perfect, even on the underside, I ripped it out and began again. Do you have any idea how much time it takes to create a French hand-sewn garment?"

"I can't say that I do."

"I'm not talking about throwing something together the way most people do when they sew. What I am talking about is the delicate precision of hand sewing the finest garments using only the highest quality fabrics, threads, and trims. All of this work, and now we are here. It's embarrassing." Olivia sobbed, "Can you teach them how to act properly?"

"How are children supposed to act?"

"They're supposed to behave and follow the rules. How difficult is that?"

Dr. Klesel raised an eyebrow and continued to make notes.

"I had no way of knowing when we adopted Samantha Leigh and Steuart James that the three of us would be deserted before Steuart's second birthday. I was young. I had no idea that I would find myself a single mother trying to raise them on my own." Again, Olivia cried. Steuart reached for the tissue box and handed it to his mother. She took a tissue, wiped her tears and handed Steuart the box. He placed it on the table.

"This is not easy." She looked at each child, and then paused for a moment before starting again, "Especially when you have rescued children from…" Olivia cleared her throat, took a deep breath, looked away and continued talking as if her children were not in the room. She whispered, "…especially when you have rescued them from God only knows what." She cleared her throat, smiled and looked nervously at Steuart. She took a deep breath, frowned and looked at Sam.

"I cannot believe the way these two have been behaving since we moved to Maybell. I know little about their true backgrounds if you understand what I mean." Olivia raised her left eyebrow and frowned again. She shook her head and continued in a deliberate voice before breaking into sobs. "I should have known better. This is not what I planned. This is certainly not what I expected. I'd like to know why these things always happen to me?"

"What things?" the doctor asked.

Olivia shook her head in distress. Dr. Klesel looked at the tissues. Steuart reached for the box and handed it to his mother. She took a tissue, wiped her tears and once again returned it to her son. He placed the box on the table.

"There is nothing I can do about biology," Olivia said.

"Do you believe...?"

Olivia interrupted, "I do the best I can in all situations. Believe me, I've done absolutely nothing wrong here."

"Is someone suggesting that you're done something wrong?"

"Of course not, why do you ask that? You hear me, but it appears that you're not listening. I'm more than a good parent. I'm a great parent, but that doesn't matter. No matter what I do, or how hard I try, this is what I end up with." She turned, looked at both of the children and then back at Dr. Klesel. She spelled the word in a soft, but distinctive whisper, "b-r-o-k-e-n. Do you understand?"

"Please try to be less provocative."

Olivia nodded.

"What do you want me to understand?"

"Fill in the blank, repair, I said."

Dr. Klesel looked puzzled.

"Beyond fill in the blank," Olivia threw her hands in the air. "How can I tell you if you won't allow me to tell you? This is frustrating."

"What?" Steuart asked.

"Quiet Steuart. It's Mother's turn to talk." Olivia let out a sigh, opened her arms and nodded, "See?"

Dr. Klesel made notes. He looked up at Olivia.

"I asked for them. I am responsible. I wanted children. I did. They're my responsibility and I do not take my responsibilities lightly. No. I'm not ready to give up—yet." Once more, she turned left, and then right, this time looking at each of the children sternly before turning back to the doctor. "Something has to be done." She put her elbows on her knees and her head in her hands. "Can you help me? Samantha Leigh and Steuart James are completely out of control." Olivia cried. Steuart reached for the tissue box. He handed it to his mother. She took a tissue and wiped her eyes. She handed the box to Steuart who, this time, decided to hold the box ready.

Looking over the top of his glasses Dr. Klesel asked, "Ms. DuBoise, what are you looking for me to do for you?"

Steuart had a sudden vision of his mother jumping up and going for the doctor's neck, ripping him from his chair, throwing him against the floor and screaming loud enough to crack the windows throughout the building.

Instead, Olivia raised her voice, "I keep telling you—fix my children. F-i-x. Are you not listening?"

"I'm listening."

Steuart handed Olivia the tissue box. She took a tissue and wiped her tears. She handed the box to Steuart. This time he refused. She handed the box to Sam. Sam held the box ready.

The room became quiet. Dr. Klesel looked at Olivia. He leaned forward, looked at the children and nodded. "I think this would be a good time for me to take a few private minutes with Sam and Steuart."

"No," Olivia responded. "Absolutely not," she shook her head. "I disagree. It's too early. This is our first session. I'm not comfortable with that idea."

Dr. Klesel nodded and leaned back in his chair. He looked at the children and asked each of them a question. Neither Sam, nor Steuart found an opportunity to speak as their mother monopolized the appointment. She talked, she whined and she cried. She told the story about the white gloves and the handbook. She talked about Steuart's behavior on the day of the move. She talked about Sam's unacceptable behavior on her special day and about how Steuart joined the mutiny. Tears flowed. Sam handed Olivia the tissue box. She took a tissue and handed the box to her daughter. Sam refused. Olivia held the box and whined, "This is what I go through daily with my children. I cannot even depend on them for something as simple as a facial tissue."

"They're children," the doctor responded. "This is more than a tissue issue."

Olivia put her head in her hands repeatedly; her elbows on either side of the tissue box and asked several more times, "Why do these things always happen to me?"

Dr. Klesel said little. He watched and he listened. Sam and Steuart looked both bored and depressed. Then, something magical happened. Dr. Klesel leaned forward again. "I'd like to schedule private sessions with Sam and Steuart twice a week. Also, I believe it would be beneficial to schedule them back-to-back. This will allow for shared sessions when we feel the need."

"Did you actually say what I think you just said?" Olivia asked.

"I did."

"Without me?"

"That's how it's done."

"*What?*" Olivia shouted. "This is ridiculous. Who do you think is paying your bill? How can I help my children if you'll not allow me to participate in their appointments?"

"Ms. DuBoise, you're asking for my help. In order for therapy to work, the children need to be seen privately. They need an opportunity to share their feelings openly without fear of repercussion. That means I will not be reporting what is shared in our sessions."

Olivia held her head in her hands once more, "I don't believe this. I came here for your help, and this is what I'm getting? What kind of physician are you?"

"The best."

The room was quiet. Olivia sat with her head in her hands. Steuart and Sam smiled at the doctor.

"Ms. DuBoise, if you're not comfortable I can refer you to another physician."

Olivia sat silently before speaking in a softer voice, "No—you'll do."

Steuart leaned back, looked at Sam, and winked. Sam smiled, unintentionally catching the doctor's eye. Something felt right. For once, Sam felt safe. Steuart did too.

"Why can't I be with my children for their appointments?"

"Sam and Steuart must have a place to come where they're able to speak openly and freely about the things that are on their minds."

"How can you help my children if I have no idea what they're telling you? This makes me uncomfortable. I should be aware of what's being discussed."

"Ms. DuBoise, do you want my help? Do you want me to treat your children?"

"Yes."

"Are you certain?"

"I think so."

"In addition to Sam and Steuart's sessions, I would like to see you."

"That's not necessary. There's nothing wrong with me. My children need your help."

Dr. Klesel looked at Olivia, "Behavioral problems in families are often symptomatic of deeper problems within the family. The best results happen when parents are well trained."

"I beg your pardon. I am not a dog. I do not need to be trained, nor do I need anyone to teach me how to be a good mother."

"We need to stop for today and arrange for next week." Dr. Klesel scheduled two back-to-back sessions for each of the children.

Olivia nodded.

"It'll take a few weeks before we can find a regular appointment slot. Until then, we can go week to week. Olivia reluctantly agreed to see Dr. Klesel twice a month under the guise of "parental updates."

The family stood to leave and told the doctor good-bye. Before walking out of the office, Sam handed her mother a tissue. Olivia threw it into the trash.

* * *

Dr. Klesel's office was located in River Towers, a group of two residential high-rise buildings on the north side of the river; about one-quarter of a mile from the DuBoise's new home. He had a view of the Preserve, the Maybell Hospital and the downtown Maybell skyline. From his office, there were great sunsets and breathtaking views of the Saugahatchee River. His office was a comfortable place for the children to visit. In a short time, they felt safe, relaxed, and looked forward to their appointments, which were beginning to feel more like visits than therapy.

At home one day while playing with anagrams, Steuart became excited. "This is a good one," he said. "Sam, I like this. Look at Dr. Klesel. He's a shark yeller."

"What's that?" Sam asked. "What's a shark yeller?"

"Well," Steuart began, "It could mean that he sees the sharks and he knows how to keep them away." Steuart waited for Sam's response while she looked at the anagram.

"Like a light house?"

"Yeah, that's it. Exactly, that's what I was thinking too." Steuart rolled his eyes, and leaned forward with a laugh. "Harry Klesel is a shark yeller."

"Do you think he knows?" Sam asked.

"Maybe. I don't know."

Deciding to give the doctor a gift, Steuart and Sam spent hours working on an art piece. Using pencils, markers, cutouts from old catalogs, stickers, crayons and a bit of glitter too, they worked for hours. They stitched on the paper with a needle and thread, glued beads and shells, and added photos of themselves with cryptic clues in the margins of the artwork. The piece became more of a collage than a drawing. Satisfied with their work, Sam loosely rolled the picture, and tied it with repurposed gold ribbon found in her mother's gift-wrap closet. Steuart held his finger on the knot as Sam finished making the bow.

"What a fun surprise," Sam said. "This was a great idea."

SEVEN

On good weather days, Steuart and Sam rode their bikes to see the doctor. They enjoyed having appointments one behind the other and enjoyed that his office was close to their house.

A kind man who listened and talked easily with the children, Dr. Klesel was tall and thin. He had curly gray hair, and wore dark framed glasses. His voice was soft and deep. Sam, Steuart and Dr. Klesel quickly became friends. Often, instead of sitting on the sofa, the three of them sat on the big rug in the middle of the room and played games. Dr. Klesel had a variety of interesting games and seemed to enjoy them as much as the children. One day when they were together as a group, Steuart shared their surprise. "Sam and I have something for you."

Dr. Klesel untied the ribbon, unrolled the picture and spread it on the floor. "What is this? Did you make this wonderful artwork?"

Sam pretended to be the doctor. "What does it look like to you?"

"Well, let me see," Dr. Klesel bent down and analyzed the artwork with a brass lizard-tail magnifying glass. "I see your initials. You both made it, so we know this is your work of art." He paused, and looked at the children. "I think I'd like to hear your interpretations."

"We were hoping you'd play along," Steuart said. "We want to know what you think about it. What comes to mind?"

"Okay, I'll try. Please remember, this is your creation. What matters the most is what you think." Dr. Klesel started to say something and then he stopped, "I can't help it," he laughed. "What comes to mind is that I'd like to know what this means to you."

"Okay," Steuart pursed his lips and looked at the doctor before letting out a deep sigh. "If you insist—we call it *Shark Yeller.*"

"It's you," Sam added.

"I'm a *shark yeller*? What's a shark yeller?"

"It's not a realistic portrait of you," Sam explained. "It's our interpretation. Think about it Dr. Klesel." Sam looked at Steuart, "Should we play the question game, or should we just explain?"

"He's not so young and our sessions don't last that long. I think he needs our help."

"Okay," Sam nodded, "Shark Yeller is the anagram for Harry Klesel."

"I had no idea."

"Steuart found it."

"I did," Steuart nodded. "We liked it and decided to make this for you as a surprise."

Dr. Klesel cocked his head and smiled as he looked at the picture. He pointed and asked questions. "Shark Yeller, I don't understand. What makes me a Shark Yeller? That's me?"

"Yes," Steuart answered.

"Okay, but where am I? Am I hiding someplace? I see two children, but I don't see myself."

"No, you're not hiding," Steuart blurted. "You need to look harder. You're the lighthouse with the face at the top. You're holding the big red bullhorn. See the initials S.Y.?"

Dr. Klesel nodded and listened.

"We're the kids in the boat," Sam added.

"That's a small boat. What can you tell me about the boat?"

"Sam and I are in the boat together," Steuart explained. "See the sharks in the water?"

"I do. I see a large number of sharks out there." Dr. Klesel studied the art piece. "The water looks rough and choppy to me." He stopped for a moment before pointing to a shark wearing pearls. It was jumping towards the boat. "I'm curious about this big shark, the one lunging so close to your boat; the one on the giant wave, wearing bright pink lipstick."

Sam and Steuart ignored the question.

"The sharks," Sam explained, "the sharks are the danger all around us. You're like a lighthouse. You're helping us see the sharks in the water. You're helping us stay away from the danger." She waved her arms around as if she were rocking a boat. Steuart stood up and joined his sister.

Dr. Klesel stood. He joined the children rocking, and then wrinkled his forehead. "Are you in danger?"

Sam and Steuart became quiet.

"Is there something you want me to know? That water looks very rough."

Steuart sighed, "You understand these things." He walked across the room and looked out the window.

Dr. Klesel turned to Sam, "Would you like to explain?"

"You understand. There's nothing to explain." Sam joined her brother at the window. "We just wanted to give you a gift. Do you like it?"

"Very much. Thank you."

Steuart walked back towards the sofa, "Let's not spend our entire visit talking about your picture. It's just a gift. In a minute you'll say *Sam, Steuart, our time is up for today.*" He looked at his sister, "I think we should talk about the colors and the words."

Sam agreed. She joined Steuart on the sofa and sat comfortably. Dr. Klesel stayed on the floor, leaning back against his chair. "What did you have in mind?" he asked.

"May I go first?" Sam asked.

"Sure."

"The colors call me. It's a kind of magic. Only nothing has happened lately."

"What do you think about that?"

"I don't know."

"If you did know, what might it be?"

"It makes me feel sad. The colors had more magic on Atchison Bay. It's not the same here."

"What kind of magic?"

"Grandmother helped. She said that the colors led me to important things and that I should pay attention to them for that reason."

"You miss your grandmother?"

"You know the answer to that question. I miss her very, very, very, very, very, very much. I miss her every morning. I miss her every day. I miss her more often than I don't miss her. I always miss my Grandmother."

Steuart joined in, "Me too. I miss her too. She helped Sam with colors. She helped me with my words."

"In what way?"

"Grandmother taught us to pay attention to words and names. *Look at the words, look for anagrams, you'll find hidden messages and meanings*, she said."

Dr. Klesel listened.

"She said *they'll take you places*."

"What did she mean?"

"I'm not sure," Steuart became quiet as his thoughts drifted to sitting on the pier and looking out over the bay. He remembered being home with Ida.

"What'd she say about it?" Dr. Klesel asked.

"She said the anagrams would show me things if I wanted to see them."

"Yep," Sam said, "just like she said the colors would lead me. They're puzzles."

Steuart nodded, "We enjoy puzzles."

"Grandmother likes for us to figure things out."

"I see."

Steuart looked at the doctor, "Grandmother says that we all need to find our own way."

Dr. Klesel, Sam and Steuart sat quietly for a few minutes. The doctor looked at the children. "I was thinking," he said before standing up and excusing himself. He went into an adjoining room and returned with his hands behind his back. "I also have something for you."

"What is it?" Steuart asked.

"You're not the only people who can have surprises." Dr. Klesel nodded towards the door.

By this time, Sam was also standing. "What's your surprise? Is this a game?"

"No, but I believe you'll like what I have." He pulled his hands from behind his back and showed the children two dolls. At first glance, Sam felt a chill in the air, and the breath taken from her lungs. She saw Steuart hold his arms. He felt it too.

"It's the *Wayward Gifted*," Steuart whispered and reached for the dolls.

Dr. Klesel looked curiously at Steuart. "Where did you get that name?"

"Look at them," Steuart gingerly held the dolls and inspected them. "They're bright and gifted, artistic types. This one, the boy, he's a comic." Steuart's voice picked up a bit. "I can tell by looking at him."

"How do you know that?"

"Just a feeling," Steuart looked at Dr. Klesel and Sam. "He looks like a comedian. Comedians know comedians. I'm a funny guy. I can also tell because of the way he's dressed. It's his hair, the striped pants and the plaid beret. He looks like he has a good sense of humor to me." Steuart handed the female doll to Sam.

"She feels so real in my arms," Sam hugged the doll closely. "She's cuddling me." Sam hugged her again. "She's wonderful. I love the way she feels."

"What do you think?" Dr. Klesel asked.

"This one," Sam said, "this one, she's an artist, no doubt about it. She's a painter. She makes beautiful pictures."

Dr. Klesel pointed to the dolls feet. "But she's wearing ballet slippers. You don't think she's a dancer?"

"No," Sam shook her head, "that's not a problem."

"No? Are you certain?"

"An artist might wear a beautiful pair of ballet slippers like these to a gallery opening, or even a street fair."

"That makes delightful sense to me," Dr. Klesel stood with the children as they held the dolls and looked at them. "I need to let you know that these dolls are unusual."

"They're wonderful," Sam added.

"I wonder why you call them *wayward."* Dr. Klesel looked at Steuart.

"Wayward ... they're whimsical, unpredictable and perhaps a bit rebellious or irreverent. They're not bad. It's mostly because they're from another place ... a different world ... sort of like Sam and me."

"Steuart, I'm consistently impressed with your vocabulary."

"Thanks SY. I enjoy finding new words."

"Can we take them home?" Sam asked.

"Yes, you may. Just remember that you're responsible for their care. I don't share my dolls with many people."

"Can we bring them to our appointments?" Steuart asked.

"Yes," Dr. Klesel nodded, "Steuart, tell me more about your words."

"There isn't much to tell. It's something grandmother taught me once I was old enough to read. When I find a word, hear a word, or see a word that I like, I collect it here." Steuart pointed to his valise.

"Nice antique. I wondered what that was for."

"It belonged to my great-grandfather, Matt."

"I've noticed that you always have it with you. What's your process?"

"Process?"

"Do you carry a dictionary or a thesaurus? Do you research when you first hear the word?"

"No."

"No? Why not?"

"For the same reason that Sam doesn't carry a color wheel."

"Why's that?" Dr. Klesel turned to Sam.

"Boring."

"Really?"

"Yes, we like to investigate and figure things out on our own. It's fun." Sam looked at Steuart, "I think our time's up for today. We need to get going." She looked at Dr. Klesel, "We can talk more about these things at our next appointment."

"Also," Steuart continued talking, "when I find an anagram I know that it's a word I have in my vocabulary. By doing that I'm always interested in learning new words."

Sam yawned.

"Do you ever look things up?" the doctor asked.

"Eventually, but I like to wait until I've taken a little time to see if I can figure it out on my own. Then I check to see if I'm right or not."

"Interesting."

"Dr. Klesel, thank you for sharing your dolls with us." Sam reached out to give him a hug, but changed her mind and stepped back. "Please don't throw out any of your magazines before we see you again. There's a color on one of the pages that I'd like to have if that's alright with you."

Dr. Klesel looked both pleased and puzzled, "Sam, I want to hear more about your colors when you come back. We can look at the magazine together."

Sam and Steuart walked towards the door.

Steuart stopped, "Thanks Shark Yeller. Thanks for the doll." He nodded in an appreciative manner and then grew concerned. He stood close to the doctor. "I need to be absolutely sure about something—before we go home."

"About the dolls? What's your concern?"

"About the dolls. He..." Steuart looked away, and then back, "...this one is okay for a boy, isn't he? You get my meaning?"

"Yes, why wouldn't he be?"

"My mother, you know, she thinks that boys shouldn't have dolls."

"Oh," Dr. Klesel stopped for a moment before kneeling down to Steuart's eye level. "Steuart, you're doing good work. This guy is part of that work. He's okay. He'd be okay even if he wasn't part of our therapy."

Steuart looked at the doll and smiled, "Just wanted to be sure about this. Mother may give me a bit of a time about having a doll."

"I see."

"I like this guy."

"I'm glad you do. You and your sister are doing great work."

"I'm doing work. This guy's part of my work."

Dr. Klesel patted Steuart on the shoulder. He looked at Sam. "Thank you both for the lovely picture. I'll see you on Thursday."

EIGHT

At first sight, Olivia quashed her children's excitement over the dolls. The expression on her face told them what they already knew. "We do not need these things in our house. They are going back to Dr. Klesel tomorrow."

"What's wrong with them?" Sam asked.

"They look like *wayward trash*."

"Don't say that."

"Sometimes the truth is painful."

Sam and Steuart stood silently holding the dolls as they listened to Olivia's rant. "I'm serious, they look like garbage. There is nothing *gifted* about these ugly things. Why would you even come up with such a silly name? Wayward, maybe, but gifted—I don't think so. They belong in the trash."

"I think they're beautiful," Sam said.

"Because you don't know any better. If you read your handbook you would know that these are not acceptable." Sam winced as her mother spoke, "*Right, Good, and Appropriate* states that *while toys are appropriate for children, they are inappropriate for others*. Dolls, even the highest quality dolls are ridiculous at your ages, unless you are a collector. Even then I would prefer that you collect something more interesting than a doll. What the hell was that man thinking?"

Steuart and Sam quietly listened. They waited for their mother to take the dolls away. She reached for Sam's doll, shook her with both hands and then carelessly threw her against the sofa back. "Stupid damned doll."

"Mother, why are you using that language?" Sam asked.

"There is a time and there is a place for everything. However, there is never a time or place for you to correct your mother. I cannot understand why that man would give you dolls like these, especially you Steuart. Boys do not need to be playing with dolls. It could lead to things that are best left ignored. I don't want to raise you to play with dolls. Do you understand me? At this rate you'll be in therapy for the rest of your life." Olivia walked into the kitchen with the children following behind. "Maybe that's his plan. It's not going to work."

Steuart reached for his doll. "Dr. Klesel says this is therapy. He says I'm doing good work. The dolls are part of my work. He said there is nothing wrong with dolls—even for boys."

Olivia opened the refrigerator, took out a bottle of wine and reached for the corkscrew. "Dr. Klesel and I are going to have a talk."

"And you wonder why we need therapy?" Sam muttered under her breath.

"What was that?" Olivia poured a glass of wine.

"Nothing, Mother. I need to do my homework."

* * *

The following afternoon Steuart stayed with Nanny Claire while Sam and the dolls accompanied Olivia to see Dr. Klesel.

Olivia talked nonstop, "Dr. Klesel, I'm returning your dolls. I strongly believe it is my place, not yours, to decide what types of toys come into my home. Samantha Leigh is too old for these things. It makes no sense to give her a doll, but I find the situation with Steuart absolutely distressing. What possessed you to do this? What exactly are you trying to do to my son?"

Sam, too embarrassed to look at the doctor, fantasized that the floor would open wide enough to swallow and carry her down a long tunnel leading home to Point Taken. Then she fantasized that the same floor would swallow and carry her mother off to the Galapagos.

"Are you okay?" Dr. Klesel asked Sam.

"Yes," Sam nodded and walked to the window while her mother ranted about the dolls.

Dr. Klesel listened and remained calm. "What's the problem Olivia? Why don't you want the children to have the dolls?"

"You are the problem. Dolls are the problem. Why are you giving my children toys? Why aren't you prescribing medication for my children? How are dolls going to fix their problems? What type of psychiatrist are you?" Her words grew sharper and louder. "What have I hired you for? Was I not direct enough when we came here on the first day? How did you ever get through medical school? My children are broken. They do not need toys."

"That's enough. You're being abusive."

"*Abusive?* You are not doing a thing to help my children. You cannot even have this conversation with me. You're completely unemotional."

"Strong and bitter words indicate a weak argument. When you decide to settle down we can talk."

"What type of psychiatrist are you?"

"What are you afraid of?"

Olivia stopped. Sam moved closer to the window and held her breath as she waited for her mother to annihilate Dr. Klesel. She prepared for a tirade so awful that not only would he throw them out of his office, refusing further service, he would also call for security backup. They would be escorted from the building and thrown into the snow.

"We're not having this conversation," Olivia said softly.

"Why are you afraid of the dolls?" Dr. Klesel pressed.

"That's ridiculous. I'm not afraid of toys."

"If not the dolls, what?"

* * *

Sam didn't understand why her mother decided to allow the dolls, but she was thankful for her decision. Upon returning home, Olivia laid out the rules. "For reasons that are beyond me, your psychiatrist feels strongly that you need to have these things that he has given to you. I've decided to allow them because he feels that they are going to help you in some way. However, I want to make myself absolutely clear so that there are no misunderstandings. I do not want to see those nasty, ugly pieces of trash—ever. Am I making myself clear?"

Steuart and Sam nodded.

"I'll keep her in the closet or under my bed," Sam said.

"I don't care where you keep them as long as I never have to see them. I do not understand why he insists on wasting my time and precious money with toys."

"Mother," Sam said, "I thought insurance and Grandmother were paying for our sessions. What exactly are you afraid of?"

Olivia slapped her hand against the kitchen counter and screamed. "I'll find plenty for you to be afraid of if I ever hear you speak to me in that tone again. How dare you. You do not know enough to understand what you are saying. For that reason, and that reason only, I am letting you off the hook. If that man does not do something to fix your behavior soon, I may be forced to find a psychiatrist who knows what he's doing—one who'll allow you stay in a special hospital for badly behaved children. Now, go to your rooms."

NINE

Steuart couldn't sleep. He was awake, hungry and bored. Remembering a chocolate bar on Sam's dresser, he tiptoed quietly from his room into the bathroom and on into his sister's room. Illuminated by a tiny night-light that was partially hidden beneath her desk, and a sliver of moonlight peeking in through an uncovered windowpane, Sam's room was dark. In the middle of the night, everything looked just a little purple.

Steuart found Sam lying face down, across the bed, and on the top of her comforter. She didn't move. He noticed a slipper on her left foot. The right one lay on the floor by the side of the bed. Sam's head dangled so far down that she looked to Steuart as if she might roll off the bed at any moment and do a somersault. Her hair flipped over her head and covered the carpet. The dust ruffle, pinned up under Sam's body, allowed her to peer underneath at her doll. Sam's face was completely obscured, not only by the mass of hair, but also because of the darkness. Steuart couldn't tell if his sister was awake, or if she'd fallen asleep in that position.

Quietly, he moved closer, stood for a moment, and stared. His sister didn't move. Steuart cleared his throat. She didn't move. He coughed a little. She remained lifeless. Then he walked around to the foot of the bed and coughed once more. Still no reaction, he thought about how Sam would be cranky and unwilling to share if he woke her from a sound sleep. He wanted her attention, but not at the expense of a bite of chocolate.

Steuart put his index finger against his forehead and then opened and looked at his palm. He devised a plan. He caught a glimpse of himself in the mirror, and smiled. He extended both arms and closed his eyes. He turned around three times and began walking. Steuart walked forward and then sideways; he walked forward, sideways again, and around in a circle. He walked two steps back, sideways two steps, and forward once more before bumping against Sam's chest of drawers.

He walked backwards two steps, continuing his game until he finally backed into the foot of Sam's bed, tripped and fell onto her mattress. Steuart landed next to his sister.

"Ouch! What are you doing Steuart?"

"Oh, oh, where am I?" Steuart yawned.

"You're in my room. What are you up to?" Sam shook her brother's arm.

Steuart opened his eyes slowly and yawned again, "Sorry, I must've been sleepwalking again."

"Sleepwalking—*again?* You're kidding me—right? When did this start?"

He continued to yawn. "It's just something I do from time to time. It's occasional."

"What are you talking about—time to time? Occasional? What are you up to?"

Steuart ignored Sam's questions. "This time I was dreaming. I was dreaming. I found myself in here."

"Dreaming?"

"Dreaming," Steuart nodded. "I was dreaming about being hungry. I had a dream about something to drink. No, that's not it. I was dreaming about getting something to eat."

"What was it?"

"Vegetables, no, not vegetables." Steuart sighed, and looked at his sister. "It's vague. Dreams are so hard to remember."

"You should go back to bed now. I need to sleep."

"No, wait..."

"What was it?"

"It was brown."

"What?"

"Chocolate!"

"Chocolate?"

"Yes, it's coming back to me. I was dreaming about chocolate." Steuart yawned.

"Shh," Sam looked under the bed. "I think I hear something."

"Mouse?"

"Don't say that!"

"Shh, don't be so loud, you'll wake Mother." Steuart jumped up, walked to the doorway, put his head into the hall and listened as his mother snored softly. Looking back at Sam, he teased, "Or upset a mouse?"

"Don't do that. Stop it! Do not say mouse. That's not what it sounds like."

"How do you know what a mouse sounds like? Have you ever heard a mouse in the house?" Steuart was wide-awake, and in a mood to tease.

> Mouse in the house
> A house mouse
>
> Houses have *mouses*
> Well, houses have mice
>
> Mice can be nice
> But there's always a price
>
> What is the price
> A mouse might have lice
>
> Throw dice
> Or be very nice
>
> If you have a cat
> He'll make your mouse scat
>
> Does this make sense
> Or make you feel tense
>
> Sorry dear Sam
> You don't give a...

"Steuart, please hush." Sam put her fingers into her ears. "You're acting like a child."

"Acting like a child? Sam, I am—I am a child. Surely you realize that I'm little more than one year past fifty-percent of becoming an adult. I'm supposed to sound childish. You should be having fun too. You're only sixty-six percent there."

"This is not fun."

"Now you're sounding like Mother."

"Fighting words Steuart, say that again and I will not-so-kindly ask you to leave my room. I'm going to tell Dr. Klesel what you said."

"You're right. That was unkind of me." Steuart stopped. He bowed his head briefly. "I apologize. However, you must remember that I'm a boy. Besides that, I'm your brother—not your friend."

"I don't think it was a mouse. Please don't tease me. I don't like the thought of anything unwanted in my room, or anywhere else in the house. Being ten doesn't excuse you or give you the right to be mean to me."

"No? Being twelve doesn't give you the right to boss me around."

"You know better."

"Okay, but I'm hungry. Do you have anything?"

"What?"

"To eat." He looked towards the hall. "You know a lot of kids like mice, some keep them as pets."

"Stop it," Sam pushed Steuart's shoulder. "Right now. We both know that I have a chocolate bar."

"Will you share?" Steuart added extra sweetness to his voice. "Please, please, please," he put his hands together in a prayerful motion, "cherry on the top and all of that stuff."

"If I share my chocolate will you hush and go back to your room? I have a history test in the morning."

"Who's being mean now? Can't you hear my stomach growling?"

Sam rolled her eyes.

Steuart looked towards Sam's closet, "If there's a mouse in here..."

"Okay, okay, okay—*okay*, go ahead and help yourself. It's in that drawer." Sam pointed to her nightstand.

Steuart reached to take out the chocolate bar. Sam turned over and began looking under the bed at various items. Just as she reached for the artist doll a wee voice said, "Please, I'd like a small bite too."

Sam dropped the doll onto the carpet and bolted upright. "Steuart! Don't do that!"

"Do what?" Steuart had the chocolate bar halfway to his mouth.

Sam looked at her brother, "How'd you do that?" She looked around the room and asked again, "How did you do that?"

"I didn't do anything."

"Down here, please. I've not eaten all day."

Sam looked at Steuart. Steuart looked at Sam. They looked at the doll. "What's happening here? Sam asked.

Sam and Steuart sat looking at one another in the darkness. They looked at the bedroom door. They looked at the bathroom door, the closet door and the bedroom window.

The voice spoke again, "What are you doing? All I did was ask for a bite of chocolate. It's not as if I could eat the entire bar."

Sam looked at the doll, "No," she whispered, "dolls do not talk." She walked to her closet, opened the door and came out with a box. She walked to her bed and looked underneath at the doll.

"Chocolate? Share? Please? Hello? Are you deaf?" the doll asked. "I know you speak English. I've heard you. I'm starving."

Sam picked up the doll, put it into the box, and closed the lid. The doll yelled and kicked as Sam shook with fear. She looked at Steuart and laid the box on the bed.

Steuart set the chocolate bar on the nightstand and ran out on tiptoe leaving Sam alone with the talking box.

Sam's heart raced. She jumped under the covers, turned tummy first onto the mattress and moved down so that the covers were over her head. She locked them tightly under her body and shook with fear. She felt the box roll over. The top came off and hit the floor. The doll came out and sat on Sam's bedspread. Sam continued to hide. "Sam," the doll said, "we need to talk."

"I must be the sleepwalker," Sam whispered to herself.

* * *

Eventually, Steuart returned to his sister's room. Wide-awake, Sam was calmer, but still afraid, and still hiding. "Don't be scared. It's okay," Steuart said. "I promise. It's okay."

"No, it is not okay," she whispered and pulled the covers tighter. "I'm scared. Go get Mother."

"I will not," Steuart whispered. "Mother will make us get rid of the dolls. She can't know about this."

"I don't care. We should get rid of them. I'm scared. I think I'm going to scream."

"Don't scream. Please don't scream. Listen Sam," Steuart sat on his sister's bed.

"Steuart, I'm going to scream!"

"No! You owe me. Remember the tree house? You cannot scream. Listen to me."

Sam lay silently under her covers.

"I took my doll out from the closet. I had a feeling that everything was okay. I knew there was something magical about the Wayward Gifted. Sam, they're magical because they're alive. You don't have to be frightened. They won't hurt us. They're like you and me—just smaller. Come out Sam. Come on." Steuart tried pulling the covers away from his sister. Sam continued to struggle. Steuart pulled at the covers and accidentally pushed Sam off the bed. She landed on the floor underneath the box. She stared up at her brother. He held the boy doll.

"Steuart, What are you doing? I don't like this. We're in some sort of weird, crazy dream. Dolls cannot be alive."

"These are," Steuart grinned. "These dolls are alive. I am not teasing with you."

"No."

"They are. Sam, I'm sure-as-Matt."

Sam stared at Steuart. She glanced at his doll.

"Sam, this is my friend, the comedian, Ed Camino."

Sam watched as the doll moved, bowed from the waist, and threw her a kiss. It was magical. The doll extended his hand towards Sam and then spoke, "Hello Miss DuBoise. Steuart says that you have a bit of chocolate. Is it possible that I might have a tiny bite?"

Sam watched carefully as Ed continued, "I understand that you've already met Trista Petrina."

Sam glanced at the girl doll seated on top of her covers. Trista put her hand up and waved, "Hi Sam, I'm Trista. It's lovely to meet you." Sam's mouth hung open. "I apologize for frightening you tonight. We're alive—we're also hungry." Sam grabbed the covers and pulled so hard that Trista lost her balance and rolled away.

"Stop that!" Trista yelled. "I thought you were nice."

Again, Sam jumped in the bed and pulled at the comforter. Again, she covered herself completely. "This is a dream," she repeated to herself, "This is a dream. This is a dream. This is a dream. This is a dream. This is a dream. I don't believe this. I'm dreaming. I'm having a dream. This is a dream. I'm in a dream. No—I'm in a nightmare. This is a very bad dream."

Olivia entered Sam's room, turned on the light, and yelled, "What is going on in here?" She pointed towards her son, "Steuart go to your room—right now! I've had it with both of you. Go to sleep and put those nasty dolls away."

"Sorry Mother," Sam knew this would be better discussed with Dr. Klesel.

"Sorry Mother," Steuart walked towards his room.

Olivia turned out the lights, walked down the hall, got into her bed and then screamed, "If I come back, I'll return with my wooden spoon."

Sam lay stiffly under her covers and wondered exactly what was going on. Steuart looked at Ed. He reached down, picked Trista up and whispered, "Let's go to my room."

"But, what about the chocolate?" Ed whined.

* * *

People say that children often learn things more quickly than adults. Perhaps that's because it's okay to embrace magical thinking when we're small. As children, we're encouraged to believe in things unseen. Fairies, giant bunnies, elves and other magical creatures are known to visit, leaving gifts and trinkets as we sleep.

As children, our minds are open to *what if* and *why not*. We believe the idea that anything is possible. Perhaps this is because we live in a time when new discoveries occur daily in our lives, proving that anything can happen and quite often will. We are young enough to realize that we do not know what we do not know. We are bright enough to realize that it might be foolish to say something does not exist strictly because we've never seen it. As children, we know better. For whatever reason, children tend to accept things sooner than adults. And then, sadly, as we grow, our fears grow also. With each year, our ability to believe in things unseen becomes more fragile and fades much too soon. Eventually, we are fully-grown.

As the younger sibling, Steuart was immediately comfortable with his new knowledge of the Wayward Gifted. Sam, however, was not only skeptical, but also frightened. She came around more slowly. Her mother's comments, *my children are broken* and *they need to be repaired*, played repeatedly in her head.

The fact that Sam knew nothing about her biological family added to her troubled feelings. She wondered if something terrible could be wrong with her and with her brother. She wondered if the two of them had snapped. Did they need medication? Were they b-r-o-k-e-n? If so, what exactly did that mean? Were their actions indicative of a bizarre, childhood *folie a deux?*

Eventually, Sam came out from under the covers. She found Steuart, Trista and Ed conversing in Steuart's room. For a moment, she stood silently watching the group before turning around. She walked into the bathroom, turned on the faucet and splashed cold water across her face. She returned to

Steuart's room where nothing had changed. Steuart and the dolls sat quietly talking.

Again, Sam turned around. She walked to her room and picked up the chocolate bar, returned to Steuart's room and seated herself at the far edge of his bed. "I'm ready to talk. I brought chocolate."

"I knew I liked her," Ed smiled and held out his hand.

Olivia's voice came from the end of the hall. "Are the two of you still awake? Don't make me come in there."

At that, Steuart, Ed, Trista and Sam decided it was time to stop for the night. Ed stayed with Steuart. Trista accompanied Sam to her room where the two got under the covers. Neither girl said a word. Sam smiled at Trista and Trista smiled back. No longer afraid, the girls slept.

TEN

Olivia woke Sam and Steuart early the following morning. "What in the world were the two of you doing last night?"

Sam, half-awake, remembered the excitement. *Did it happen? Did the dolls come to life? Was it just a strange, wonderful dream?*

Her mother's voice brought Sam back to the moment. "You are not allowed to keep me awake like that. I'll be a zombie all day because I didn't get a fraction of my required sleep. And now, I'm running late. There will be consequences."

Nanny Claire arrived as Olivia left for work. Sam listened as the garage door closed.

Steuart walked into his sister's room, "Can you believe it?"

"No, I thought it was a dream."

Steuart shook his head, "That wasn't a dream. That was definitely not a dream."

Sam brushed her teeth and combed her hair. "I have to think about my history test."

Nanny Claire shouted from the kitchen, "You'll miss your bus if you don't get moving,"

Sam put her comb away and looked at her brother, "We'll figure these things out when we get home."

* * *

Steuart and Sam did not care for Nanny Claire. The feeling appeared to be mutual. The woman was happy to see the children leave for school and less than thrilled upon their afternoon arrival home. Claire preferred reading mysteries in privacy and quiet. "I dislike interruptions," she'd say, "Your mother tells me that you're accustomed to amusing yourselves. That's a good thing." The upside to Claire's disinterest was how easy it became for Sam and Steuart to get out of the house. After a snack, with the dolls in their backpacks, Sam and Steuart asked permission to go out to play.

Hiking to the tree house, Steuart asked his sister, "Do you think she was always so large, or do you think it's because she's an Éclair?"

Sam giggled. "That's not a nice thing to say. Maybe she can't help it."

"It's a perfect anagram. Maybe I'd feel differently if she were nice."

"Maybe. You're probably right. Let's keep her around—she doesn't care what we do."

After climbing to the top of the tree house, Steuart and Sam carefully pulled the dolls from their backpacks and seated them on the floor. They readied for a frank and sincere discussion.

"Hi," Steuart said. "We're sorry that we couldn't spend the day with you, but we had to go to school."

The dolls said nothing.

"Don't be angry," Sam said. "We didn't have a choice."

The dolls didn't move.

"Why aren't they talking?" Steuart looked at Sam.

"I don't know."

Steuart tapped Ed on the shoulder, "Hey, Ed, it's okay, you can talk now."

Ed did nothing.

"Was it a dream?" Sam asked.

"How can two people be in the same dream?" Steuart shook his head. "I don't think that's possible?"

"How can dolls talk? Is that possible?" Sam turned to Trista, "Hi Trista. How are you today?" Trista did nothing. Sam turned and looked at her brother, "This is not good."

"They were alive last night. I know they were."

"They're just dolls. They're not alive. It was some wild, absurd, unbelievable, strange, dream."

"Is that what you think?"

"Yes," Sam nodded, "I do. Maybe it was something we ate."

"We didn't eat the same things." Steuart spoke to the dolls again. "Hello. Ed, Trista, come on guys, let's talk."

Sam shook her head. "I don't know what happened, but something caused you and me to have the same dream."

"I don't believe that."

"I've heard this sort of thing happening when people eat rabbit."

"We've never eaten rabbit."

"I'd rather think that we're having terrible dreams than think that we've lost our minds."

"We're not nuts."

"Mother says that we're broken."

"Mother says a lot of things."

"Maybe she's right. Maybe she sees something we're missing. Maybe we are mad." Sam stared at the dolls.

"We don't act like we're crazy."

"What do you think this is? We both think that we had a conversation last night with two inanimate objects."

Sam and Steuart sat in silence looking at one another.

Steuart frowned. "Do you believe we're broken? Is that what you think? Are you listening to Mother now?"

"We're seeing a shrink. That's not a good sign."

"We're seeing a shrink because Mother has this obsessive thing about perfection. It's not us."

"I don't know."

Steuart sighed. *"Raw Eye Czar."*

"What?"

"Are we crazy?"

"Could be," Sam frowned.

"No," Steuart shook his head, *"Tone Wary Car Zone."*

"I don't know that. How do two kids figure out what it means to be crazy? What's crazy? It's like asking what it means to be creative."

Steuart tried talking to the dolls again. They didn't move. He looked at his sister and frowned. "I don't know. I think it's something else."

Sam nodded. "We should talk with Dr. Klesel."

"Maybe." Steuart looked away, "You're probably right. I didn't eat my lunch today. I feel hungry and confused. Do you have anything?"

"Help yourself," Sam reached into her backpack for the remainder of last night's candy bar. She handed it to Steuart. "You can have it."

"Are you sure?"

"I don't want it. I'm not hungry."

Steuart unwrapped the bar. "Chocolate makes everything better."

"Finally..." Ed jumped up and laughed. "They're speaking our language!" He looked at Steuart, "Can we have a bite too?"

"What?" The children were shocked.

"Practical joke! Ha! Ha! Good one, huh? How'd you like it?"

Trista stood, looked at Sam, and shook her head. "It was his idea—not mine. He's in charge. I didn't think it was funny. Seriously, I tried to talk him out of it."

"What's going on?" Steuart asked. "Why would you do that?"

Sam looked at Ed. "You're not funny."

"That was mean," Steuart said.

Ed continued laughing, "Get over yourselves. It was just a little joke, that's all. Why is everyone always so serious around here?"

Sam looked at Ed, "That wasn't nice. You should be ashamed of yourself for scaring us like that."

"Come on kid," Ed pointed to Steuart. "Look at your size. Now look at me. Look at Trista. Who do you think should be afraid here?"

"We're not afraid. That's not the point. We don't like being teased." Sam looked at Steuart, "I don't believe this."

"Oh, for God's sake. Get over it already." Ed continued laughing.

"You shouldn't play jokes on friends," Steuart said. "It's a terrible way to behave."

"Oh, come on," Ed chuckled, "We have to get our thrills where we can find them. Now, please, share some chocolate."

"You think I should share with you?" Steuart asked. "Why?"

"Because you're a nice person." Ed smiled, "Look at the bright side—you're not nuts. Would you rather we become quiet again?"

"I'll share the chocolate," Sam said, "but if we're going to be friends you're not allowed to do that again. Also, we need answers."

Steuart nodded, "She's right. Where did you come from? Are you space aliens? Are you from another planet? Does Dr. Klesel know?"

"Okay," Ed began. He took a deep breath and exhaled slowly. "No more dead doll games."

"Where did you come from?" Steuart persisted.

Ed took a piece of chocolate, bit down, chewed, and swallowed. "I love chocolate. We don't have it at home."

"Where did you come from?" Steuart asked again.

"I'm not sure how to describe us." Ed reached for the chocolate bar.

"Just tell us," Steuart said, handing Ed another bite of chocolate.

"We are—from another place."

Steuart rolled his eyes. "Oh, that's great. Why not tell us something obvious."

"Where?" Sam asked.

"In some ways it's a lot closer than you think."

"Does Dr. Klesel know who you are?"

"I'm not allowed to answer that question."

"You're being vague," Steuart argued. "I'd appreciate answers."

Sam stared at her brother, "Steuart, we're talking with dolls."

"Yeah, we are, and they're talking with us too. We're not crazy."

Steuart turned from Sam to Ed, "Are you dangerous aliens?"

"No."

"What can you tell us?" Sam asked.

Ed reached for the chocolate bar, "Just a small bite this time."

Steuart broke off a small chunk of chocolate and handed it to Ed, who bit and chewed as he spoke. "Look here's the thing. We can travel from where we live to where you are. We use dolls as placeholders. Yes, we're aliens, but not in your traditional, dangerous, weird, *we're going to cook you and eat your for dinner*, fictional sense. If we wanted to hurt you, we could have done that days ago."

Sam gasped.

"It's okay," Trista said. "We're harmless."

Ed looked at Sam, "Don't worry. We haven't hurt you. You can stop being afraid."

"What about Dr. Klesel?" Sam asked.

"I don't know."

Sam folded her arms, "Keep talking."

"Yes, keep talking," Steuart nodded.

"It's not an exact science."

"What?" Sam asked.

"If you don't remember anything else that I tell you, remember that this is not an exact science. It's one of the rules."

"What rules?" Steuart asked.

"The rules of comedy."

"Now I'm really confused."

"The rules of comedy. They apply to everything we do. One, know your audience; two, timing is everything; three, it's not an exact science."

"Are you serious?" Sam asked.

"Very serious," Ed nodded. "Always remember the rules."

"Why are you here?" Sam asked. "Are you looking for something? Are you here to take something back to your planet?"

"Right," Ed smirked. He looked at Trista, "She's cute." He looked back at Sam and shook his head, "No. We're not here to deplete your resources."

"Then why are you here?"

"If you had the means, would you travel to other places?"

"Yeah," Steuart nodded. "Definitely."

"There's your answer," Ed reached for more chocolate. "I never tire of this stuff." He tried to give a piece to Trista.

"I don't really like sweets."

"Scary," Ed said.

"How does it work?" Steuart asked. "Tell me how you travel."

"It's complicated. I'll give you the simple part for now."

Sam and Steuart nodded and listened.

"I'm here at this moment, but I have a doll back home. My doll acts as a place holder when I'm here."

"What?"

"Just listen for a bit. When I go home, my doll and I switch places."

"How do you do that?"

"It's sort of like going to an airport or a bus station. We travel from portal to portal."

"How does that happen?"

"The doll acts as my placeholder."

"I don't understand," Sam said.

"Don't worry. It takes a while to put it all together. It's a straightforward travel situation—most of the time."

"Most of the time?"

"Yeah," Ed took a deep breath. He scratched his head. "Portal to portal. That's the way it generally goes. Easy, simple, and you're there."

"That's it?" Steuart asked.

Ed took a deep breath, "Most of the time. However, there are occasionally odd situations. For instance, my doll and I can end up in the same place and sometimes if that happens, the only way that I can travel is to make certain that the doll is with me, in my possession, at the time of transport. When we do that, only one of us will actually travel. The tricky part about that is not knowing which one of us is going to transport and which will stay behind. It's not a big deal in most situations, but if you can avoid it, it's best to make sure that you and your doll are at opposite sites. It can be messy if I'm in a hurry."

"Huh?"

"He's right," Trista said.

Ed looked at Trista, "Things usually go smoothly. I'm here now, but my doll is somewhere else. When I decide to travel I go to a transport station and we switch."

"Is it dangerous?" Sam asked.

"I wouldn't say it's dangerous, but it's not without risks."

"Such as?" Steuart asked.

"Such as what happens if a doll becomes lost or damaged."

Trista grimaced.

"Yikes," Sam took a deep breath.

"It's okay," Ed reached for more chocolate. "I'm giving you worst case scenarios first. We're talking about things that almost never happen. I've only known of a few people who've had a bad experience and every one of them eventually made it home."

Sam and Steuart stared at Ed.

"I've never lost a traveler."

"This sounds silly to me. Can you prove any of this?" Sam asked. "Can everyone travel?"

"Sometimes I can prove it, but not always." Ed shook his head. "No, everyone does not have a doll. Only a percentage of the populations travel."

"I want to do it!" Steuart said.

"No," Sam snapped.

"Why not?"

Sam looked at Ed, "What do you mean by *populations?*"

"You're getting ahead of me. Let's take one thing at a time."

Sam thought for a moment, "I might try it, but I'd have to know a lot more before I did anything."

"Okay. We can tell you a little more." Ed took a deep breath and became serious. "But, before we can go any further we need to talk business. Let's talk about our needs. You're going to have to do something for us."

"Needs?" Trista questioned Ed.

"Shh!"

Steuart looked at Sam, "Needs?"

"My brother and I are just kids. I don't know how we can help you."

"We have needs," Ed insisted.

"Ed, did you hear Sam? We're kids. Older people call us children. We're *future* adults."

"So?"

"That means our resources are limited."

"Yeah, yeah, I heard. I heard you. You don't need a lot of money. You need a brain." Ed nodded, "We need cigar boxes."

"What?" Steuart asked.

"Cigar boxes."

"Our mother doesn't smoke. What do you need cigar boxes for?"

"That doesn't matter. You need to find them. We need two—one for Trista and one for *moi*."

Trista gave Ed a puzzled glance. "Cigar boxes?"

"Shh," Ed looked at Trista before turning to Sam and Steuart. "Some things are personal. We need older boxes. I can't deal with the smell of cigars. The brand doesn't matter." Ed scratched his head and frowned. "Is this going to be a problem for you?" He looked from Steuart to Sam and then again at Steuart, "We can always talk with someone else."

"It's going to be a challenge," Sam said.

"I don't know. I don't know," Steuart repeated. "I don't know if we can find cigar boxes. I don't think I've ever even seen one."

Ed let out a sigh and stood to leave. "I see. The two of you want me to teach you about the magnificent wonders of travel from one universe to another, but you're going to whine like little babies about the difficulties of locating something as small and insignificant as a cigar box?" Ed paced the floor. He shrugged his shoulders, "If you can't find a cigar box, I'm going to have to question whether or not you have the right personality for this kind of adventure. Maybe this is a—mistake."

"No," Sam insisted.

"I think it's time for you to take us back to Dr. Klesel." Ed looked at Trista, "It's time to stop wasting their time—and ours. Obviously the good doctor made a mistake. We weren't intended to visit with these two. Let's go now. I'll call a cat." Ed snapped his fingers and began calling, "Here kitty, kitty, kitty, kitty."

Steuart turned to his sister, "Do you think we can locate the boxes?"

"We can try."

Steuart turned to Ed, "Okay, we'll get your boxes."

"Are you sure? Because it's okay if you can't do this—we can all shake hands and say good-bye now—no hard feelings."

"We'll find them," Sam said, "sure-as-Matt."

"Is that code for something?"

Steuart smiled and nodded, "It's a family thing. Don't worry, we'll get your boxes."

"Good—tomorrow?"

Steuart nodded, "Tomorrow."

Ed clapped his hands together, "That's great. Well then, that's it for today."

"It?" Sam asked.

"There's no reason for us to continue until you have the boxes."

Trista stood and walked towards Ed. "Aren't you are being a little tough on the kids?"

"Who's in charge here?" Ed snapped.

Trista bit her lip and threw her hands into the air. "Sorry kids. This is new to me too." She shook her head and sat down.

"Don't worry Trista. It's okay," Sam insisted. "We like a challenge. We'll get them tomorrow."

"So," Steuart looked at Ed, "Where are you from?"

Ed shook his head, and put his hands in his pockets, "Sorry pal, boxes first, answers second. I think it's time for us to call it a day."

ELEVEN

The following morning, with Trista in Sam's backpack and Ed inside of Steuart's, the children set out on their bikes for an appointment with Dr. Klesel. Once at the doctor's office, Sam and Steuart sat on the floor and leaned back against the sofa. They removed the dolls from their backpacks and placed them on the couch as they watched for the doctor's reaction.

"Well, what do you think of the dolls?" Dr. Klesel asked.

"Magic," Sam said.

"Yes, authentic magic." Steuart agreed.

"What does that mean?"

"It means they're a lot of fun," Steuart said.

Sam nodded, "We like them."

"A great deal," Steuart said.

"Yes, we do," Sam smiled. "A great deal."

Dr. Klesel sat quietly and wrote on his clipboard before looking up. "What do you like about them?"

"We like everything," Sam said.

"Exactly," Steuart agreed. "Everything."

The three sat quietly for a few minutes. Sam reached over and held Trista in her hands. "Trista's a good friend." Sam looked at Dr. Klesel and asked, "Is there anything you'd like to tell us about the dolls?"

"What would you like to know?"

"Maybe you should tell us," Sam said.

Sam and Steuart watched the doctor closely. He gave no indication of understanding the question.

* * *

Leaving Dr. Klesel's office, Sam and Steuart were two children on a mission. With everyone in place, the team hopped on their bikes and started pedaling as they began the trek towards downtown.

Heavily bundled, wearing down winter coats, matching wool hats and bicycle helmets, Sam and Steuart stayed warm in the below freezing temperature. Their boots were bright, shiny and new. Sam's were fire engine red while Steuart's were a dark glossy black. Their hats, gloves and scarves were colorful and thick, all perfectly hand-made by their mother.

A cloudless sky allowed the sun to reflect harshly against the day's fresh accumulation of snow. With Steuart leading the way, he and Sam biked onto the bridge and noticed the river, now mostly covered by winter. Across the river, three huge snowmen stood happily, each one wearing a black top hat and scarf. This was a day most children wished for, especially two little southerners experiencing their first winter in cold temperatures. Neither Sam nor Steuart realized how bitter cold the winter day actually was.

They continued biking along the path and through the Preserve before turning to move onwards towards the hospital. They followed the western circle onto the hospital grounds, pedaled up the hill and around the sharp curve by The Women's and Children's Center where construction continued night and day on a new building.

Not far from the Emergency Room entrance, but far enough to be officially off hospital property, a group of smokers huddled together under a bus stop shelter. One member of the group stood as if at a cocktail party, holding an IV pole in one hand and a cigarette in the other. The patient's hospital gown hung inches below a bright plaid car coat. Large white bandages covered most of her head. An emergency helicopter, just yards away, hovered low as it prepared to land.

The children rode alongside the dental school, next to the student art gallery, through the dormitory quadrangle, and beside the engineering school before crossing in front of the North Union building and finding themselves in downtown Maybell on day two of the annual ice festival. A large banner hanging across Main Street proclaimed: *Maybell Winter Ice Festival—35 Years—Coolest in Town.*

The children raced to see who would make it to their destination first, stopping only once for a small group of protesters. Signs carried by the group implied they were upset because of a recent campus policy regarding red meat and a drum group. Once the protesters crossed Main Street, Steuart noticed Sam's attention still focused on the crowd. He surprised his sister by taking off quickly and increasing his lead. Sam tried to catch up, and at one point, was close enough to see Ed climbing out from Steuart's backpack. Ed stood on Steuart's shoulder and began waving to Sam and Trista. His long red and black scarf trailed in the air.

Steuart hit a bump. Ed lost his balance and began to slide down and across Steuart's shoulder. Ed caught himself by thrusting his arms up and under Steuart's hat and then hanging onto Steuart's earmuff. Sam and Trista watched in horror. Sam called out to her brother, her voice drowned by the sound of construction workers and ice carvers. "Slow down! Ed's falling!"

Sam raced to catch up with her brother. Steuart, determined to win the race, pedaled harder. Ed hung onto Steuart's ear with both hands—his legs dangled in the air as he worked to regain his balance. Trista peered from Sam's coat, "I don't believe he's doing this!"

Again, Ed pulled his feet up and jumped on top of Steuart's shoulder. Maintaining his balance by holding onto the back of Steuart's hat, Ed swung his legs out, pulled his body up, and sat on top of Steuart's head. He waved at Sam who prayed aloud, "Dear God, don't let him fall!"

Trista watched from inside Sam's coat, "This is insane."

Steuart pedaled harder and faster along the winter path, still unaware of what was taking place. He was so heavily bundled that he didn't feel or hear a thing. Sam's heart pounded. Her breathing became labored.

Most of the bicycle trail was shoveled and clear, but black ice caused both Steuart and Sam to slide first on the right side and then on the left, both of them almost falling more than a few times. Again, Ed jumped up and stood on top of Steuart's head. Steadying his balance, Ed looked like a surfer riding a wave that was Steuart's helmet.

Steuart hit another bump. Sam gasped. Trista screamed. Ed lost his balance and tumbled, this time free-falling through the air, sucked dangerously close to Steuart's racing spokes. Ed grabbed onto the bottom side of Steuart's wire basket, which sat just above his back wheel. Holding on with both hands, he worked to pull himself up into the basket. Steuart's speed made this impossible. To passersby, Ed looked like a small windsock whipping about on a blustery day.

Thin sheets of ice continually forced Sam to lower her speed. She continued efforts to catch her brother while remaining aware of the need to protect Trista and herself. She pedaled extra hard, aware she could go down at any moment. Trista peeked cautiously out every now and then, looking up and around before ducking back into Sam's jacket.

The race was close with Ed and Steuart finishing first. Steuart stopped his bike at a downtown corner next to a polar bear ice sculpture. Trista and Sam were a close second. The group locked their bikes in front of an ice cream parlor where they stopped to watch a busy artist painting a winter scene on the inside window; a snow couple enjoying an ice cream sundae.

Ed laughed. He bragged to the group. "Wasn't that the most amazing shoulder walking, head surfing, basket racing, acrobatics act that you've ever witnessed? Impressive, huh? Have you ever seen anything so exciting?"

Sam looked at Ed and then doubled over as she tried to catch her breath. "Yeah, right, that was one amazing shoulder walking routine." She coughed and stood. She moved directly in front of Ed's face. "I don't think so. What I saw was a scared little man who had a series of close calls."

"You don't have to yell," Ed whispered.

Sam turned to her brother and yelled, "What's wrong with you? Ed's your responsibility. You don't know how close things were back there. You couldn't see what we saw. Ed could have been killed!"

"What'd I do?" Steuart asked. "What are you talking about?"

Sam reached into her coat and helped Trista out. "What's your opinion?"

Trista placed her hand over her heart and took a deep breath, "I'm just a student. I came here to check out the light and find inspiration for my art. If you don't mind, I'd appreciate going home in one piece. Do you think that's possible?"

Walking around the corner, the group arrived at the East End, an historic part of downtown Maybell. This area, only recently rediscovered, housed a number of new restaurants and boutiques. Tucked in among these were a few of the original stores. It was time to think about business.

* * *

The first store on the corner was Ivy's, a place long ago known as the finest antique store in the city. Now more flea market than antique, Ivy's stood as a memory of something that once was. Faded wallpaper, dusty chandeliers and velvet oil paintings of old movie stars hung high above moth-eaten mink coats, and yellowed, tea-stained silk gloves. Milk glass vases, boxes of chipped Christmas ornaments and silver plate Chihuahua ring holders sat beside tarnished menorahs, stacks of silver plate coasters, and a large bowl of curled black and white photos—all on top of an old ladies vanity—memories long ago forgotten. Empty perfume bottles, stacks of orphaned kitchen utensils, deviled egg platters, and an entire wall of ceramic cookie jars stood beside a dried out player piano. Standing tall in the corner and guarding the room was a fourteen-foot, hand-carved, wooden, Jamaican giraffe. A sign around its neck read:

>Delightful, my things
>Oh, so lovely to hold
>Break a thing
>Poor, poor you
>I'll mark it as sold

A sizable front portion of the shop held buttons and political memorabilia. This is where Steuart and Sam met her for the first time. A stench was obvious; a mixture of body odor, urine, mothballs, honey-coated bath powder and perfume. "Old person smell," Steuart whispered.

"Shh, Grandmother doesn't smell that way."

A woman came from a door at the back of the store. She was tall and thin with a drawn face that looked as if it had seen the plastic surgeon more than a few times.

"Puppet face," Steuart whispered. "She's a lot older than Grandmother."

"Hush," Sam said. "That's rude."

The woman's eyes bulged out. Neither Sam nor Steuart had ever seen lower eyelids that were such a tense and frightening red color. The woman wore multiple strands of pearls and three or four brooches; all of this on top of a heavy ultra-marine swing coat. She had a short bob that was white with streaks of yellow and long ago in need of a wash. Her hair was pinned back on the longer side with a ruby and sequined hairpin. The woman didn't see Sam. She saw Steuart. She looked his way, stopped, and then spoke.

"Oh, a little darling is visiting my shop today." She began waltzing down the center aisle towards the front of the shop on a well-worn Oriental rug. She moved smoothly, kicking up dust in her wake. Sam coughed.

Before the children were able to step back and run out the door, the woman stood over them. She bent down and scooped Steuart into her arms.

"Lady, what are you doing? Let me down," he yelled.

The woman twirled around, hugged Steuart tightly, and planted a sloppy, wet, neon-pink kiss on his right cheek. She continued dancing with

Steuart and then, in full melodious voice said, "Don't worry about me dear, I'm a kisser. I'm a kisser. I kiss all the gentlemen who enter my establishment."

Steuart's eyes bulged. He shook with fear. He struggled to get away from the woman, gasped for air, and tried to wipe her lipstick from his face. "I'm not! I'm not a kisser! I'm not! I'm not! Let me down! Let me down—now!" He turned and called out to his sister, "Sam, help me. Please!" Steuart's legs and arms flailed about as he struggled to get away.

"That's okay dear. You can calm down," the woman said. She brushed Steuart's hair away from his face. "Everything is fine. I'm a kisser and I've always been a kisser. I never fight the urge."

"Fight the urge," Steuart screamed. "Fight the urge!"

"I don't believe there's a thing that can be done about it." It was as if the woman didn't hear Steuart. "Some people say it's a problem, especially at my woman's group." She paused for a moment, looked up towards heaven and then at Steuart. She brushed his hair away from his forehead again and gave him another kiss. "I've been told that I should *air kiss,* but I can't do that. I can't help myself. Have you ever heard of anything as foolish as an air kiss? Imagine? She shook her head, frowned, and stopped to consider her words. She shook her head again, kissed Steuart, and began once more. "No, I don't think so. It's not the same. No, it's not the same at all. Did I tell you I'm a kisser?"

Sam didn't move. Instead, she stood stunned and watched helplessly while the woman gave Steuart three more big kisses and counted them aloud. "One, two, three, kiss, kiss, kiss, I just enjoy men so very much. I'm not even particular."

The woman peered at Steuart. She held his head in one hand and forced him to make eye contact. "You know I'm completely harmless, don't you? It's true." She pressed her index finger into Steuart's cheek. She smiled and spoke in a singsong voice. "Sweet little fella, if you would smile, I could see those dimples all the while. Sweet little fella, give us a smile?" The woman pouted. She dropped her voice, and then demanded, "Come on kid. Let me see those dimples."

Steuart yelled and refused, *"Evil lady!"*

The woman stopped. Her affect went flat, "...or not." It quickened as she began to giggle. "How embarrassing this is. I think I failed to introduce myself. How awful of me. How rude I've become. The name's Della Ivy," the woman's voice was now deep and rich. She cooed as she spoke, "Miss Della Ivy." That's what you may call me." She put another wet smooch on Steuart's cheek, stopped again, looked at him and asked, "What can I do for a little darling like you? What brings you into Della Ivy's today?"

"Harmless?" Steuart gulped. He looked at Sam, made a crazy face, and then went limp like an antique rag doll.

Della laughed, shook Steuart, laughed some more, and kissed him again. "Young man, you are adorable. You are beyond cute. Truly, I believe I am in love. I do." She paused, "Did I mention that I'm a kisser?"

Sam stood in one spot, "Miss Ivy?" Della was not listening. "Miss Ivy?" Sam tried again, "Miss Ivy?" Sam was invisible. She raised her voice slightly, "Miss Ivy, down here, Miss Ivy, Yoo-hoo. Miss Ivy," she demanded, "We need boxes! We're looking for boxes Miss Ivy, can you help us please?"

Steuart stared at his sister as if she should forget the boxes and rescue him. Sam tried to think of what to do. Trista squirmed inside of Sam's coat. Sam put her hand over her chest and encouraged Trista to stay still. Whispering to Trista, Sam said, "We'll get the boxes and then we'll all get out of here."

Steuart continued to struggle. He reached out with his leg and tried to kick Sam. He missed.

"Miss Ivy?" Sam tried again.

Della, now annoyed, whirled around, looked at Sam and barked, "What? What is your problem kid? What do you want?"

Stunned, Sam recoiled and began to shake.

"Did anyone teach you to wait your turn? Can you not see that I am engaged?" Della gave Steuart a kiss as he continued trying to get away.

"Let me down lady," he twisted and squirmed. He demanded, "Let me down. Let me down!" He looked over at Sam, *"Sits bits unhitch!"*

Della kissed Steuart again before speaking to Sam. Her sentences became rapid. Della spoke so quickly and fast that it was difficult to tell where one word stopped and the next began.

"Well, my dear. I didn't realize you were standing there—you two must be together. Boxes you say? What size do you need? I have many options for you to see. You want boxes. I have boxes." Della's voice dropped again. "Why would you want boxes when you can have buttons? Little girls usually like buttons." Della walked to the back of the store and then back to the front where Sam stood waiting.

Della held onto Steuart as he continued struggling and demanding, "Let me down right this minute."

Again, Della walked towards the back of the store. She turned and looked at Sam. She didn't speak, but Sam felt Della's eyes asking the question: *What's wrong with you? Don't you know what you should be doing?* "Well? Come on. What are you waiting for? Come on."

Della began showing boxes of every type, size, and price, throwing her index finger purposefully in the direction of the boxes as she pointed to them one by one. She became insistent that Sam purchase boxes filled with music scrolls from an old player piano. "These are my absolute favorites." Della began humming an old tune and continued to dance, waltzing with Steuart as he struggled to escape.

"Just look at these," Della pointed to a barrel of boxes. "The ones with the pictures are the most valuable." She danced, "One, two, three, one, two, three, you can have, fun with these." Della continued her waltz and then stopped. She looked at Sam, "These would be more fun for you. Why not buy one or more of these lovely items? Do you make art projects?"

"We need cigar boxes," Sam explained as she followed Della and Steuart throughout the store.

Sam's attention was briefly diverted to a shelf of antique eggbeaters and shoehorns. She looked directly above at an old sign advertising *Bitter Balm, a ladies nighttime remedy*. Her eyes traveled down below to a crate of signs where she noticed an advertisement for *Fresh Peach Ladies*. The paper was beautiful with flowers and leaves, but Sam was only interested in the colors. Briefly, she forgot herself and stood transfixed, aware that she wanted to add that particular peach color to her collection. Sam stood in the same spot until she noticed a pair of yellowing, white gloves.

She heard Steuart's voice, "If you don't mind, Lady, I'd like to get down now. You're cutting off my circulation. Lady, I can't breathe. My arm's asleep." Steuart went limp again like a rag doll and pretended to be dead. He opened his mouth and hung his head towards his chest. Della acted as if she didn't hear Steuart and continued to tote him around the shop, pausing occasionally to plant another kiss on his cheek.

She pointed to boxes. "Lunch box, match box, music box? I have no cigar boxes." She shook her head. "No, no, no, I have buttons. Buttons are much nicer than boxes, especially cigar boxes, although some of them have lovely graphics, that is true, but if you absolutely must have boxes you children should choose these." She pointed towards boxes holding music scrolls for player pianos. "The graphics are superior and the paper rolls are wonderful for art projects. I'm sure you realize that children need to be creative." She cocked her head. "Young lady, do you make crafts? You can do all sorts of things with music scrolls. The only thing you can do with a cigar box is clutter the damn thing with stickers and junk." Della kissed

Steuart again. "Oh, you are so irresistible, you dear, sweet little man-one-day-to-be."

This time Steuart turned his head and pretended to vomit. Trying to keep Della on topic Sam composed herself, "No, ma'am, we're only looking for cigar boxes. We need them for our dolls."

"Dolls?" Della stopped. "Dolls? *Dolls*?" She moved closer to Sam. "You have dolls? What type of dolls? I love dolls. Why didn't you tell me? Dolls are important..." her voice trailed into a whisper, "I'm not certain why." Della's voice became sharp, "What've you got kid?"

Quietly, Sam pulled Trista from her coat. "This is my doll." Trista and Sam held as still as the broken grandfather clock leaning against the far wall. Della's eyes lit up as she leaned in close for a look. For the first time since entering the shop, Della was interested in Sam.

"Little darling, little dear, oh, my darling, please come here and tell me, please…" Della moved closer, "Where did you get this doll?" Della stopped to compose herself. She lowered her voice and bent down reaching for Trista with her left hand while continuing to hold Steuart with her right arm.

Sam took a step back. Della inched closer and asked, "Where did you get this lovely treasure, so beautiful and so..." Della took a deep breath, pursed her lips and looked as if she might faint. Her skin became even whiter than white; all the while she moved closer towards Trista, reaching to take her from Sam, "Let me see her," Della demanded as Sam stepped back. "Let me see her...."

Sam and her brother were frightened. Trista was mortified. Ed was hiding. The children looked towards the door knowing they had to leave right away. Sam stepped back and held Trista close to her chest. Trista sneezed. Della reached for the doll while holding Steuart. Steuart managed to pull his arms free. Sam prepared to run but knew that she would not leave her little brother or her friends. *Pop!* The front door slammed. *Ding!* The bell on the counter pinged. A man stood at the counter. "Good morning," he said in a cheerful voice. "I was told this is the place to visit for buttons. Is the button lady here? Sapphire blue, circa 1922, I'm told that you..."

Della stood straight and whipped around to respond. Steuart pushed his elbows into Della's ribs and finally broke free. He ran from the shop. Sam immediately followed.

"Sapphire blue," Della repeated. "My dear man, you are in luck today."

* * *

Steuart ran hard, stopping at the end of the street to catch his breath. Once she caught up, Sam couldn't help staring at her brother who was covered in vulgar, garish pink. "Are you okay?" she asked.

Steuart rubbed his face across the arm of his jacket. He looked at Sam and sneered, "No thanks to you."

"I was doing my best."

"To help me get kidnapped? Why didn't you help me?"

"I was trying to help."

"That woman's crazy. She needs to be locked away. What were you thinking? Why didn't you help me?"

"I didn't know what to do. I was trying to help. I didn't know if I should grab you and run, or if I should stay and look for boxes."

"Forget the boxes—*Grab and run.*"

"Trista peeked from the front of Sam's jacket, "Don't bicker you guys. We were all scared. I thought she was going to snatch me from Sam's hands."

"I thought the same thing," Sam said.

"Grab and run. That's all you need to remember. Grab and run."

"I'm thankful she didn't grab me," Trista looked at Steuart. "I'm sorry you had to go through that, but at least you're bigger than Ed and me."

Steuart stared down the alley and whispered, "Not—big—enough."

"I was frightened too," Sam said. "Trista, did you see how she looked at you?"

"What about me?" Steuart asked.

"I was confused. I was worried about helping you. I was worried about protecting Trista. I didn't know what I'd do if she got Trista too. I've never chased after an old person before."

"She's a strange lady." Trista said. "I'm sorry that I sneezed. I thought we were done for."

"You couldn't help sneezing. The dust in that place is terrible. I think she wanted you more than she wanted Steuart.

Ed pushed open the front pocket of Steuart's backpack, and peered out. "Are we safe?"

"You're safe," Steuart said.

Climbing out, Ed walked across Steuart's shoulders, slid down his arm and then jumped into his hands. Looking up at Steuart's face, he laughed, "Whoa. That's a picture."

"Where were you?" Steuart asked. "Why didn't you help me?"

"I was doing what I'm supposed to do in a crisis situation."

"I didn't see you do anything."

"Exactly. I was hiding. There was nothing I could do." Ed pointed his finger at Trista, "You should have stayed hidden too. I'm responsible for you." He looked at Sam, "In the future, heed your brother's words—*grab and run.*"

"We were in danger Ed. You should have helped. That woman's dangerous," Steuart said.

"What would you have had me do—tell her a joke? She's such a lovely dear thing."

Sam, Steuart and Trista scowled at Ed.

"She's dangerous," Sam said.

"Dangerous," Trista agreed.

"Awe, come on girls. Lighten up. How can you talk that way about Steuart's new girlfriend?" Ed looked at Steuart and frowned before continuing, "Seriously mate, I think ruby red is a much better color for your complexion."

"That old skeleton isn't my girlfriend and I don't wear lipstick."

"Hey," Ed put his hands up. "Don't get upset with me." He put his hand across his mouth and spoke to the girls in a stage whisper. "Obviously the kid has yet to see a mirror."

"Hush," Steuart said.

Ed laughed. "There's nothing like an actual skin test. I'm not trying to hurt your delicate feelings. I just think you'd look better in red."

"Be quiet," Steuart said.

Ed continued laughing, "I think your new lady love has different ideas, huh?"

"Ed, I am not amused. *Pot sit!*"

Ed looked at Sam, "What's he saying now."

"He wants you to stop."

Ed glanced at Steuart, "Our communication might be easier if you would speak a language I can understand."

"*Mat a rue.*"

"I give up." Ed threw his hands in the air, and looked at Sam, "I think it's amusing. Perhaps you're being a little overly sensitive." He turned to the girls, "Don't you think it's amusing?"

The girls frowned.

Ed laughed again. "We know I'm right. See, ruby red is a much better color for you Stew Boy. You're blushing pal. If you weren't wearing that cap, I'm sure we'd see ruby red ears."

"Ed, stop it," Steuart raised his voice. "That's enough!"

"The ruby red doesn't go too well with that nasty hot pink."

"I said *stop it*. I'm a lot bigger than you."

"You look good in lipstick. It's not your fault that Della chose a bad shade."

Steuart tensed, "I just realized something. You're not a real comedian."

"What? Not a comedian? What do you mean?"

"You're not. You're an obnoxious little man."

"Stew Boy, Comedians are supposed to be obnoxious. So, be honest with me, how'd you like that dance?"

Ed's teasing continued until Della's voice was heard coming up the street behind her last customer. "Wait, sir. Wait! Don't leave. You've not seen my complete selection…"

Ed clung to Steuart's arm, "Quick! *Dragon Burn Awn!*"

"What?" Steuart asked. "I don't understand."

Ed screamed, "*Grab and run—now!*"

Steuart held onto Ed while Sam helped Trista move safely into her jacket pocket. The group of four ducked inside the closest shop. A sign hanging above the door read: *I.M.Felphul—Used Books and Items of Interest*.

A bell was triggered as the children entered. Other than that, the place was quiet and appeared to be empty. Sam let out a sigh of relief. She checked to see that Trista was okay.

"Fine down here. What about you Sam?"

"I'm okay."

"Let's go home," Ed whispered to Steuart.

"I thought you were doing all of this for the adventure. Where's your spirit of adventure?"

"Some adventures should never be repeated."

"I understand." Steuart smiled. "It's okay. You can apologize now."

Ed rolled his eyes and chuckled, "*Girth*."

Sam glanced around the store, "Maybe we should leave."

"Just be cautious," Trista whispered.

"See what you can find." Steuart said. "Ed and I've had more than enough excitement. We're going to stay close to the front."

"You don't think Trista and I were frightened?"

Steuart looked at his sister, and whispered, "I don't believe you were being held captive by a crazy woman with a puppet face and dinosaur lips."

"At least it doesn't smell like pee in here," Ed whispered. "I could barely breathe at Ivy's."

Sam pointed to a sign, "Look: *items of interest.* I'll ask if they have cigar boxes." She unzipped her jacket and reached in for Trista. "Ready?"

Trista gave Sam a squeeze, "Let's do this."

* * *

I.M. Felphul's bookstore was narrow and deep. Located in a cold, older building with high ceilings, exposed pipes, and vintage institutional green walls, fluorescent tube lighting buzzed and occasionally crackled overhead. Dark, heavy bookshelves stood tall guarding a community of stools and ladders that waited patiently for visitors. Worn plank floors held stacks of books. Towards the back of the shop, a small area was devoted to comic books and graphic novels.

It's true that a good bookstore can help a child forget even the worst of days. Steuart eagerly dove into the shelves of books and was soon lost inside the fantasy hub as he began searching for new words. He climbed around the shelves. He opened and closed books. He read paragraphs, looked at inscriptions, and then stopped to write several new words on his cards. *Lanate, flibbertigibbet* and *moribund* were three of his favorites.

A clerk sat reading at the back counter. Moving towards the clerk Sam stopped briefly to flip through a couple of art books. She found a museum catalog with a new colors floating inside. She looked at the clerk. His head was still down. Sam reached into her backpack, pulled out a small pair of scissors and snipped a corner sample from the loose page. She slid the color into her satchel. "That's good," she sighed. It was a cool teal, more blue than green, with a light hint of red that added a beautiful depth to the hue.

"Shouldn't we be getting down to business?" Trista whispered.

"You're right. Sorry." Sam walked to the desk and stared at the man who sat reading. "Hello Sir, we have a particular interest today. I'm hoping you can help us."

He didn't look up until after Sam completed her sentence. He was a large and gruff looking man with a bulbous nose and smallish blue eyes that were a bit too far apart for his tiny round wire frames. His hair, pulled into a ponytail, disappeared behind his back. The man wore a wrinkled surplus army jacket over a brain zap t-shirt. He looked in need of a haircut, shave, and maybe a shower. Sam imagined him as a person who arrived for college, forty or more years ago and stayed. She pulled Trista from her coat. She held the doll with both hands. "Can you help us? This is my doll. She'd like a cigar box. Do you have any?"

The man looked at Sam. He put his book down. He reached across the desk, taking Trista into his hands before Sam realized what was happening. Trista remained motionless. Sam wondered if she should grab Trista and run.

The man examined Trista and then looked at Sam. He placed the doll back into her hands. He stared at Sam for what felt like several minutes before speaking. "I can see what you have here. Are you new in town?"

"What do you mean? Why do you ask?"

"My name is Mr. Felphul. I.M. Felphul," he pointed to the sign above the door. "I've never seen you here."

Sam nodded. Mr. Felphul reached into his pocket, unwrapped a piece of hard candy and put it into his mouth. "This is my bookstore. First time visitors are usually here for a football game—or they're new in town." He shook his head, "There's no football game today."

Sam nodded again, "We just moved here. That's my little brother," she pointed towards the front of the store where Steuart continued climbing and looking at books. Her voice began to shake, "Did we do something wrong? We weren't trying to do anything wrong." She touched her backpack.

"No." Mr. Felphul shook his head. Biting his candy he stopped and looked at Trista and then at Sam. He leaned in as closely as possible without getting up from his chair. "Sam," he whispered, "your doll is nice."

Sam nodded, "She is."

"What you have here is a treasure."

"Thank you," Sam pulled Trista close.

"There are people in Maybell who would love to get their hands on this doll. These dolls are quite special and unique." Mr. Felphul looked towards Steuart. "Little brother came from Ivy's?"

"Yes, sir." Sam lowered her head.

"You need to understand that Miss Ivy is one such..."

"One such?"

"One such," Mr. Felphul nodded.

"One such?"

"Exactly."

Steuart continued looking at books. He stepped down to browse a lower shelf and then climbed across to pull a book from the other side. He paid no attention to Sam or Mr. Felphul.

Sam asked again, "One such *what*, sir? Miss Ivy is one such what?"

"Just that..." Mr. Felphul replied, "one such."

"I don't understand."

"Mr. Felphul leaned in again, this time he lowered his voice. "She is one such who would like to get her hands on your doll."

"Oh, she already saw my doll."

Steuart climbed over to pull down another book. This was closer to the front of the store and up a little higher.

Mr. Felphul leaned back in his chair, laced his hands across his stomach. He pursed his lips, shook his head and raised his left eyebrow. He looked over his glasses at Sam, "You are fortunate that doll is still in your possession."

"Fortunate?"

"Yes," he nodded. "Does little brother have one too?"

"His name is Steuart, sir." Nervously, Sam asked "One what?"

"Doll—does little brother have a doll?"

"Steuart?" Sam asked with extra emphasis.

"Steuart." Mr. Felphul nodded, "Does little brother Steuart have a doll too?"

"Yes, he does, but we don't call them dolls."

"What do *we* call them?"

"The Wayward Gifted, sir. Steuart has Ed Camino."

Mr. Felphul leaned closer. Well, I'll tell you Sam, these dolls are hard to come by. I know these dolls. Only special people are given these dolls."

Sam pursed her lips. She looked at her brother and then at Mr. Felphul. "So, you know they're real?"

"Real?"

"Alive," Sam said believing that Mr. Felphul understood. She wanted him to tell her what he knew. "Do you take care of any of them?"

Mr. Felphul was silent. Fearing she had said too much, Sam bit her lip and held her breath. Mr. Felphul stared at Sam. Sam showed no expression and stared at Mr. Felphul. Trista did not move. Steuart continued looking at books and making notes.

Mr. Felphul smiled. He almost laughed. "Oh, my, you have quite the imagination little Sam." He removed his glasses, wiped a lens, and chuckled as he put them back on his head. "I understand why you were given a doll. You have a true creative gift."

Mr. Felphul stood, turned, and then motioned Sam towards a hallway. He invited her to "Come on back. I'll show you what I have."

Sam stood silently. She looked at the dark hallway.

Mr. Felphul continued, "I think we have something back here that will work beautifully for you and your doll."

Sam turned and looked towards Steuart who was still looking at books. She looked again at Mr. Felphul, and again down the long, dark hallway. Mr. Felphul turned away from Sam and began walking towards a door. Sam followed. Again, she turned and looked towards Steuart. She could feel Trista's arms wrapped around her hand. Sam stopped. She stood back. Mr. Felphul opened the door to a room that was as dark as a cave. He walked inside, "Join me?"

Sam gasped and backed away.

"I prefer to stay out here."

Mr. Felphul flipped the light switch and pointed towards a wall of cigar boxes. Sam relaxed, but remained in the hall. "These are perfect," she whispered. "How much are they?"

"Seven-fifty each."

"No," she shook her head. "That won't work."

"No?"

"We've found them and now we can't afford them. We don't have enough money."

"How much do you have?"

"Together, or separate?" Sam looked towards Steuart.

"Together."

"Less than five."

"What about books? Do you have any books you might like to bring in for a trade? If we can come up with a trade, you can keep your money."

Sam smiled, "Oh, yes, Steuart does too." Sam and Mr. Felphul talked about her books and came up with an agreeable figure. She considered trading her copy of *Right, Good, and Appropriate*. "Do you accept books that are signed?"

"By the author—always!"

"No, I was talking about a book that has an inscription—a gift."

"It depends on the book and the inscription. Is the signer famous?"

"Only in her mind." Sam looked away, "I shouldn't trade that one anyway. I might get into trouble. I have plenty of others."

"I'm curious about your need for the boxes, Sam. What are you going to do with them?"

"I'm not sure."

"Not sure? Why are you buying them? Who buys something without knowing the intended purpose?"

"They're not for us. The dolls made a request."

Mr. Felphul chuckled and nodded, "I should have known. It's a secret?"

"Exactly. They didn't give us the reason."

"Let's look through this stack and see what we can come up with. You like pretty colors?"

"I collect them. I love colors. I have this folder. It's where I keep my swatches. Do you have anything this color red?" Sam opened her folder and pulled out a red that she liked. "I think Trista would like this one." She turned, looked at Steuart and asked, "Are you okay out there? Do you want me to choose a box for Ed?"

"Go ahead. I'm finding new words."

"Does Ed have a color preference?"

Steuart shook his head. "I think I've found my new favorite place in town."

"What color do you want for Ed?"

"Anything, as long as it's not pink."

Mr. Felphul looked through several stacks and showed Sam various options. "What about this one? Do you like this? Is this color close?"

"I think that one has too much orange. Can we continue looking?"

"Sure. We'll look until we find one you like. These dolls must be important to you. I'm curious to know more. How'd you come by them?"

"Our doctor gave them to us."

Mr. Felphul stopped and listened.

"That's not right," Sam corrected herself. "He didn't give them to us. He lent them to us. We're using them. We play with them at home and take them with us to appointments. Do you know Dr. Klesel?"

"Oh, yes, Maybell's a small place. I know almost everyone. That's why I asked if you were new in town. I've known the good doctor for years."

"He's very smart. We like him a lot."

Mr. Felphul nodded.

"Does he buy books here?"

"He buys, and also sells books from time to time."

"We call him the Shark Yeller."

"Shark Yeller? That's an odd name, care to explain?"

"It's an anagram. I'm Samantha Leigh DuBoise—ghoulish abased inmate."

"Where will you use that one?"

"Halloween."

"It's definitely good for ghosts and goblins. Are there any others you like?"

"Imaginable head shout," Sam frowned. "None of mine are very interesting."

"That's how it goes. Some work better than others."

"I like yours."

"It doesn't provide many options, but I find that it works well for my profession." Mr. Felphul picked up a cigar box, lifted the lid and looked inside. "And, purists might argue against it." He held the box for Sam to see. "I'm serious about your need to be careful with these dolls. My friend Ceil lost one several years ago. She never found it. You should be cautious."

"Ceil Nunstern?"

"Yes, do you know Ceil?"

"She's our friend. We play in her tree house. Ceil had a doll?"

"Now that I think of it, I may be confusing her with someone else. You know, perhaps I'm thinking of another customer."

"But you said Ceil Nunstern."

"I know what I said, but I was wrong. Maybell's a big place."

"It's not that big. Besides, you just said it's a small place."

"*SAAAAMMMMMM!*" Steuart called out to his sister. Books flew in multiple directions as he reached for the closest shelf. Steuart hit the floor with a loud *thump*. The room became silent before Steuart let out a groan. Sam and Mr. Felphul raced to the front of the store in time to see Della Ivy with her face pressed against the window. She exchanged glances with Mr. Felphul, turned, and walked away. Sam and Mr. Felphul quickly turned their attention to Steuart who lay on the floor holding his arm. "My arm, my arm."

"Don't move him." Mr. Felphul looked at Steuart, "Don't move. I'm calling for assistance."

TWELVE

Olivia pulled Sam out of bed before the sun was up. "Dress quickly. We overslept."

Sam yawned, "Yes, ma'am."

"We should be in the car now. If we don't hurry we'll miss seeing Steuart before his surgery." Olivia walked into the hall and turned back, "Bring your hairbrush with you. Don't worry about your bed." Sam leaned down for Trista. "And leave those nasty dolls here."

"I'd like to take them with me."

"Samantha Leigh, leave them here. We don't want to contaminate the hospital."

"I'd like to take you with me," Sam whispered to Trista.

"You don't want to get into trouble."

"I'm already in trouble. She blames me for Steuart's accident."

"It wasn't your fault."

"Doesn't matter," Sam shrugged.

"Samantha Leigh," Olivia called out. "Let's go."

"It wasn't your fault," Trista smiled at Sam. "Tell Steuart I'm thinking about him. We'll see you tonight."

* * *

Visitors came, went, sat, stood, paced, and walked around the busy surgical waiting room. Some were alone, others in groups; each waiting to hear about a friend or loved one. Sam and her mother sat together. Olivia talked on the phone while Sam sat quietly thinking about Steuart. One family, seated just across from Sam, alternated between praying and arguing. The group discussed religion so loudly that she found herself unable to think. She shook her head, closed her eyes, and wished they would go away. Three seats over, a lady with two friends sat eating snacks, reading tabloid magazines, and talking, "We have a family rule," one of them said giggling. "We're only allowed to read trash at the hospital or the lake. The rest of the time we glance at covers in the check-out lane and look forward to weekends up north." Up front, a woman and an older man, both wearing pink vests, sat at a counter shuffling small stacks of paper, answering the phone, and providing information to visitors. Sam yawned.

After surgery, but before Steuart was out of recovery, Olivia handed Sam money for the cafeteria, "I'm going to see Dr. Klesel."

"When?"

"Now."

"Can I go?"

"No, I'll be back in a few hours."

"What am I supposed to do?"

"Stay here."

"When can I see Steuart?"

"When I get back. Don't worry. Whatever you do, do not leave the hospital grounds."

Sam sat for a long while watching the crowd. Ready to close her eyes and about to nod off, she opened them quickly when a deep purple gift bag grabbed her attention. She jumped from her chair and followed the bag-carrying stranger, turning and moving throughout hospital corridors onto the elevator, and up several floors. She walked through a skywalk and into another part of the hospital before entering the cafeteria.

Keeping the bag in sight, Sam bought a small carton of milk, a sandwich, and a cupcake before finding a seat by the window where she waited for the bag-carrying stranger to finish lunch. One behind the other, the stranger and Sam exited the cafeteria. Sam continued following the stranger down another hall and then waited quietly outside a ladies room before following further towards the elevator, up two more floors, and midway down a long corridor where the woman finally entered a hospital room. Careful not to be seen, Sam walked past the room, turned back, and silently waited. Eventually, the woman, no longer carrying the bag, exited the room and disappeared.

Sam peeped into the room and saw a young girl sleeping. She had a large, brightly colored bandage across her head. The purple bag sat on a bedside table at the far end of the room. Quietly, Sam walked towards the table, sat next to the bed, and unzipped her backpack. An aide walked into the room just as Sam took out her scissors and began reaching for the tissue. Sam held her scissors and smiled as she pretended to be a visiting family member. The aide walked out. The little patient, now slightly awake, looked at Sam and asked, "Are you from my school?"

"No," Sam answered. "My name is Samantha Leigh DuBoise. I'm a volunteer."

"I'm Dotsie Caples. I guess you know that."

Sam nodded, "It's a pretty name."

"Do you deliver cards or flowers?" Dotsie looked around the room. "I don't see anything new."

"No," Sam shook her head.

"You said you're a volunteer."

"I am. Actually, I'm visiting my brother. He broke his arm. I decided to do a little volunteering while I'm here."

"I'm sorry about your brother. I hope he gets well very soon."

"Thank you."

"What do you do?"

"I deliver songs."

Dotsie smiled. "Do you know the song *Love Makes You Feel Happy?*"

"No," I don't know that one."

"How about *I'm Happy Today?*"

Sam shook her head, "No."

"*Sing, Sing, Clap Your Hands?*"

"I don't know that one either."

"What songs do you know?"

"I have one that I made up just for you."

"What's it called?"

"*Love Is Here With You.*"

Dotsie smiled. Sam took a deep breath and sang,

Please don't feel bad
Please don't be sad
Love is here with you

Don't feel lonely

You're not only
Love is here with you

Days can be sad
Days will be bad
But there are happy days too

You're not only
Please never feel lonely
Love is here with you

With Dotsie once again sleeping, Sam bent down and snipped the color, slipped it into her pocket and stood to leave the room. A nurse watched from the doorway. Sam walked slowly to the door, looked up, and whispered, "I'm sorry. It was just a color snippet."

"It's okay," the nurse nodded. "Your song was sweet, but I think you should go now."

Sam walked quietly down the hall. Along the way, she stopped an aide and asked directions to surgical waiting.

* * *

The first three minutes were silent as Dr. Klesel waited for Olivia to speak. Time for her family update, she sat miserably on the sofa, her feet side by side, elbows on her knees and her head in her hands.

The doctor began, "How's Steuart?"

"He'll be fine."

"What did they do?"

"Two pins and a plate in his right arm. It was a terrible break."

"Sounds like it."

"We're looking at a lengthy recovery." Olivia shook her head and sighed, "I don't understand these things."

"You spoke with his surgeon? He didn't answer your questions?"

"I'm not talking about the surgery. I'm talking my life. I'm talking about why these things always happen to me."

"What things?"

Olivia looked up. She let out a deep sigh, "You know, the broken arm."

"He's fortunate it wasn't worse."

"True enough, but there are families who sail through daily life without ever confronting these types of issues; families where things never go wrong. I don't understand."

"We don't always see what others are dealing with."

"I know that. I'm not brain dead," Olivia let out a sigh. "I'm just saying that a lot of people never have to deal with the type of things that are continually thrown on me. I never get a break. It never stops."

Dr. Klesel listened.

"I love my children. You know that, don't you?"

"I do."

"I do my best every day. I give more than one hundred percent. But, it doesn't seem to matter because things continue to happen." She sighed again. "I don't understand why everything always happens to me."

"Is there something you're not telling me?"

"You know exactly what I'm talking about," Olivia snapped. "Why do you always insist on giving me this crap?"

"What crap?"

"That crap. The *what things*, the *what crap*. The *what comes to mind*, and *how does that make you feel crap?* I feel like you're running me in circles. I'm completely exhausted. I'm tired. This move has not been easy for me. I am totally worn out, spent—do you hear what I'm saying?"

"I hear you."

"Why don't you just tell me how to keep them from doing these things?"

"You're talking about the children?"

"Who do you think I'm talking about? Why don't you tell me what I need to do? I want my children fixed. Better than that, why don't you just do what a *real* doctor would do?"

"I'm not a real doctor?"

"Of course you're a real doctor."

"What do you want me to do?"

"Write prescriptions. Give me a prescription. Real doctors write prescriptions."

"I just told you I'm a real doctor."

"And I just agreed with you. Why are you so defensive."

"You seem combative."

"I'm saying that most doctors actually write prescriptions."

"I write prescriptions."

"Not for me. You refuse. You never write prescriptions for me."

"Are we talking about you or the children? I'm confused."

Olivia exhaled loudly, "Steuart has a broken arm. This is a nightmare. I am completely exhausted. We need drugs."

"What does Steuart's broken arm have to do with your wanting prescriptions? What type of prescriptions do you want?"

"I have no idea. You're supposed to decide what type of prescriptions we need. Why are you asking me to diagnose myself? You just told me that you're a real doctor."

Dr. Klesel pointed to the diplomas and certificates on his wall.

"Write a real prescription for my children. Give me a prescription—or both. I need to relax."

"I thought you were here for family updates."

"No—maybe—no," Olivia sighed again. "Forget it. I don't know. I'm tired of these things always happening to me."

Dr. Klesel didn't say anything.

"You know *what things*." Olivia raised her voice, "I'm telling you *what things*. You're not listening to me."

"You're talking in generalizations."

"No, I am not."

"You're all over the place."

"I'm explaining things."

Dr. Klesel listened.

"I'm telling you that my children are making my life a walking, breathing, hellish nightmare and they're both individually and collectively driving me nuts. I'm serious. I think they want to kill me."

"That's a very strong statement."

"It's true."

"Why do you say that?"

"Samantha Leigh and Steuart James have morphed from sweet little angels into scary little monsters. They look normal to you and they look normal to everyone else, but there is nothing normal about the way they've been carrying on these past weeks. Underneath everything, they are wild children possessed by demons. They waited for me to adopt them just so they could ruin my life."

"Do you honestly believe…?"

"I do. They're trying to kill me."

"No hyperbole? No sarcasm?"

Olivia shook her head.

"Perhaps you're overly tired."

"I'm exhausted. I'm not feeling well today."

"And you're worried about Steuart?"

"Of course, I'm worried about Steuart, but he's being taken care of. I'm the one carrying the load. Samantha Leigh and Steuart James are the stressors in my life that are going to finish me off early. I won't make it to forty. I know it. My adopted children are killing me with stress."

Dr. Klesel stared at Olivia.

She nodded vigorously, "They are. I'm serious." She shook her head, "Don't look at me like that."

"Like what?"

"That. You think I'm exaggerating."

"I do."

"I'm not. Okay, maybe a little bit. Maybe I'm exaggerating to a degree, but that doesn't alter the facts. Samantha Leigh and Steuart James know how to behave, but they refuse. I continually tell them what they need to do. I drill these things into them every single day. I spend hour upon hour teaching them how to act properly, but they roll their eyes and refuse to listen. I'm getting exactly nowhere. I'm accomplishing nothing."

"Perhaps Sam and Steuart need an opportunity to be children."

"They *are* children. They are badly behaved, uncontrollable children who refuse to listen. No one listens to me. I'm begging for your help. There are people in the world with children who not only manage, but also thrive as they maintain a normal, peaceful, and loving existence. Why can't I be one of those people?"

"What do you think?"

"I don't know. That's why I'm asking you. Why can't my life be all perfectly wrapped up and tied with a beautiful bow like a lot of other people I know? I always put my best foot forward. Why do these things always happen to me?" Olivia stopped. "Don't say it." She stood and moved towards the door.

Dr. Klesel waited.

Olivia returned to the sofa and sat down. "Don't look at me like that. I'm having a rough day. I feel like you are making everything much harder than it has to be."

"What do you feel like I'm doing?"

"My children need help now. Why do you refuse to give them medication?"

"They don't need medication."

"I want my children fixed."

"You continue telling me that the children are broken and that I need to repair them; that they need medication."

"So, you are hearing me?"

"Your children are not machines."

"Steuart James has a broken arm."

"I feel certain that his attending physician has prescribed medication for his arm. Would you like for me to talk with him? I'll be happy to give him a call. What's his name?"

I'm not asking for medication for Steuart's arm. I'm asking for medication for his broken behavior. Broken behavior is *your* responsibility."

"Olivia, medication is not going to repair your children's behavior. We go through this every time you're here. Their actions are symptoms. They are not the problem."

Olivia shook her head.

"The encouraging news is that parents can be trained."

"Oh, great. Here we go again. I don't know what you're getting at. I continue to tell you that I do not need training. I do not need to be taught how to be a good parent. I am a good parent. You talk about training. You want to teach me things that I already know. For some incomprehensible reason you not only refuse to prescribe medications for my children, but you also think that dolls are the answer to our problems. I don't get it."

"What's confusing you?"

"Dolls—dolls are confusing me. Dolls are not going to fix our problems. I don't understand why you encourage my children to play with those ridiculous things." Olivia pointed to her chest, "It's my responsibility as their only participating parent to choose the toys that my children play with. Why do you continue wasting my valuable time and money with dolls?"

"You've not been charged for the dolls. You know that. I'd like to know why you find the dolls so repulsive."

Olivia stared towards the door.

"If you were here more frequently, we could talk about this in greater depth. These are issues that we need to address and explore."

"They're repulsive."

"What do you find repulsive? Why are you so focused on the dolls?" Dr. Klesel stared at Olivia, "What is it about them that upsets you?"

"I'm not upset. I don't like them. Is there a written rule that says I have to like everything?"

"Not that I'm aware of."

"So, I do not like the dolls. That's it. I don't like them."

"Why don't you want your children to have relationships with anyone other than you?"

"What? Where did that come from?"

Dr. Klesel reached for the water bottle on his side table. "It appears that you may not want your children to have relationships with anyone other than you." He unscrewed the cap and took a sip.

"Who *are* you? Where do you get off saying these sorts of things to me? Of course I want my children interacting with people. We're not talking about people. We're not talking about relationships. We're talking about stupid, dirty, disgusting, nasty toys. Toys and people are not the same thing. How do you make the leap?"

"Why are you so upset?"

"I am not upset!" Olivia balled her fist and began to shake as she put it against her teeth and bit down. "I'm asking that you do something other than provide toys for my children—toys that I do not find appropriate, or stimulating."

"Why do you feel so strongly about the dolls?"

"I don't know."

Dr. Klesel waited.

"I don't like them." Olivia looked away.

"What do you dislike about them?"

"I don't know."

"Your reaction seems a bit intense not to know."

"I don't like them."

"If you knew, what might it be?"

"That is a ridiculous question."

"Not when you're blocking—I think you know."

"I don't."

"Olivia, the dolls allow your children an opportunity to practice relationships with others. They need the experience. This is safe and healthy for them."

"I can teach my children how to behave. I can teach them how to interact with others. They do not need dolls for that. My handbook teaches everything they need to know about functioning properly in our society."

"Handbooks don't provide practical experience. The dolls provide Samantha and Steuart with an opportunity to play, practice, and apply ideas. They need this." Dr. Klesel took another sip of water, looked at Olivia and asked, "Don't you want your children to have relationships with people other than you?"

"Dr. Klesel, you are insulting me." Olivia looked at her feet, "Of course I do."

"Then, what is your problem with the dolls?"

There was a long silence before he repeated his question, "What is your problem with the dolls?"

"I don't like them."

"Okay," he nodded, "You don't like them. Tell me the first thing that comes to mind. What exactly do you dislike?"

"I, I, I," Olivia stuttered. "They're extremely unattractive."

"What else?"

"They look rough around the edges. The workmanship is poor. I prefer handmade items that are perfectly crafted, finely crafted. I want my children to be exposed to fine quality. Perfection is our goal in all that we do. We are intended to strive for perfection."

"Who defines perfection?"

"*Right, Good and Appropriate*. It's all there. You should read it. When I create something for my children, I make sure that everything is perfectly matched and perfectly stitched. I've told you all of this before. If I make something and it is not one hundred percent right, I will take it apart and begin again. I do not take it partially apart—I am telling you that I take it completely apart. I handle everything in my life the same way whether I'm at home or at work. No matter what I'm doing, I continue until I have an end product that is perfect."

"This is a recurring theme with you."

Olivia nodded.

"It's very important?"

"Certainly," Olivia relaxed. "I believe it is impossible to live life properly unless one follows all the rules. We get one shot at this. There is no room for error. Perfection is my personal benchmark. It dictates everything that I attempt. If I take on a responsibility, or accept an assignment, I do it only after I am certain that I can do it correctly. I'm doing my best to pass this philosophy along to my children. Those dolls are an insult to my value system and to all the things I hold dear. There is nothing uniform about the dolls."

"Life is not uniform. People are not perfect."

"Of course, I know that, but these dolls are beyond imperfect."

"What do you mean?"

"They remind me of something my mother would make."

"What about your mother?"

Olivia stiffened, "We're not going to talk about my mother today." She shook her head, "No, I'm not going there."

"Why not?"

"You are not about to make this all about me. I know where you're heading."

"Where's that?"

"This is an attempt to pressure me into scheduling extra appointments." She raised her voice, "Listen to me. Hear what I am saying to you. I am not here to pay for your new sports car, nor am I here to finance your next exotic vacation. I am here because of my dear, troubled, children. I am here because I want you to help them." She looked towards the clock, "Is our time up?"

"We have a few more minutes."

"I say it is. Dr. Klesel, our time is up for today."

* * *

Trista was napping comfortably on Sam's bed when Olivia burst into the room. "I'm going to have a talk with that girl." Olivia turned off Sam's bedside lamp. "Maybe I should insist she pay for electricity." Ed sat on the windowsill watching the snowfall. Olivia watched Trista, "Dr. Klesel may be brilliant, but he has no idea what he's talking about as far as you go. I know what you are, but I don't understand what he's trying to do. Doll therapy is a joke. How dare he suggest that I have issues with my mother." Olivia picked Trista up, waved her around and then pulled her in close. "That man has no idea with whom he is dealing."

Olivia stared at Trista. "You are, without question, the ugliest thing I have ever seen in my life and you do look like some pathetic piece of garbage that my mother would throw together." She dropped Trista onto the bed. Trista didn't move. "Why does he want my children to have dolls like you? How can you make anything better? I have a child in the hospital with a broken arm. You stupid dolls did nothing to keep that from happening. *Practice relationships with dolls*? The last thing they need is to practice relationships with trash. You should be locked away." Olivia looked at Trista, "*ick*." She reached down, picked the doll up again and squeezed tightly before drawing back, and, with full range of motion, throwing her into the bathroom. Trista hit the tile and screamed on impact. Olivia stood shocked.

Ed sat helplessly as Olivia rushed into the bathroom. Trista's head was crushed. The entire left side of her skull was broken. Olivia sank to the floor, "What have I done now?" She looked at the mess, "I broke you stupid doll. I was correct about your crappy construction." She took a deep breath, "My daughter will be a wreck." Olivia began picking up the pieces, "I can do this. I'll repair you." She studied the mess. "No, I can't. Mother could do this." Ed sat stunned.

"Pull yourself together," Olivia lectured herself. "You're upset and emotional because of Steuart's accident. I can't believe that I did this. What's wrong with me?" She sat on Sam's bed and stopped herself as she began to cry. She took another deep breath and began again. "Pull yourself together. This was an accident. You didn't do it on purpose. Who are you kidding?" She shook her head as she spoke to Trista, "This wasn't my fault." She took a deep breath, stood in front of the bathroom mirror, pulled a tissue from the box, and wiped her eyes. She studied her reflection. "Stupid doll. This is about Steuart's accident and your visit to Dr. Klesel." She looked down at Trista. "I think that man has a lot of nerve upsetting me on such a stressful day. He should have been supportive. He put me in this frame of mind. This is his fault—not mine. I'll see to it that Samantha Leigh understands. All I've done is make the world a neater and cleaner place."

Olivia forced another deep breath, turned sideways, and straightened her clothes. She straightened her hair. "It was a doll of no value—a silly, useless, toy." She checked her hair once more, "What is Dr. Klesel going to say?" She checked her teeth, "Why do I even care what he thinks? It serves him right. What would *Right, Good, and Appropriate* advise?" Olivia sighed, "It would tell me that *I* am the mother in charge. Crap. I hope Harry doesn't try to charge me." She picked at her teeth, "Just let him try. I'll have a word for him. I'll fire him. It was a toy. It was an accident. I don't care what he says. He works for me. The point is that I can fire him anytime I decide it's in the best interest of my family. Maybe that's what I should do. Fire Dr. Klesel—it was just a doll."

"She wasn't just a doll," Ed whispered through his tears.

Olivia went into the kitchen and returned with a dustpan and broom. She swept up the broken pieces and dropped them into a plastic bag. She laid the bag on Sam's dresser before leaving for the hospital.

Ed wept.

* * *

The following afternoon Ceil walked into Steuart's hospital room. "Hey you, how are you feeling?"

"Ceil, I broke my arm. I had an operation."

"I know."

"They put metal pens in my arm," Steuart pointed to the spot.

"That's what I heard."

"You knew? How did you know?"

"I ran into Mr. Felphul at the grocery store. He told me about your accident. That must've been scary."

"I don't know. It happened too fast."

"How does it feel now?"

"It hurts bad sometimes, but not so much. It's already feeling better."

"I brought you a surprise. I hope you like it. I tried to find something extra special." Ceil handed Steuart a wrapped box that he quickly opened.

"Captain Crandall Comics! This is great. He's my favorite! Did you know that Captain Crandall is the greatest superhero of all time?"

Ceil smiled, "I think I heard that somewhere. You'll let me read it when you're finished?"

"Of course I will. I'll be happy to share. I'll even read it to you if you like."

"Perfect," Ceil looked around the room. "Where's Sam? Where's your mom? Are you here alone?"

"Mother had an appointment. She'll be back in a while. Sam's here, but she's off exploring."

"That's okay. You're the person I came to visit. I'm so sorry to hear about your accident."

"Why are you sorry? It wasn't your fault."

"Because you're my friend and I never like seeing bad things happen to the people I care about."

After a while, Ceil stood up to leave, "I'm sorry that I missed your mother and Sam. I'll try to get back over here tomorrow. Do you know when you'll be going home?"

"Maybe tomorrow but they said it depends…."

"On what?"

"I don't know."

"Don't worry about any of that. You just need to concentrate on feeling better. Can I get anything for you before I leave?"

"I'm fine. Thanks for asking. I think I'm going to sleep for a while before I read my new comic books."

"Good idea—sweet dreams. I'll call tomorrow before I head over."

THIRTEEN

Steuart was unable to ride his bike with a broken arm, but that didn't keep him from getting out and having fun with his sister. Sam borrowed an old purple, twin, child carrier from a neighbor. She hooked the thing up to her bicycle and put Sparky in the back for extra padding. Because he was small, pulling Steuart was a breeze. He sat eagerly in the carrier and held a rolled drawing for Ceil. He leaned next to Sparky, after carefully moving him to the side, "I don't want my pal to get squashed."

Even with his broken arm, Steuart had great fun. He enjoyed riding in the carriage behind Sam's bike while he pretended to be royalty from another world. He imagined himself busily surveying his personal kingdom. "Faster Sam."

While she found Steuart's imperious attitude a bit annoying, Sam also enjoyed the time with her brother. She was thankful he was out of the hospital with nothing more than a broken arm. If only things had been so good for Trista. Sam continued to grieve over Trista's accident while keeping the information secret from Steuart. She and Ed had agreed that it was a bit early for Steuart to hear the bad news. Sam realized her brother was going to begin asking questions soon. While she looked forward to visiting with Ceil,

Sam was also hoping for information. She was on a mission and needed to find a doll maker who could repair Trista.

"First stop, Ceil's house," Sam said.

"Our ETA?" Steuart asked.

"Soon."

"I look forward to visiting with Ceil. I wish to thank my loyal subjects for visiting me whilst I was in the hospital."

"Whilst? Get over yourself. Keep talking like that and I'll drop you off here in the gutter."

"Just playing, sis. I prefer to stay in character."

Sam tried to keep the conversation light and happy, but her heart was breaking as she thought about Trista. *Why did she break into so many pieces?* Sam wondered.

"Oh, come on, come on. Let's play," Steuart said. "This is fun. Do your part. If you don't, I'll be forced to banish you—to the dungeon."

"You're kidding me?"

Sam looked back at her brother and stuck out her tongue.

With the bike carrier attached, the biggest challenge Sam faced was the route. Because of the snow and ice along the paths, she decided to stay on paved roads, however, this made a number of trips longer than usual. Instead of biking through the preserve, Sam rode across the bridge towards the hospital and then over to the street that ran behind the children's clinic. She continued back one more street, and then next to the dental school where she finally turned into a neighborhood. Taking another left Sam continued along the opposite side street before turning into a cul-de-sac. She stopped in front of Ceil's driveway and turned towards her brother, "Sir, your taxi stops here."

"What? What do you mean? You're stopping here?"

"I am."

"Why? You're not taking me to the door?"

"I am not."

"Why not?

"The drive is too steep."

"How will I get to the house?"

"The same way I will. Use your legs."

"But, I'm just out of the hospital. You can't do this to me."

"Yes I can. You've been out for weeks. Your legs work fine." Sam began walking up the hill.

Steuart refused to leave the carriage. "You're kidding me? Right? This is a joke. Ha. Ha. You are kidding me?"

"Nope," Sam shook her head and continued walking up the drive. "You need the exercise. It'll do you good."

"You are a spoilsport. Royalty should never be treated in such a careless manner. You're forcing me to punish you. It's your choice. You'll be made an example of for others. I will have to throw you into prison—or worse. Maybe I'll send you to the Galapagos Islands to work with the Pirates."

"Steuart, I'm tired. Go ahead, send me to the Pirates and see if I care. The Pirates would be easier to work for than you. At least I'd get a bowl of soup. All I get from you is complaints."

"Don't bet on it. The soup-maker's position is taken. They'll make you clean the head. You'll have to scrounge around for your food and eat out of compost bins."

"I don't believe this. Sometimes you're a real brat. It's hard work driving you all over the city. You're so ungrateful. Maybe you should just walk home."

"You're right," Steuart stuck out his lower lip and frowned. "Thank you, Sam. I appreciate you."

"That's better." Sam stood and waited for her brother. "Come on. Let's go."

Steuart didn't move. "Now will you pull me up the drive?"

"You can walk."

"I said *thank you*. Doesn't that count for something."

"Of course it does. I appreciate being appreciated. But you can walk."

"I'm taking back my thank you."

Sam stopped. She turned around and looked at her brother. "Too late. It's out there and it's non-retractable. But, if you want, I'll let you have it anyway. It won't make a difference because you still have to walk. Come on, it's cold out here. Come on, let's go see Ceil."

* * *

Visiting with Ceil was a favorite pastime of the children. She was always happy to see them and they were equally happy to see her. Sam and Steuart were especially eager to share their art with a friend.

"It's called *Lectern in the Sun*," Steuart explained. The drawing contained a reading podium inside the sun with the name Ceil Nunstern pasted in the middle.

"The sun is smiling," Sam said proudly.

"Oh, I like that. How lovely. I've never had a picture like this one before." Ceil thanked Sam and Steuart. She gave each of them a hug. "How about a cup of nice hot tea and a ginger cookie?"

"Do you understand the symbolism," Steuart asked, "about the picture?"

Ceil shook her head, "I'm going to have to give it a bit of thought. But, please don't tell me. I want to figure it out on my own."

"Do you really like it?" Steuart asked.

"Yes, very much. You are very talented."

Steuart blushed, "It was nice of you to visit me in the hospital."

"My pleasure."

"Your visits made me feel well and I appreciate the Captain Crandall comics."

"You're not the only one. It made me feel better. I like to see things for myself. And, I'm delighted that you like Captain Crandall. How's your arm today?"

"Better."

Sam interrupted, "Mother said she wanted to meet you, but you were gone before she made it to the room."

"I tried, but it never worked out that we were there at the same time." Ceil opened the cabinet and removed three cups and saucers. "I wanted to meet her too. Perhaps we should arrange a visit?"

"That's a good idea," Steuart said.

"I was thankful when Mr. Felphul told me about what happened. I had no way of knowing."

"Mr. Felphul's been kind to us," Sam said. "He called for the ambulance and drove me to the hospital."

"I rode in an ambulance," Steuart said proudly.

"He stayed with me in the emergency room until Mother arrived. I think he would've stayed longer, but Mother wasn't feeling very friendly."

Ceil picked up a wooden tea box and let the children choose their flavor. "Mr. Felphul is a good person to know."

"I like his book store," Steuart said. "I'm looking forward to visiting him again soon."

"Mother says that we can't," Sam added.

"Why would she say that?"

"She blames Mr. Felphul for Steuart's accident."

"Oh dear, that's dreadful."

"She says that his bookstore is dangerous. She also blames me for not watching Steuart more carefully."

"She called it a firetrap," Steuart said.

"That's such a shame. Mr. Felphul does have books everywhere, but that's the nature of a great bookstore."

Steuart nodded, "I love that place."

"I wish you could help Mother understand," Sam said.

Ceil looked at Steuart, "You need to be careful anytime you're climbing, no matter where you are. If you can't reach something, ask for help. That's what I do all the time."

"It wasn't the height of the books," Steuart shook his head and looked away.

"No?"

"It was the button lady," Sam said.

"The button lady?"

Sam and Steuart told Ceil about their misadventure with Della Ivy. "We thought we'd lost her." Steuart touched his face. "I was looking around the shelves at Mr. Felphul's and then I saw her again. She glared at me through the window. All I could think was *she found me*. She tapped on the window and we were suddenly eyeball-to-eyeball. It happened fast. I was afraid she was going to come inside and grab me again."

"My goodness."

"That's when I fell. She startled me." Steuart shook his head, "I don't remember falling."

"Oh dear, poor, poor, dear. Did she come inside?"

"No, Mr. Felphul said she knows to stay out of his store."

"But she still frightened you?"

"I didn't know she wouldn't come in." Steuart scratched his head. "Wait a minute. What do you mean, *poor dear*? Poor dear *me*, or poor dear *Della*?"

"Both of you."

Steuart raised his voice, "Why poor dear *her*? She's a scary person."

"I understand. I can see that. I say *poor dear Della* because she can't help herself. But you didn't know that. I can only imagine how the two of you felt."

"Petrified," Sam said.

Ceil shook her head, "I can understand. Della is a sad, misunderstood, and terribly confused woman. I'm sorry that you had a bad experience with her. She was a very nice lady in her younger years."

Sam took a bite of cookie, "Mr. Felphul doesn't like Della."

"Is that what he told you?"

"No, but he told me to be careful around her."

"I see," Ceil sipped her tea.

"He said she might try to take my doll. I don't think Della and Mr. Felphul get along."

"Maybe not. He's such a nice man. I can't imagine that he would have a problem with anyone."

Sam stared at Ceil. "Do you have a doll?"

"What type of doll?"

"Like Ed Camino…" Sam turned towards her brother, "Steuart, show Ceil your doll."

Steuart removed Ed from his backpack and placed him on the table. Ceil glanced at Ed and then back at Sam. "Do you have one too?"

Sam nodded, "I do. I have one, but she got hurt." Ceil stood with her back to Ed and asked, "What happened?"

Sam told Ceil and Steuart about Trista's accident. Ed stood and began walking around behind Ceil as she was talking with Sam. Steuart listened quietly.

"I left Trista on my bed the morning of Steuart's operation. That's where she got hurt."

"What?" Steuart asked.

"Got hurt?" Ceil asked.

"When I got home from the hospital," Sam began to cry as she told the story, "I found Trista in a plastic bag on my dresser. Her head was in pieces. She was badly broken."

"Oh, honey," Ceil put her arm around Sam, "We all have accidents. I'm sure you didn't do anything on purpose. Don't feel bad."

"I didn't do it," Sam shook her head and looked at Ceil. "It wasn't me."

"What?" Steuart asked.

"It was Mother. She told me that she dropped Trista in the bathroom."

"She dropped her?" Steuart asked. "That's what caused her head to shatter? What was Mother doing with Trista?"

"She told me that it happened because Trista was poorly made."

Ceil wrinkled her forehead and continued to listen.

"Mother hates our dolls."

"Don't you think the word hate is a little strong?" Ceil asked.

"No, she called them *the wayward trash*."

"Does Dr. Klesel know?" Steuart asked Sam.

"That your mother dislikes the dolls?" Ceil asked Steuart.

"No," Steuart shook his head. "Does he know that Trista was in an accident?"

"No, I haven't told him yet. I want to get Trista well before I tell him."

Steuart swallowed his cookie, "Why?"

"I don't want him to know. I want her fixed before I say anything."

"Dr. Klesel?" Ceil asked. Ceil turned and looked at Steuart. Ed quickly sat down.

"The dolls belong to Dr. Klesel. They're not ours."

Ceil turned back towards Sam. Ed turned and looked at Steuart who put his fingers on Ed's shoulder. Ed reached up and held onto Steuart.

Ceil poured more tea. "Sam, I'm sorry to hear about this. Surely, Dr. Klesel will understand."

"It's more than that. I'm worried about Trista."

"Worried? In what way?"

"Mr. Felphul told us that you have dolls. That's why I'm telling you what happened."

"He said that one of yours got lost." Steuart said.

"You have to understand. You must know that they're alive, don't you?" Sam looked Ceil in the eyes.

"Alive?" Ceil asked. "Of course they're real to you. I have no doubt, but..."

Sam cut Ceil off, "I see. Will you show us your doll?"

"Honey, I'm afraid Mr. Felphul was mistaken. I don't have any dolls. I wish that I did. They can be quite fascinating and wonderful. Would you like another cup of tea?"

"You just poured another cup for all of us," Sam looked harshly at Ceil. She wondered if Ceil was being truthful and remembered how Mr. Felphul suddenly changed his story about Ceil's dolls.

"Ceil, you have such a beautiful house," Sam said. "How long have you lived here?"

"About ten years."

Ed and Steuart sat straight. Sam saw tears in Steuart's eyes.

"Was the tree house here when you moved in?" Steuart asked.

"No," Ceil stopped and corrected herself. "No, I mean yes, it was here when we moved in."

"We? I thought you live by yourself," Steuart questioned.

"Oh, I was just speaking in the third person. We, as in me, the royal *we*."

"Ceil, sometimes you're strange," Sam said.

"Do you think so?"

"Yes."

"I guess we all have our little quirks."

Steuart broke into the conversation. "I do the same thing. *We* should like another cup of tea, please."

"We should?" Ceil smiled.

"Yes, we should. Please."

"Then we shall have it." Ceil poured another cup of tea for Steuart, "How is your arm feeling, really?"

"You've already asked twice, but since you asked again, we, are feeling fine, thank you for asking."

"This is ridiculous," Sam stood and walked towards the back door. "You're..." Sam stopped. She turned around and gave Ceil a stern look.

"What's wrong, Sam? Is there something you want to say?

"You don't want to let on that you know anything about the dolls. *Pa my leg again.*"

"I don't understand the game you're playing. You know I'm not good with anagrams."

Sam let out a deep sigh. She looked at Steuart and shrugged her shoulders. "It's time for us to go."

FOURTEEN

Leaving Ceil's, Steuart and Sam agreed that something was odd.
"I think she knows a lot more than she's saying," Steuart said.
"I don't understand why she won't tell us what she knows."
"Maybe she doesn't know anything."
Sam gave her brother a hard look. "You are kidding me, right?"
"Do you really believe she's hiding something?" Steuart stepped into the bike carrier with Ed.
"That's what it feels like to me. She's evasive about too many things." Sam shrugged her shoulders. "Why would Mr. Felphul tell me that Ceil has dolls like ours?"
"He backed off," Steuart said. "He changed his story."
"I don't believe Mr. Felphul either. I think they both know things that they're not saying."
"Sam you are paranoid."
"No, I'm not."
"You may be right—or not. I can't think of any reason that Ceil wouldn't tell us the truth about things, especially if she had information that might be helpful. Maybe that's it—maybe she doesn't know anything."

"That doesn't make sense. If she didn't have any information that could help us, she could still tell us what she knows. You weren't standing there when I was talking with Mr. Felphul. One minute he told me that Ceil had a doll that was stolen. The next minute he said he was confusing her with someone else."

"They're not bad people. Maybe that's exactly what happened."

"I'm not saying that either of them is bad, all I'm saying is that I think they have a secret. I think they both may know something they're not telling us."

Ed sat quietly and listened to the conversation. "Ed, what can you tell us?" Steuart asked.

"Not much."

"You never tell us much. It's frustrating. You were supposed to tell us more about things as soon as we got your boxes. We've been through a lot and still don't know much more about where you're from."

"It wasn't my fault that you decided to take a swan dive onto a giant pile of books."

"Can you tell us more now? It might help us help Trista."

"All you had to do was ask."

"Really?"

"Yep."

"Does that mean you'll tell us anything we want to know?"

"No. It means that I'll tell you what I can."

"Where'd you come from?" Sam asked.

"Bellamy. Any thoughts? Let's see how smart you are."

Steuart and Sam conferred with one another. Ed refused to give clues.

"I've got it," Steuart shouted. "I know the answer. Sam does too."

They shouted the name in unison, "Maybell!"

"Correct. You're the big winners, *ding, ding, ding, ding, ding, ding, ding!* You guys are quick."

"Where's Bellamy?" Steuart asked.

"Not far," Ed laughed, opened his arms and said, "Sam, Steuart, welcome to the wonders of the Anagrammatic Universe."

Steuart and Sam gasped in unison.

"Anagrammatic Universe," Steuart whispered.

"Do a lot of people travel from Maybell to Bellamy?" Sam asked.

Ed shrugged, "I couldn't say. Probably more than you might imagine, but not a high percentage."

"What does that translate into as far as numbers?"

"Here we go again." Ed mumbled to himself, "They always have the same questions. She wants numbers. He wants to know who and how many." He grew serious, "Kids, these are good questions. The problem is I'm not allowed to say."

"Not allowed to say? What? Why?" Steuart demanded. "We've answered your questions. We found your boxes."

"Ed," Sam asked, "Do you know the people who travel?"

"I know some of them."

"Who are they?" Steuart asked.

"I just told you. I'm not at liberty to tell you."

"You're not telling us anything. I think you're teasing."

Ed growled, "I hate this part of the talk."

"What do you mean, *the talk*? How often do you do this?" Sam asked.

"It's how I make my living. This is my job."

"Job?"

"Yeah, I work as a guide."

"What about Trista?" Sam asked. "Do you and she always work together?"

"Trista isn't a guide. She's a student. She came here for the cultural experience. I'm her guide, too." Ed looked off in the distance.

"So, Dolls are place holders?" Steuart asked.

"Yes and there are defined holding areas in communities that keep the dolls safe."

"Dr. Klesel? What does he know?"

Ed shook his head, "Dr. Klesel's office is a holding area."

"What does he know?" Steuart asked.

"It's unclear."

"You're kidding us."

"No, and if I knew anything more, I'd still be unable to tell either of you."

Sam stretched and took a deep breath, "It's so secretive. Where did Dr. Klesel get his dolls?"

"The Doll-maker."

"Is that where you came from?"

Ed nodded, "Dolls come from the doll-maker."

"Where's the doll maker?"

"Where's God? You might as well answer that question."

"When did you arrive?" Steuart asked.

"About a week before we were introduced."

"You seemed different—not like you were alive. You didn't seem real," Sam said. "Explain, please."

"I can't."

Steuart looked at Sam. "This is frustrating."

"The absolute most important thing you need to remember is that this is not an exact science. Also, we occasionally get surprised."

"You won't tell us who travels?" Steuart asked.

"It's against the *Code of the Guide*."

"What?"

"There's a code we guides live by. I follow the code. I took an oath. I live under strict orders."

"From whom?" Sam asked.

Ed shook his head. "Look, I sincerely apologize for my vagueness. It's not by choice. I'm bound by my oath. Believe me, I feel your frustration."

"Do you?" Sam asked.

Ed nodded. "You can feel confident that I won't tell anyone about you."

"What will you tell us?"

"I'll tell you everything that's allowed—nothing more. That's how it works."

Sam let out a huge sigh and walked to her bike.

"Where are we going now?" Steuart asked his sister.

"I'm not sure. Let's bike downtown. Maybe we can figure things out when we get there." Sam got on her bike and began pedaling.

* * *

Sam biked towards town. Steuart and Ed sat with Sparky and enjoyed the trip. Sam thought about Trista's accident and wondered how it all came about. *What was Mother doing with Trista?* Sam felt angry and sad—she also felt responsible. "Trista, I'm going to help you get well. You have my promise," she whispered.

Snow fell and the temperature dropped as Sam continued pedaling towards downtown. A small number of people walked in and out of buildings, some using umbrellas, others wearing hoods or hats. Cars inched along on the snow-covered roads. A yellow city truck, preparing for icy evening conditions, dropped salt as it passed the bicycle. The day was becoming one of those grey, dreary days that Midwesterners often complain about—cold, slushy, icy, wet, and dull.

The children learned early that Midwesterners care little for cold or snow. For some, complaining about the weather seemed to make them feel better. For others, it appeared to be a hobby. Sam didn't understand. *It's snow. It's beautiful, wonderful, gorgeous snow*, she thought. She loved the snowy days, even days like this one. She fantasized about standing in the middle of the street screaming, "Be thankful for these beautiful days! They are treasures for you to enjoy." Sam also realized that one man's richest blessing is often little more than another man's daily complaint. She felt sad and grateful at the same time. She felt sad for the people who hated the season. She felt grateful for the ability to recognize and appreciate every day. Then she wondered, *what do other people see and appreciate that I miss?*

Sam slowed her bike as she noticed a little coffee shop diagonally across the street. A heavy velvet curtain was installed at the entrance for the winter months. The color of ripe, juicy, raspberries, it was pulled around to keep the cold and wind out of the shop.

"What are you doing?" Steuart asked. "Why are you stopping?"

Sam pulled up to the curb. "Let's go in here. Are you hungry?" she asked. Steuart stepped onto the snowy pavement with Ed. "Watch your step." Sam reached to help her brother with his good arm. "I was thinking we could get a muffin and a cup of tea."

"Chocolate," Ed insisted. "Let's get a chocolate muffin."

"Ed, sometimes you have to eat food other than chocolate," Sam said.

"Blasphemy!" Ed shouted.

"Please, don't yell," Sam whispered as the people walking in front of them turned back to see who was yelling.

"Sorry, I can't help myself. I'm enthusiastic about good flavor. That said, I'm going to recommend we save poppy seed for another day. My vote is for chocolate."

"You can't always eat chocolate. At least I can't." Sam looked at her brother for reassurance.

"She's correct," Steuart said.

Ed shook his head, "What's wrong with you people?"

Inside the coffee shop, Sam asked for a booth away from the crowd. "How about that one?" the hostess asked as she pointed to a booth located in the far, back corner.

Sam leaned close to Ed, "This is perfect. You can talk without being noticed."

"Hi, I'm Christy. I'll be your server today," the young waitress looked like she had just popped from a toaster. "What would you like?"

"We'd like a muffin. Do you have lemon poppy seed?" Steuart asked.

Ed made a noise. Sam nudged him with his elbow.

Christy nodded, "We do. What to drink?"

"Two cups of tea with cream please."

"I'll be back with one lemon poppy seed muffin and two cups of tea. Is Earl Gray okay?"

"Yes," Steuart responded.

"I'd like peppermint..." Sam said. "If you have it."

"I'm not sure about the peppermint, I'll have to check on that. What's your second choice?"

"Green. Green is good."

"And that muffin—would you like it heated?"

"Yes, please," Sam smiled. Steuart nodded.

As soon as Christy was out of hearing range, Ed frowned, "What's wrong with our server?"

"I think they call it a tanning addiction," Sam said.

"I thought you were going to tell me she ate too much pumpkin. Why the sudden problem with chocolate? I really wanted chocolate."

Steuart looked at Ed, "What's wrong is that we've never seen you eat anything other than chocolate. We're concerned about your health. Sam's right. It wouldn't hurt you to try something new and different."

Christy returned with tea and muffins. She looked at Sam and shook her head, "Sorry, no mint today."

"That's okay. I like green. Do you know of any place in town that repairs dolls?"

Christy shook her head, "I'm not much help today. I don't know of anything like that around here. I'm a new student—probably not the best person to ask. I'll ask in the kitchen and see if anyone knows of a place."

A young woman approached the children from a booth across the aisle. "I overheard your conversation with our server. Did I hear that you're looking for a doll hospital?"

Sam nodded, "We are. Do you know a place?"

"The Purple Doll House is well known. It's in Hytumpol. They do great work, but it's at least fifteen miles from here. You'll need to ask your parents to take you."

"Does the bus go to Hytumpol?" Steuart asked.

The woman thought for a moment, then nodded, "Yes, I think it does, but not the local bus. You'll have to get on the transit."

"Where do we do that?" Steuart asked.

"The bus station. It's about two blocks from here. You can't miss it." The woman wrinkled her forehead, "I wouldn't go alone. You should probably ask your parents."

The children nodded. The woman said good-bye and walked away.

Sam and Steuart began talking with Ed about how they would make their way to Hytumpol. "I don't know," Steuart said, "that's a long way from here. Taking the bus sounds risky. Mother will ground us for the rest of our lives if we get caught."

"I know," Sam sighed. "You're right. But I think we can figure out a way to make it happen. We have the day off on Thursday. If we leave early enough, we might be able to make it back in plenty of time. Nanny Claire won't care."

Steuart nodded, "She never misses us."

"I know. Aren't we lucky."

"What about our appointments with Dr. Klesel?"

"We can cancel."

"Let's go to the bus station after we leave here. We can find out how much it's going to cost."

* * *

The children left the coffee shop and biked the two blocks to the bus station. "Bus schedules are confusing," Sam said.

"Expensive too," Steuart nodded.

The children sat on a bench and discussed their options. A man stopped in front of them. "Hello, young people." The man was as round as he was tall. "Did I hear you talking about The Purple Doll House?"

"Yes sir. Do you know it?" Steuart asked.

"Oh, yes—yes indeed," the man nodded. "You're in luck if you want to go now. I'm headed in that direction."

Steuart reached for his sister and looked up at the man, "No thank you."

"I'm going that way," he said. "Are you certain that you won't let me drive you over?"

"Certain," Sam nodded. "We haven't decided to go."

"Well, if you need a doll hospital, that's the one you want. The place has an excellent reputation."

"No, thank you," Sam said, this time in a more forceful voice. She stood to walk out the door. "Steuart, we have to go. Daddy's waiting for us."

"Oh, your father is here?"

"Yes, he's outside." Sam and Steuart exited the building. Steuart ran towards the bike carrier. Sam followed.

Steuart yelled to his sister, "What is it with these people? I wish they'd leave us alone."

"I'm glad you didn't let him drive us," Ed said.

Sam pedaled until she felt safe and certain that the man was not following behind. "Look," she slowed briefly and pointed to a pink sign in the distance, "I'm going there. I have a good feeling. I'm going to follow that color."

Reaching the sign, Sam slowed and looked in the distance at another pink sign.

"What are you doing?" Steuart asked.

"I need to keep going. We need to follow that color." Again, Sam pointed in the distance and continued pedaling.

At the corner, Sam stopped and looked to her right. This time she pointed in another direction. "We're going over there."

"Will you please make up your mind," Steuart shouted. "I'm getting tired. This is silly."

"No, it's not." Sam kept moving. "It's *that* pink. That's the one." She pointed to a pink building and continued up the block until she arrived. She smiled as she stopped her bike in front of a large pink house with white gingerbread trim. A sign hung from the porch, "Girren Herd, Attorney at Law." Disappointed, Sam frowned. "I was certain this was a dollhouse."

"You can't win them all," Steuart said.

"Thanks." Sam looked back at her little brother. She let out a heavy sigh. "I might as well start back. We'll have to worry about this later." She pedaled the bike up the street four blocks before stopping to catch her breath.

Steuart became animated, "Sam, I don't believe this. Look, Sam, look up the walkway. I think you've found it!"

Sam turned and saw a tiny pink house with a sign above the entry that read, "Lars Abot Doll Hospital."

The children walked inside with Ed and Trista. They stood in a small room and waited ten minutes before a young man entered from the back. "Have you been here long?"

"Just a little while," Steuart responded.

Sam took Trista from her backpack and placed her gingerly on the counter. "This is my friend Trista. Do you think you can help her?"

The young man opened the bag and looked inside, "I don't know. I really do not know." He shook his head, "This looks serious. I'm not sure. What happened to her?"

"Someone threw her against a tile wall." Sam felt tears coming, "She's extra special. I hope you can help her."

"The only promise I can make you is that we will do our best. I'll call you as soon as we know something."

Sam and Steuart said good-bye to Trista. "We'll be back for you soon," Sam whispered. "I love you."

FIFTEEN

Five days later Sam received a call that Trista was ready to come home. Immediately following school, she and Steuart headed towards the doll hospital. This time an older man greeted them. "I think you will be pleased," he said as he laid Trista on the counter.

Sam gasped, "She looks perfect. Oh my goodness, thank you for doing such a wonderful job."

"I had my doubts when I saw her. I'm pleased with our work."

Sam paid the man, put Trista into her backpack and walked outside with Steuart. She let out a huge sigh and smiled. "I'm so thankful. I'm relieved." Sam took Trista from her backpack and looked closely at the doll. "Trista, you look beautiful. I don't see any trace of your injury. How do you feel?"

Trista didn't move.

Sam and Steuart sat on a bench. Steuart held Ed. Sam held Trista.

"Trista?" Sam looked at her brother. She looked at Ed, "Is she playing a joke?"

Ed shook his head, "I hope so. Trista?" Ed reached over and touched her arm, "Are you teasing us?"

Trista didn't move.

"She wouldn't play that kind of joke," Steuart said. "Something's wrong."

Tears rolled down Sam's face. "It didn't work."

* * *

Sam and Steuart decided to visit with Ceil. "Are you okay?" Ceil asked.

Sam shook her head.

Ceil looked at Steuart.

"We just picked Trista up from the doll hospital."

"How does she look?"

Sam removed Trista from her backpack and sat her next to Ed.

"She looks wonderful," Ceil said.

Sam shrugged her shoulders, "I don't know what to say. I'd rather not talk about it if you don't mind."

"That's okay. Is there anything I can do to help?"

"No," Sam held back the tears. "I should probably go home."

"Is that what you want to do?"

"No. I don't know what I want to do."

"I understand." Ceil changed the subject, "How about going to the tree house?"

"You're forgetting, Steuart can't climb."

Ceil smiled, "I have a surprise that I think you'll both like. Come on. Let's take a walk."

Ceil pointed towards the tree house, "Steuart, check this out. Roger, my handyman, has been working on this since you were in the hospital." She showed the children an elaborate system of pulleys—a sort of dumbwaiter designed to lift Steuart up into the tree house.

"This is way too cool" Steuart exclaimed. "It's identical to the one that Captain Crandall made for Baby Bonner Blaster!"

Ceil nodded, "That's where we got the idea."

"Cool."

"There's only one thing you have to promise before you do this. You must promise that you'll not go up or down without help from Roger or me. You need an adult. Understood?"

Ceil turned towards Sam, "Sam, you can go ahead and climb to the top. I'm going to need your help."

Steuart leaned into the basket. Ceil strapped him into the seat and secured the safety belt. "Sam, when he gets up to the top, we'll pull the hatch shut, I'll come up and show you how to do it. After that, I'll show you how to unhook his seatbelt."

"Are you sure this is safe?" Sam asked.

"Roger's a retired engineer. He's worked nonstop getting things just right for you."

Ceil looked at Steuart. "Pay attention, please. I don't want you getting back into the basket without assistance. You need adult help. Do I need to repeat myself again?"

"No," Steuart was eager to ride to the top. "Now I feel like a true king," he said.

Ceil followed Sam up the ladder and prepared to meet Steuart.

"Ready?" Roger asked. "Ready on the count of three."

Steuart gave Roger a thumbs-up.

"One, two, three," Roger counted. He pushed the button and began pulling ropes. Steuart was lifted up. Once inside the tree house, Ceil pulled the hatch closed and helped Steuart exit the basket.

"This is great," Steuart said laughing. "It's so much fun to be back up here."

"I've heard the two of you talk about names," Ceil said. "What are we going to name this one? Did I hear *Sam-Steuart*?"

"Yes, you did," Steuart said.

"It's okay with you if we give it our names?" Sam asked.

"I like the name. I think it's perfect."

Steuart and Sam looked out the window towards the river.

"That's it," Steuart said to his sister.

Together they both said the name aloud several times, "Sam-Steuart."

There was a burst of snow over the river—a white out.

Steuart turned towards Ceil. "Wow, the snow's coming down now. Look..." Ceil was gone. "Where did she go?" Steuart turned back towards Sam, "Did you see her leave?"

"No."

"Why didn't she tell us?"

"Maybe she forgot something and had to run."

The snow settled as quickly as it began. Steuart and Sam continued looking at the river. "Ceil's nice letting us play here. I wonder why she never had any kids."

Sam shrugged.

"Why would you build a tree house when you don't have children?"

"She said it was here when she moved in."

"Maybe, but that's not what she said first. I don't know about some of the things she says."

Sam shrugged again, "I do like having a place to bring Ed. It's nice to be able to talk without worrying about who's listening. I still have a million questions. Maybe this is a good time. Where's Ed?"

"Oops, I left him at the house with Trista."

"Would you like for me to go back and get them?"

"No, don't worry about it. He's probably taking a nap."

Looking out the window, Sam noticed a bench on the side of the river. "Did you see that earlier?"

"Huh? No, I've never seen it before. Where's our house?"

Sam let out a big sigh. Steuart continued looking out the window. They looked at one another and smiled. "It's hard to see from here when there's so much snow."

The children continued looking, "Steuart, we have a tree house. It has our name. This is so much fun." Sam's smile turned to frown, "I just wish Trista were well."

"We won't give up. We'll continue looking until we find someone who can help."

"Are you sure-as-Matt?" Sam asked.

Twice again the children said the phrase together, "Sure-as-Matt. Sure-as-Matt." The snow and the wind picked up.

"How would you like some furniture in here?" Ceil asked. "Now that we have that basket I think we could pull up a few chairs and a little table."

Sam and Steuart looked at one another, "Where did you come from?" Steuart quizzed Ceil.

"The stork brought me."

"No, not that," Steuart rolled his eyes. "Where did you go?"

"What do you mean? I haven't gone anywhere."

The children exchanged glances.

"This is weird," Sam said.

"It's getting a lot colder," Ceil said. "Anyone care for another cup of hot tea by the fire?"

* * *

"You were gone," Steuart insisted. "Ceil, I'm not playing with you. One minute we were all in the tree house and the next minute, you weren't there. Where did you go? You disappeared."

"I didn't go anywhere. All I can say is that you were excited and completely immersed in the moment. I'm certain that's what happened."

Steuart shook his head and pursed his lips. "I don't know. I looked and I didn't see you."

After enjoying tea and a few minutes by the fire, Sam asked Ceil, "Is it okay if we go back to the tree house for more playtime?"

"I'll ask Roger to walk with you and help Steuart use the lift. When Steuart's ready to come down you can walk up and get Roger or me. Please do not try to do it without us."

Walking towards the tree house Steuart asked, "Sam, do you think Ceil's confused like Della?"

"No, not at all. We all forget things from time to time."

"What do you mean? I don't forget things."

"We just left Ed and Trista in the kitchen for the second time today. What do you call that?"

"Should we go back?"

"No. This won't take long. I'd like to try an experiment."

Roger helped Steuart into the basket and hoisted him up. Once inside, Sam held the sign. "What were we doing just before the white out?"

"We were saying our names. We said *Sam-Steuart, Sam-Steuart*. Why?"

"I have a suspicion."

"What are you talking about?"

"I just want to try something. Let's do it again and see what happens."

"Sam-Steuart," They said the name together once. The tree shook just a bit. Nothing else happened.

"Oh well," Sam said.

"What were you expecting?"

"Nothing really. Not expecting, just hoping. I thought I figured things out." Sam shrugged her shoulders. "I'm disappointed."

"I'm bored. Let's go back to the house. Better than that, how about a quick ride downtown? I'd like to say hello to Mr. Felphul."

"Good idea. I don't think we need their help. I can do this by myself."

The process was a bit challenging, but Sam was able to work the pulleys successfully. At the bottom of the tree house, Steuart exited the basket and removed his sling.

"What are you doing?"

"I don't need that stupid thing."

"What are you talking about? Of course, you need it."

"I don't," Steuart shook his head. "My arm's okay. Look, I don't need it."

"Don't be stupid. You have to wear it until the doctor tells you it's okay to stop using it."

"Look," Steuart waved his arm with no difficulty. "My arm is fine."

"Are you sure?"

"...as Matt," Steuart smiled.

"Mother will be have a fit if you're injured again. I'm getting tired of having her angry with me all the time."

"Seriously, I'm *sure-as-Matt*."

"Where's my bike?" Sam asked. "I left it here."

"No, you didn't. We left it at the house. Remember?"

"Oh, yeah. Would you rather ride or walk?"

"We can get the bike when we come back," Steuart moved his arm about. "This is great. Mother's going to be amazed that my arm is okay."

"She'll probably make you wear the sling until you see the doctor."

"I hope not."

Walking into town Steuart suggested stopping at their favorite coffee and sweet shop—Franklins.

"I don't have much money," Sam said.

"Every time we come downtown things look different. I'm turned around."

"It's just the snow, that's all. We've had so much snow this week."

"Do you see Franklins?" In its place stood Kinnflars Florist.

"We're on the wrong street," Sam pointed to a sign. "Franklin's is on Ashley."

They walked one street over and then two more streets before walking another two blocks. Sam stopped and looked in the opposite direction. "I'm completely turned around." She stopped a woman on the street and asked for directions.

"Oh, dear. I'm sorry. I don't know that street. What are you looking for?"

"Franklin Sweets and Coffee."

"I'm sorry dear, I've never been there. Bellamy has so many coffee houses. I have trouble keeping up with all of them."

"Bellamy?"

"Of course," the woman nodded. "Are you okay? Are you lost?"

"No." Sam shook her head. "We're fine. My brother and I just moved here a few months ago. We're learning our way around."

"I see. Just remember the city is laid out like a grid. It's easy to get around once you do a little exploring. Are you certain you don't need help?"

"We're fine," Steuart said.

Sam nodded, "It's okay. We can retrace our steps."

"Okay then. I hate to leave you, but I need to move along. I have an appointment around the block and I'm already fifteen minutes late. You children stay safe. Be careful. We're expecting a lot of snow this afternoon and tonight."

"Steuart," Sam looked at her brother.

"I know what you're about to say."

"We traveled."

For several minutes, Sam and Steuart stood in the snow and looked at the town. Sam felt the chill around her feet. She finally broke the silence, "Let's walk to Dr. Klesel's office."

"Good idea."

Sam and Steuart passed several people as they hiked through the snow. They walked through town, down the path, across the bridge and over to the towers. They found two tall buildings, but these buildings didn't look like Dr. Klesel's. They were older and maybe, not as tall. The children walked in and looked at the front register. Dr. Klesel's name was missing. A guard asked if he could help. "We're here to see Dr. Klesel," Steuart said.

"I don't believe we have a resident by that name."

"Resident?" Sam asked.

"Yes."

"What is this place?" Steuart asked.

"River Towers Retirement Community."

"I see," Steuart said. "Sam we need to retrace our steps."

"Are you lost?"

"No, sir," Sam said. "We're new in town. We're just exploring things and learning our way around."

"You've chosen a heck of a day to be out. This might not be the best time for you to be exploring. Bad weather's coming. You'd be wise to go home and save your exploring for another day."

The children walked outside and decided to go to their house. It wasn't there. A vacant lot sat on the river.

"We should find a place to sit where we can sort things out," Steuart said.

"Let's go back to town and sit in a coffee shop."

Along the way, Steuart stopped and read a shop sign, "Davey Ellis—toys, games and stuffed animals." He looked at the window, "Oh my gosh, Sam, look."

Sam stopped and stood speechless. Steuart didn't move. Sam moved in closer. Della Ivy's doll stood in the back corner of the window.

"Let's go inside," Sam said.

"No, let's not. This is close enough."

Sam looked at her brother, "I just had a thought."

"I'll listen as long as it has nothing to do with Della."

"Not about Della. I'm thinking about Trista."

"I don't know what more we can do."

"I'd like to know where she came from." Sam reached into her backpack and pulled out a business card. It read *Trista Petrina, Works of Fine Art*. Sam took a deep breath, "The address is on Halsey."

"That's where we were."

"Can we go back? I'd like to see where she worked."

"I wish they were with us."

Sam and Steuart walked to Halsey and counted the numbers until reaching Trista's studio. It was just above a local restaurant. Sam reached for the exterior door, "It's locked."

"What did you expect? She's not here." Steuart peered in through the glass door and looked at a stairway leading to the second floor.

Sam let out a big sigh, "I was hoping another artist might be here, maybe a friend of hers working in the same studio. I thought we might be able to talk with someone and get some answers. I wish we could go inside and see her studio. I wish we could see Trista." Sam began to cry.

"Me too." Steuart put his arm around his sister. "It's okay."

"No, it's not. I still don't understand what happened. I should never have left her alone in my room."

"It's an awful thing, but there isn't anything we can do about it today. We need to go back to the tree house. It's getting dark. You know how upset Mother gets if we're late coming home."

SIXTEEN

"Get in the basket," Sam said. "I'll pull you up."

"I'm fine. I can climb."

"Okay," Sam sighed. "I wish Ed was with us. He could explain what's happening.

"We need a guide."

"I wish Trista was here, too. I wish she hadn't gotten hurt. I'll never understand what happened." Sam climbed up the steps and stood in the middle of the tree house. "Steuart, do you remember what we were doing when we traveled?"

"We used the sign."

Sam moved to the back of the tree house and opened her backpack.

"I made it here on the floor." She pointed to the sign, "While I was looking at colors, you worked on anagrams. What did you come up with for Sam-Steuart?"

"You've forgotten? How could you forget?" Steuart huffed.

"It's been a long day."

Steuart placed the Sam-Steuart sign on the floor. He rearranged the letters. They recited the words together, "sure-as-Matt."

Sam gasped. "*Sure-as-Matt*, that's it."

"*Sure-as-Matt,*" Steuart nodded. They repeated the phrase three times. The tree house became quiet.

* * *

Sam stood alone in the tree house, and gasped. The train was passing. She looked outside and down the ladder. She walked up to the house.

"Is Steuart ready for me?" Ceil asked.

"Not yet. We'd like to play a while longer. I came to get our dolls."

"Are you sure it's not too cold to be out there?"

"We won't play much longer. We're just finishing a game."

"Okay then, let me know when Steuart's ready to come down. I'm going to be leaving for an appointment, but Roger will be here. He can help you. Don't let Steuart come down without our help. Understand?"

Understood." Sam picked up the dolls and walked to the tree house. Climbing up the steps she pulled Ed from her bag and explained what happened. "I've lost my little brother."

"I don't believe you two. What made you think you could travel alone? Are you completely nuts?"

Sam began to cry, "We're not nuts. We're not broken. It was an accident. I didn't realize what I was doing. I was playing. Ed, I have to get Steuart home now. Can you help me? Please?"

"Calm down," Ed leaned against the wall. "I'm sure that Steuart's fine. There's no need to worry. I didn't mean to upset you."

"Are you supposed to say that because you work as a guide?"

"It is true that I have extensive experience calming travelers during times of distress and great difficulty. However, there is no need to catastrophize."

"It seems like a good time to me. My brother is missing. He's lost."

"No," Ed shook his head, "Steuart is not lost. He's in Bellamy. We know where to find him."

"Let me try to explain that to my mother. We need to find Steuart and go home before we get into trouble."

"This is not a problem. We'll go back for him now and have you both home in time for dinner. What's your password?"

"Password?"

"What are the words you and Stew Boy used to transport?"

"Sam-Steuart, Sam-Steuart, Sam-Steuart."

Sam found herself standing alone in the tree house. "Oh great. I'm alone, again."

Sam heard a rumble behind the door, "You should have waited for me. We have to say the words together. Did you find Steuart?"

"He's not here."

At the bottom of the tree house Sam and Ed searched the area. Steuart was gone. "I'm guessing that you did the same thing with Steuart," Ed said.

"What's that?"

"I think you were out of sync when you chanted. He probably traveled at a different rate of speed."

"What does that mean?"

"My guess is that Steuart is now back in Maybell looking for you. He probably walked home while you were at the house talking with Ceil."

"Really?"

"I'm a guide. I understand these things far better than you think I do."

"We should just go back? He'll be waiting at home?"

"That's my best guess."

"Guess? We're guessing?"

"I keep telling you this isn't an exact science. He'll probably be back at the tree house or at Ceil's once he realizes you aren't home."

Sam was frustrated. She wanted to find Steuart and she wanted to make sure he was okay.

"Let's do this," she said.

"What's the return anagram?" Sam started to respond, "No," Ed said. "Don't say it yet. We don't want to travel separately again. Do you remember the three most important things a comedian needs to know?"

"I'm not a comedian."

"We'll go though it again."

"Why?"

"This is a teaching moment. Pay attention this time because this applies to travel as well as comedy. First, know your audience. Second, timing is everything. Third—and this is by far the most important thing—it is not an exact science." Ed held up a finger to emphasize each point.

Sam nodded.

"Now, go ahead and write your phrase on a piece of paper. We'll say it together on the count of three."

Sam reached into her backpack. "I have it here."

She showed Ed the phrase. He counted to three. They began, "Sure-as-Matt. Sure-as-Matt..."

"Wait, wait," Ed stopped Sam again. "Don't say it."

"What now? We don't have time to be silly."

"I agree. Just a minute, I need to think about this."

"What is there to think about?"

Ed cocked his head and looked at Sam, "One of us should stay here while the other one travels."

Sam raised an eyebrow, "If I'm not home soon my mother will have people out looking for me."

"That's why I should stay. You should go. I'll wait here for a while and see if Steuart shows up. If he doesn't, I'll go out and look for him. He'll probably be with you, but this is the best idea I have. We'll have him home before dark."

"I better go. Hopefully he'll be there looking for me when I get home."

"Are you ready?" Ed asked.

"I'm ready. See you in a while."

Sam clenched her fist, closed her eyes and chanted, "Sure-as-Matt. Sure-as-Matt. Sure-as-Matt."

* * *

Sam inhaled slowly, and then exhaled sharply. Instead of the crisp winter air that occasionally made her cough, this air was warm and salty. She shook her head. Instead of the quiet stillness of the tree house, Sam could hear the sounds of water lapping against the shore, the *crackle-pop* of a nearby bonfire, and the sound of people splashing in the water. These were not winter sounds; these were *beach* sounds. Sam slowly opened her eyes, looked around, and then squeezed her eyes shut again. "This can't be," she said to herself. She rubbed her eyes with the palms of her hands, blinked as hard as she could three times, and looked around once more. There was no mistaking the sleeping porch with its two summer beds that Sam and Steuart had spent many a warm evening sprawled upon. She had somehow wound up home at Point Taken.

Sam was back in Atchison Bay.

Her heart leapt at the thought of seeing her grandmother again, but just as quickly sank into the pit of her stomach. Steuart wasn't with her, and now she was a thousand miles away, unable to do anything about it. How did she even get here? Sam heard Ed's voice in her head telling her *it's not an exact science*. Sam suddenly felt dizzy, and entirely too warm.

Just then, Ida walked onto the porch with a cup of tea. She stopped as soon as she saw Sam standing there and stared at her granddaughter in disbelief. "Samantha, is that you? Thank God you're okay. What are you doing here sweetheart? How did you get here? Do you know that your mother is looking for you?" Ida paused, "Samantha, how did you get down here?"

Sam ran to her grandmother and collapsed against her, wrapping her arms around her waist. She began crying, "It's all a big mess. I've made a terrible, terrible mess."

"Sit down," Ida helped Sam out of her heavy coat and onto the bed. "Let me get you something to drink. Are you hungry?"

Sam shook her head, "No, ma'am, I'm not hungry, but I am thirsty."

Ida gave the cup of tea to her granddaughter. Sam curled up on the bed and began talking. "I'm not sure how to begin. I don't know what to say to you."

Ida brushed Sam's hair away from her face, "Just talk sweetheart. We'll put it all together. Just talk."

"You're not going to understand. Mother won't understand. This is strange and complicated. I'm not sure that I understand."

"Just tell me what you know. Where is your brother?"

"Timing is everything."

"What dear?" Ida looked puzzled.

"Sorry, I was talking to myself."

"You said *timing is everything*. Can I help you with something? Can you tell me where to find your brother?"

"Steuart's okay. He's in Bellamy." Sam yawned, "I have to help him get home."

"I need to let your mother know that you're here. I'll be back in a couple of minutes."

Sam laid on the summer bed, cried hard, and fell asleep. She woke about thirty minutes later with Ida sitting quietly beside the bed next to a small tray of fruit and a fresh glass of water. Sam worried about Steuart. She wondered if Ed had found him. She thought about what to tell her grandmother.

Ida looked at Sam, "I tried reaching your Mother."

"What did she say?"

"I got her voice mail. I left a message and let her know that you're here with me. Are you up to talking about this?"

Sam sat straight and sipped on the water. "Grandmother, you're not going to understand what I'm about to tell you, but this is what's going on." She hesitated and then began again, "Steuart and I have discovered an anagrammatic universe."

Ida listened.

"We have dolls that facilitate our transport from one universe to the other. If I'm here, my doll is there. My doll and I don't need to be in the same place at the same time because that could create difficulty in travel."

Ida nodded, "Difficulty?"

"Yes, travel is possible when a doll or person are in opposite places. Actually, it's possible if they are in the same place too. Are you following me?"

"I'm trying."

"That part's not important. That's not what's happening."

"What is happening?"

"Steuart and I discovered a tree house. It's magic because the tree house is a transportation station. We've traveled from tree house, to tree house and from universe, to universe."

"How did you get here?"

"I don't know. I thought I was going to the tree house. Maybe I used the wrong words. Ed says timing is everything."

"Ed? You were traveling with someone named Ed? Is Ed with Steuart?"

Sam shook her head, "He's one of our dolls. His name is Ed Camino. There's so much to tell you. It's going to take a long time," Sam stood, walked across the porch and looked out over the bay.

"Take your time."

"We've had a big adventure. We're still having a big adventure."

Ida looked at Sam, "Darling, you're telling me a lot, but you're not telling me how to find Steuart."

"We made a mistake today when we transported. We're still new at this and we didn't have Ed with us when we traveled. I transported back to Maybell, but Steuart didn't return."

"Why not?"

"We made a mistake... or, we didn't. I don't know. I'm not sure. Ed says that Steuart's probably still in Bellamy, but he could be back in Maybell if he accidentally traveled ahead of me. But, if mother thinks we're missing, that means he isn't home yet."

"You said Ed is one of your dolls?"

"Yes."

"He talks?"

"Yes, he does. He's very intelligent."

"Where is Ed?"

"He's in Bellamy looking for Steuart. At first he and I traveled back to Maybell together. Ed decided that it would be good for one of us to stay in Bellamy and look for Steuart while the other one went back to Maybell. Because of the mix-up, it was possible that Steuart could be in either place. I transported back because of the time and also out of fear that we would be in trouble with Mother. I thought I could make an excuse for him while Ed was helping him come home. That didn't happen because I ended up here. I don't understand how that happened. I guess I'm in huge trouble now."

Ida sat quietly and said nothing for several minutes. Then she spoke, "Samantha, you have to make a promise to me." Ida got in Sam's face. She grabbed both of Sam's hands and held them tightly, "Samantha, look at me."

Sam looked at her grandmother.

"Are you listening?" she asked.

Sam nodded.

"This is important. Tell me that you understand."

"I don't know. You haven't told me anything yet."

"Promise me that you will not share this story with anyone."

"No?"

"You must not."

"I'm telling the truth."

"Samantha, I understand that you believe this to be the truth, but you must trust me. You have to keep this between the two of us. Please understand that if you share this with anyone else you'll be in danger that you just do not understand."

"I don't understand."

"Trust me. Keep this story to yourself. I'm sorry, but if that's what it takes, that is what you have to do."

"I'm confused."

Ida sat silently and looked towards the water. "I'm worried about you and I'm worried about your brother. Do you understand Samantha?"

"Not really."

"What did I just tell you?"

"You said that I am not to share this information with anyone else. I don't understand. Don't you believe me Grandmother?"

"This has nothing to do with believing you. It has to do with other people and how they'll react. You absolutely must not share this information with anyone, especially your mother."

"No?"

"No."

"Why? Explain why I can't tell my mother about this."

Ida became silent.

"Why Grandmother?"

"I know your mother, even better than you know your mother. I raised your mother. I have no doubt that she will not understand what you're saying. I'm asking you to keep this to yourself."

"Grandmother, are you saying that you think there is something wrong with me?"

"No, darling." Ida put her arm around Sam and held her tightly. "I'm not saying that at all. I'm telling you that your mother is not going to listen to you. I do not want this to be anymore difficult for you than it is at this moment. Please, whatever you do, keep the story to yourself. Do not share it with anyone."

Sam looked at Ida, "Do you believe me Grandmother?"

Ida bit her lip and then looked down at her hands. She shook her head, "I don't know."

"Can I tell Dr. Klesel?"

"I don't think you should tell anyone."

"I'm not making anything up."

"I am not suggesting that you're making things up."

"This isn't one of our stories."

"Samantha, I don't believe that you're making up a story. We need a little time to think about this. We have to figure out what you are going to say when you go home."

"You don't want me to tell the truth? You want me to make up a story?"

"Everything will be okay. I'm suggesting that we come up with a story that will keep everyone comfortable until Steuart can be located."

"I'm worried about my brother. I hope Ed's right, but I know that things don't always work out exactly as expected. It's not an exact science."

"I'm worried too and so is your mother. I'm going to have to take you home tomorrow."

Sam let out a big sigh. She listened to the water on the shore. She shook her head, "I don't want to see Mother."

"What's wrong Sam?"

"She blames me, but Mother destroyed my doll."

"What?"

"She says that the dolls are ugly. She says they're not up to the standards of her handbook."

"That damned book," Ida whispered.

"Mother says it was an accident."

"If she says that it was an accident, it must have been an accident."

"You believe her and not me. I'm here. She's there."

"No, I'm not saying that."

"What are you saying?"

Ida took a sip of water. "I see no reason that your mother would purposely harm your doll. It makes no sense. I do think it makes sense that she had an accident. It's more logical."

"You're defending mother because she's your daughter. I'm just your adopted granddaughter."

Ida pulled Sam close again, "Do not ever say that to me again. Yes, Olivia is my daughter and you are my granddaughter. There is nothing in this world, or beyond that can change the fact that *you* are my granddaughter."

Sam began to cry. She looked at Ida, "Don't you think that Mother should know what she's done? Trista is dead because of Mother. She killed my friend."

"Samantha, your mother is going to think that you've lost your mind if you tell her that she killed your doll. If you refuse to keep these things to yourself..."

"What?"

"I worry that I may not be able to protect you. Darling, you are a bright girl and you understand a great deal, but you do not understand everything." Ida shook her head, "Samantha, you must keep this to yourself."

The phone rang. "It's your mother. I have to answer."

SEVENTEEN

The following morning Sam and Ida boarded the first available flight to Maybell. Sam fastened her seatbelt and leaned against her grandmother, "What's going to happen when we get to Maybell?"

"We're going to talk with some people about Steuart. They're going to ask you a lot of questions."

"Will you be with me?"

"No, sweetheart. I wish that I could. I'll be close by. I'll be waiting in the next room."

"Why can't you come with me?"

"Your mother feels that you'll be more comfortable without me."

"Will she be there?"

Ida shook her head, "No. Your mother will see us later. She says they're only going to ask you a few questions about Steuart and about what the two of you did yesterday. She feels confident that you'll be fine. She's already spoken with them and says these people are easy to talk with."

"You're talking about the police?"

"I am."

"What if I don't do fine? I'd like for you to be with me."

"I understand. Just walk in there and tell them that you don't remember a thing. Do not forget what I told you."

* * *

Sam was surprised that the experience was not uncomfortable. She met detectives James Foster and Duane Washington. Detective Washington told Sam that he was originally from Montana. Detective Foster, the older of the two men, was from Arkansas, but told Sam he'd lived in the Midwest since he was her age. Detective Foster said he had a son the same age as Steuart.

Sam sat with the detectives at a table in a room with a large mirror on one wall. They served cookies and fruit punch. She felt comfortable and ready to talk. She didn't understand why Ida wanted her to make up a story. Sam thought things through and decided the truth was more important than anything else. She talked about the wayward gifted. She explained to the men about the anagrams and her colors. They talked about Ed Camino, Trista Petrina, Della Ivy, Mr. Felphul and Ceil Nunstern. She told them she was sure-as-Matt that Steuart would be home soon. She explained that anagrammatic travel is not an exact science and that Ed had been doing it for years.

She went into detail as she discussed her mother's daily devotional, *Right, Good, and Appropriate*. She also talked about her special day, about wanting the paints, and about opening the box of gloves. She drank three glasses of juice, refused the cookies and then asked directions to the restroom. It was just around the corner.

Returning to the table, Sam overheard the detectives talking with a woman she had not yet met. Until that point, Sam was certain the men believed her. Detective Washington shook his head, "I'm afraid that this little girl is a real mess. I don't know what she knows—just that she believes her story. He looked at his partner and asked *what do you think James?*"

"A boy is missing. We're losing time listening to this fiction."

"What caused her to snap?"

"I have no idea, but I'm guessing it's not a good thing."

"I am curious about this Ed person."

"I agree. Find Ed and we'll find Steuart."

"Do you think she knows where they are?"

"I don't know."

"What happened to her? What has she experienced? She's sitting here calmly telling us things about traveling through the universe, playing with letters and moving from place to place. This is breaking my heart she's telling us about colors, words, standing in one place and being transported to another."

Sam realized the third person in the group was some sort of counselor or social worker because the detectives were asking her opinions about Sam's stories. "Grandmother was right," she whispered to herself.

"The child needs a therapist," the woman said.

Detective Washington nodded, "They're both in treatment."

The woman continued, "This is extreme. She's been sitting here calmly explaining all of this to both of you as if she were a little physics professor. It'd be good to talk with her doctor and find out if this time travel thing happened before or after her little brother went missing. What about the mother? Duane, did you talk with her?"

"She's an odd bird. She was quick to let us know that she's the world's greatest mother."

"She's a victim," James said. "She plays the part well."

"What do you know about DuBoise's activities leading up to her son's disappearance?"

"She's a workaholic. She's been in the office working. When she wasn't in the office, she was with other people working on work. She didn't see the kids after they left for school."

"The grandmother?"

"Down south busy with some sort of fundraiser for the community. Apparently, she was clueless until Samantha showed up at her house."

"And no one knows how she got there?"

"I know. It's insane," James said. "How does a twelve year old child travel over a thousand miles in one day without anyone knowing?"

"I hate these cases," Duane folded his arms and shook his head.

Sam walked into the room. The conversation shifted as the female member of the group turned and walked away.

Detective Foster walked towards Sam, "Welcome back. Feel better? Ready to continue?"

"I'm okay, thank you."

"Sam is there anything else you can think of that we need to know? Is there anything that you want to tell us?"

"No, I'm going to take care of things and get my brother home as quickly as possible." The men nodded. Detective Washington put his arm around Sam's shoulder and gave her a business card with his phone number. "Call us anytime. Call if you need to talk, if you have questions, or if you remember anything else."

Sam accepted the card and put into her backpack. "I prefer not to be patronized."

"What do you mean?"

"I'm a little girl, but I get it. I know you believe I'm confused."

"It's not that," Detective Washington said. "This is an unusual situation. We've never known anyone who's had this type of experience before. You're the first. That makes it more difficult."

"It's okay. I'm telling you the truth because I was taught to tell the truth. I don't know what else I can do, but unless you need me, I'd like to leave. I need to find my brother."

The detectives thanked Sam for coming in. Detective Washington knelt down and looked Sam in the eyes. "Your brother may not be coming home."

"Don't say that to me. You're not allowed to say that to me. Steuart will come home. You'll see."

"Okay, okay. I hope you're right. Maybe it would be good for you to spend a little time talking with that friend of yours, Dr. Klesel."

"Yes, I need to see Dr. Klesel. May I go now?"

* * *

Ida stood when her granddaughter walked into the waiting room. "Are you okay?"

"I'm ready to go."

"What did you tell them?"

"I told them the truth."

Ida stopped, sighed and looked at her granddaughter. "Why Samantha?"

"I know what you said, but I also know that you've always taught us to be honest. I had to tell the truth. It was the right thing to do." Sam shook her head, "But it didn't matter."

"Why?"

"They didn't believe me."

Ida put her arm around Sam's shoulder and hugged her close as they approached the elevator. "I understand."

"Do you?"

"Yes, I'm proud of you. You did the right thing. You're a good person Samantha DuBoise."

"Are we going home now?"

"Not yet. Your mother asked me to take you to see Dr. Klesel."

"That's good. We need to talk."

* * *

Snow fell heavily. Sam couldn't see the Preserve across the river as she watched the snow from Dr. Klesel's window. She touched the glass and wondered if Steuart was somewhere warm. Dr. Klesel sat in his chair and waited for Sam to begin. She knew he was concerned. Everyone was concerned. "What's going on Sam?"

"We traveled to Bellamy."

"Where's that?"

"It's an anagrammatic place."

"How far is it?"

"Think of sister cities, but not. It's another place. It's far away. Think of parallel universes. No, don't think that because you'll think I don't know what I'm saying. Just think of similar communities that are close by, but places that you can't reach using standard means of transportation." Sam looked at the doctor. She turned back to the window, touched the foggy glass and drew a happy face with her finger.

"How do you get there?"

"Tree house."

"Tree house?"

"Yes—tree house."

"Both ways?"

"Yes—yes and no. I came back by the tree house but ended up in Atchison Point at my grandmother's house, but that was a mistake."

"What was the mistake?"

"I was missing her. I always miss Grandmother. We traveled by accident and I was wishing for her because she always helps us when we have a problem."

"What was the problem?"

"It's complicated."

Sam continued looking out the window. She wondered if Dr. Klesel thought she was nuts too.

"Does this involve the tree house where you go and play?"

"Yes, it's the same place we went the night that Olivia gave me the book."

"Olivia?"

"You know, she tells people she's my mother. She adopted me when I was a baby."

"You sound angry Sam."

"I am angry. I'm worried about Steuart. Ed is looking for him now. Steuart wouldn't be there if Olivia hadn't killed Trista."

"Olivia killed Trista?"

"You're not going to believe me."

"Why do you say that?"

Sam turned around and dropped her jaw in disbelief. She gasped and rolled her eyes deliberately. "Let's try this—because even though you never look like you disbelieve me, you never look as if you actually believe me."

"How do I look?"

Sam shrugged her shoulders, "No special way." She smirked and shook her head, "Right now I feel like you don't believe me."

"I'm sorry you feel that way."

"Look, I'm just a little girl. I'm twelve years old. Everyone says that children don't know enough to know anything. Our thoughts are discounted like something at the dollar store that's been damaged or bought in bulk. Whenever anyone sees a child in the room, instantly whatever that child says is marked down because the child is a child. It happens for no other reason. The value of what comes from the mouth of a child is diminished for no other reason than the fact that it came from the mouth of a child."

"Why is that?"

"How would I know? I'm a child. That's all I am. No one ever believes children when they have something out of the ordinary to say."

"What do you want to say?"

"Aren't you listening? I've been telling you. Why would you believe me? Even if I have solid proof, how can I be sure-as-Matt about anything? You'll never believe that I can know something, or experience something that's beyond your level of knowledge because your mind forces you to wonder why a child would experience something you have not. Steuart found a good word for that."

"What's the word?"

"Arrogance. I'm a girl who collects colors and expects them to work magic. Now I'm telling you that my brother is trapped in an anagrammatic universe. Why would you believe me? Even if I were a grown up you'd probably think I'm crazy. It's just that type of thing."

"Maybe—what happened when you and Steuart were in Bellamy? Why did you go?"

"You don't want to know. You just want to think about what's wrong with me."

"I want to hear what you have to say."

Sam took a deep breath, looked down at her feet and then at Dr. Klesel. She looked over at the end table and noticed the box of tissues. She walked over to Dr. Klesel, opened her backpack and removed Trista. She held her close before handing her to the doctor. He shook his head, "I don't understand. What are you trying to tell me?"

"My mother didn't think we needed the dolls. You knew that."

"Yes, I did."

"She didn't want us to have them. I was with her that day when she told you how she felt."

"That's true. She and I've talked about the fact that she didn't want you to have dolls."

"She said it was an accident, but I don't believe her." Sam began to cry. "You trusted me to keep Trista safe. I didn't do my job. I'm responsible." Sam looked at Dr. Klesel, "I'm so sorry."

"I don't understand."

"Olivia killed her."

"Trista looks fine to me. She looks beautiful."

"She looks perfect because I took her to an expert and had her repaired. It only worked on her exterior. She looks beautiful, but Trista isn't with us anymore. She stopped talking. She stopped moving. She stopped doing anything."

Dr. Klesel looked quizzically at Sam, "How does your mother fit into this?"

"Olivia said I'm responsible for what happened to Trista because I left her on the bed when I went to be with Steuart at the hospital. I didn't take care of her like I was supposed to. I didn't put her away like I was told. Olivia said that I'm the one ultimately responsible for what happened. If I'd put her away, Olivia wouldn't have had the accident and crushed Trista's skull into so many pieces. I may be a murderer and now I'm responsible for what's happening to my brother too."

"Did you do something to harm your brother?"

"Oh, no. I would never do that."

"Did you throw Trista against a hard surface, or hit her with something like a hammer?"

"Trista? Did I throw Trista? No. I would never do that either. I can't even believe you'd ask me these questions. I left her on my bed. That's what I did. I should've taken her with me to the hospital, or I should have hidden her. I should have done something to protect her. You trusted me to. She trusted me too." Tears covered Sam's face. She had trouble catching her breath.

"Take your time. Do you need your inhaler?"

"No. I'm okay," Sam shook her head. "But, Trista isn't. I'm responsible."

"You didn't harm Trista. You've taken good care of her."

"I left her at home. I didn't put her away."

"Sam, as I understand this, you left the doll on your bed, in your bedroom. What you do not understand is that your bedroom should be a safe place to leave a doll. Trista wasn't left outside or treated in a careless manner. She wasn't left on the floor. She wasn't even left in another part of the house. A doll on your bed, in your bedroom, should be safe."

"You don't understand. I found her when I got home from the hospital. She was in a plastic bag. Her head was smashed to pieces. Olivia told me she had an accident. Ed told me the truth about what happened."

"Ed?"

"Your doll," Sam nodded, "Ed Camino, the comedian. He's the one who explained everything to Steuart and me about Bellamy."

"He explained?"

"Yes, he explained to us about traveling, about how to get there, and about how he got here."

"My dolls are talking to you?" Dr. Klesel put down his clipboard and leaned forward in his chair.

"We talk all the time. Well—Trista did until she was broken."

"You're having conversations with my dolls?"

"Yes. I know. You're thinking that I have a real problem. I can hear it now—*she's talking to dolls. The patient is talking to dolls.* You're going to suggest sending me away somewhere."

"No," he said softly and shook his head. "I'm not."

"If the dolls aren't talking to me, I may actually be crazy, but they are talking to me. I know it."

Dr. Klesel leaned back in his chair and sat silently.

"In the beginning," Sam said, "Steuart and I were not sure about things. When Ed began explaining things to us, we were skeptical too. I understand—it seems far-fetched that they came from another world, but hey, they're dolls and they talk, right? That's enough to make you realize that other things are possible too. When Trista was hurt, we found the doll hospital. When we picked her up she looked beautiful, but she didn't talk anymore. Another experience led us to realize that Ed and Trista were telling us the truth—but it took a while before everything made sense."

"What was that?"

"One time when we were at the tree house we noticed that the four o'clock train came by twice."

"What does that mean?"

"We didn't know in the beginning, but Ed explained it to us. What we know now is that we were in Maybell and then in Bellamy. We heard the train in both places."

"What?"

"Think about it. There's a slight lag in the time."

"Why didn't you know without the train?"

"Because we traveled accidentally and we were only there a short time. We didn't even leave the tree house."

"Oh."

"We saw a few things that were strange and we heard the train come by twice."

"Strange, what things?"

"I saw a bench, then I didn't see it."

"What's it like in Bellamy?"

"Just like Maybell in some ways but different in others."

"What do you mean?"

"We're getting off the track. I need to keep telling you about what happened. I have to find my brother."

"Okay."

"Olivia broke Trista. After that, we didn't know what to do. I took her to a doll hospital. They repaired her."

"That's what you said."

"Yes, but she was just a doll. She stopped being real."

"What else can you tell me?"

"Dolls change size from time to time. It depends. Ed always tells us that it can be unpredictable. It seems more unpredictable than not. Timing is everything."

"Do you think there might be other possible explanations for what you've experienced?"

"I don't know. I need to find Steuart." Sam frowned, "I wish I could have saved Trista. I think it's too late."

"For your brother?"

"No, for Trista." Sam shook her head and looked off in the distance, "I've always thought that my colors were magic, but so far they've not done a thing to help. I'm disappointed."

"You've told me the colors lead you. Colors led you to the tree house."

"Look where that got us."

For a minute, the two sat in complete silence. Sam thought about what she wanted to say, "Shark Yeller, maybe I should trust myself more, but I'm so sad about Trista. I'm worried about Steuart. The only thing that feels good is that my grandmother's here. I forgot to tell you. She's in the waiting room. She asked if she could say hello to you. She'll be going back to Atchison Point soon."

"I'd like to meet her. We have a few more minutes, let's talk more about your experience."

"Good idea," Sam nodded. "I have a few questions for you. You gave us the dolls. Certainly you know about them. What do you know? What can you tell me?"

Dr. Klesel glanced at the clock. "We can talk about all of that later. If I'm going to meet your grandmother, we should stop for now. It's later than I realized."

Dr. Klesel and Sam walked into the waiting room. Ida stood, smiled, and extended her hand. Sam introduced the two.

"Have we met before?"

"No, I don't believe we have. I'm visiting Maybell."

Dr. Klesel frowned, "You look familiar. I wish I'd known you were here at the beginning of Sam's session. My next appointment is a little late. If you'd like to step into my office, we can talk for a couple of minutes."

Ida looked at Sam, "Is that okay with you?"

"I'll be in the lobby."

"Please don't leave the building."

"I won't. I'll be close to the elevator downstairs."

With that Ida went into Dr. Klesel's office. Sam walked into the hall, got on the elevator, and rode down.

* * *

In the lobby, Sam walked to the back windows and looked out at the snow. She held Trista close as she thought about Steuart and Ed. Sam's heart was broken. She wanted to help Trista. She wondered how soon she would hear from Ed. She also wondered how soon her brother would come home. Sam wanted to cry. "Wait until you're in your room," she whispered to herself. Sam didn't want to go home. She was uncomfortable about seeing her mother.

A voice came from across the lobby, "Samantha DuBoise, do you remember me?" A young girl walked over and stood next to Sam. "Hello."

"We have an appointment. We're already running late," a woman called to the girl from the elevator.

"I know. He won't mind. I'll be upstairs in a minute. Please tell him I'm saying hello to a friend."

The woman pushed the elevator button and spoke firmly as the doors closed, "Don't take long."

The girl looked at Sam, "You don't recognize me. You were my visitor at the hospital. You sang to me. I remember you."

Sam smiled, "I remember you too."

"Do you remember my name?"

"Yes—Dotsie. You look much better today. I like your hat."

"Thank you," Dotsie reached up and touched her hat, "I'm in remission."

"That's good to hear."

"I'm happy to see you again. Your doll is very beautiful. What's her name?"

"Trista. She's an artist."

"How pretty."

"She isn't feeling well."

"I'm sorry to hear that." Dotsie looked at the doll and then asked Sam, "Will you visit me? We can have a tea party. I live on the twelfth floor of the other tower." She pointed, "Over there. I'd like to learn the song you sang when you visited. Maybe I can teach you one too. I'd also like for you to meet my doll."

"You have a doll?"

"Yes."

"You're going to see Dr. Klesel? He's my doctor too."

"Yes," Dotsie nodded. "I have a doll. He's not mine. Dr. Klesel is letting me borrow him. His name is Toriah Toroar."

"That's a name."

"It is."

"I'll see if I can come. Thank you for the invitation."

"I hope you will."

"They'll probably let me. I live over there." Sam pointed in the direction of her house. "I'll look forward to meeting your doll."

"How's your brother?"

Sam looked off in the distance, "He's missing."

Dotsie put her hand over her mouth, "Missing? Oh, no, that's awful."

"I know."

"I wish I could do something to help you." Dotsie reached out and put her hand on Sam's.

"Thank you." Sam felt a tear in her eye and worried that she was about to start crying. She shook her head, "Don't worry about Steuart. I know where he is, and I have a friend who's trying to help me get him home."

Dotsie pulled a pen and paper from her purse and began writing, "This is my number and this is the number for our condo. You must come to my house. I'll expect you tomorrow at three." Dotsie began walking towards the elevator, "I have to go now. Please come."

Ida walked off the elevator as Dotsie walked on. Dotsie turned and waved to Sam, "Promise me."

"I'll do my best."

They waved good-bye as the elevator door closed.

Ida walked towards her granddaughter, "You have a new friend?"

"I do."

Sam dreaded going home. She knew she would have a difficult time explaining things to her mother. She was wound up. She was worried and angry. She wanted to find her son and said that no one was doing what he or she should. "Just explain things to me. Where did you leave your brother?" Olivia looked exhausted. Her face was covered with tears.

"I don't know." Sam decided not to tell her mother what was happening. She remembered Ed's advice and whispered to herself, "Know your audience."

"Why is this happening to me?" Olivia asked her mother and then turned towards her daughter. "Sam, please go to bed now unless there's something more that you can tell me. I'm exhausted."

Sam nodded and said "Goodnight." She turned to her mother, "Don't worry Mother. Steuart's fine."

Olivia frowned, "What's wrong with you?"

***

"Hey Sam," Ed whispered in a quiet, happy voice.

"You're back! Where's Steuart?"

"Lower your voice."

"Did you find him?"

"Yes, I did."

"Where is he? We need to tell Mother."

"No, we can't just yet. He's still in Bellamy."

"Oh?"

"It's okay. Let's talk about it tomorrow. I'm tired from all this traveling—you must be too. It's been a long couple of days."

"I'd rather talk about things now. I've been talking with people all day. A bit more talk won't hurt. Please tell me what you know. Did you come from the tree house? Did you see Ceil?"

"No. I didn't come that way."

"How did you get here? Surely you didn't end up on the bay."

"Cat."

"Cat?"

"Yes, in times of emergency Cat is a solid means of travel."

"Cat?"

"Yes, that's what I said. Cat." Ed nodded. He raised his hands in the air and stretched, "Don't ask. It would take days for me to explain. We don't need to go there tonight. You already have too many things to think about."

"But, you saw Steuart? Is he okay? Where is he?"

"He's at a place called The Minor Protection Agency."
"That sounds terrible."
"It's not a bad place."
"How do you know?"
"That's what I've heard."

EIGHTEEN

The following morning Olivia readied herself for work. "They tell me there is nothing I can do here. I've spoken with everyone," she told her mother. "I've done all that I can. We have to wait. That's it. This is in the hands of the authorities. Where is my baby?"

"Maybe you should stay home and try to get more sleep."

"I can't sleep."

"Have you asked your doctor for something?"

"No, I'm better concentrating on my work."

"You are not going to be able to think."

"Mother—we all handle stress differently. I'm my best when I'm busy. I might as well go in and take care of business. There's nothing I can do at the moment. I will lose my mind if I stay here." Olivia started to cry. "They'll contact me if there is any news, or if I'm needed." She looked at her mother, "You have my number."

"Of course I do."

"You're right. Of course you have it. I'm not thinking."

"You have to do what feels best for you. I'd like to keep Sam here with me today. I don't think she's emotionally prepared for anything at the moment."

"It wouldn't hurt her to go to class. There's no reason to infantilize her."

"Like I said, I'd like to keep her home today."

"Do whatever you want. I don't care."

* * *

Sam waited until the afternoon before asking Ida if she could visit with Dotsie. Ida nodded, "That is a very nice idea. I think it will do you good to visit your friend." Before leaving the house, Sam turned back and gave her grandmother a big hug. "Thank you. I think Dotsie may have some ideas that'll help bring Steuart home."

Ida held Sam's face in her hands and brushed her hair back. "Enjoy seeing your friend. Do not go to the tree house."

"I won't." Sam left for Dotsie's with Trista and Ed in her backpack.

Sam entered the first tower and rode the elevator to the twelfth floor. She rang the bell and waited. A short chubby lady answered—the same woman Sam saw with Dotsie at the doctor's office. "Hello Samantha. Dotsie is expecting you. I am Anita."

"It's nice to meet you. Should I take off my shoes?"

"That would be nice. You can put them over there," Anita pointed to a boot tray and continued talking, "I can take your coat and hat too. I'll hang them here." She opened a closet door. "Shall I take your backpack?"

"No, thank you. I have some things that I'd like to share with Dotsie."

"Of course, Dotsie told me that you're new in town. Do you like the cold weather?"

"Very much. I love snow. We didn't have weather like this down south. That's where I'm from. I like getting out in the cold."

Anita smiled.

Sam tried to think of conversation, "I always wonder why more people don't make snowmen here. If we had this much snow back home, everyone would have snowmen in their yard."

"People take for granted what they have. You know that. Most children don't want to get out. They're accustomed to entertaining themselves in the house. I'm afraid we have a world of lazy little house muffins."

"You mean potatoes?"

"Did I say potatoes?"

"No."

"I prefer muffins—they're sweeter. I heard about your brother. Do you have any news?"

"No, nothing more, but I know he's okay."

"It's important to have faith. That's what my priest tells me."

"I do."

"I hear Dotsie coming down the hall."

"Sam!" Dotsie was thrilled. "You're here. Let's go to my room. Anita helped me set up a little party. We can have tea. She made scones for us."

Sam looked at Anita, "Thank you. My grandmother makes scones sometimes. Most of the time she makes biscuits."

"Which do you like best?"

"I love them both," Sam smiled.

"Today I've made apple for you ladies."

"I love apple."

"Come on Sam," Dotsie led Sam down a long hall and into her room. "Did you bring your doll?"

"Yes, well, no. I did, well, yes and no."

"Silly—either you did or you didn't. Did you?"

"Yes. I brought Steuart's doll, Ed Camino. I also brought Trista Petrina, but she's ill."

"What's wrong with her?"

Sam opened her backpack and gently pulled out both dolls. Dotsie took Ed from Sam's hands and sat him in a chair at a little table next to another male doll. Sam laid Trista on the bed.

"I feel so bad for her," Sam said.

"She looks okay to me. What happened?"

"It's awful. When you and Steuart were in the hospital, I left Ed and Trista at the house. We were in a hurry. Later that day my mother went home and had an accident with Trista. Her skull got crushed."

"That's terrible, but she looks pretty now. Who fixed her?"

"Steuart and I found a doll hospital downtown."

"I can't even see where she was broken."

"I know. They did a good job, but it wasn't enough."

"This is my doll." Dotsie pointed to a portly doll seated next to Ed. He wore a three-piece suit and carried a pocket watch. He looked as if he could bellow his name and be heard all the way across town. "I call him TT, but his real name is Toriah Toroar."

"What a name. Where did he get a name like that one?"

Dotsie shrugged, "He's an orator. He talks and talks and talks and talks and talks. After that, he talks and talks some more. Sometimes he has trouble stopping. He's long winded, but he's a long-time friend of mine. Sometimes I have to ask him to be quiet so that he doesn't disturb my mother."

Both of the dolls sat silently.

"When TT gets started, he doesn't know when to stop."

Sam stared at Dotsie. Dotsie bit her lip.

"Sam, your dolls talk to you, don't they?"

Sam stood stunned.

"They're from the anagrammatic universe. You know that—right?"

Sam's jaw dropped.

"Sam?"

Sam stared at Dotsie. She wanted to choose her words carefully.

"You don't believe me?"

Sam stood silently and considered Dotsie's words.

Dotsie became fretful, "Oh, I've done it now—great. You think I am crazy. You think I am just a crazy kid with a brain tumor who's having hallucinations. You're thinking I've had too much radiation, and too many medications. You think I have no idea what I'm saying to you. You think this is some crazy thing that I've made up. I understand. I'd think the same thing if I didn't know the things I know. I'm sorry. I shouldn't have said anything. I thought you knew." Dotsie turned and looked at Toriah, "I feel stupid. I'm so embarrassed."

Sam spoke to Ed, "She knows."

Ed stood and smiled, "Sam, this is our lucky day." He jumped up and did a happy dance.

Dotsie let out a sigh of relief. "I thought you were thinking awful things. You know, when I saw you in the lobby yesterday I felt certain that you knew. But just a minute ago you had me scared. What were you thinking?"

"I was surprised. I needed to let it sink in. You're the only person I know who knows this. Dotsie, It's a relief to talk with someone who understands. There's so much going on. Between Steuart and Trista, I have a lot of worries."

Sam looked at Trista and picked her up. Dotsie looked at the doll, "They did a good job. I can't tell that she was injured."

"She hasn't spoken a word since we got her home."

"I don't understand. You said your mother had an accident with her?"

"Mother didn't want us to have the dolls. We were instructed to put them out of her sight unless we were taking them to Dr. Klesel's office. I was at the hospital with Steuart when she came home and saw Trista on my bed. It was a hard day with Steuart having surgery and all. I'm not sure exactly how her head exploded, but I think Mother may have lost her temper."

"That's terrible. Poor Trista."

"I shouldn't have left her alone."

"You can't blame yourself."

Sam nodded, "I guess it doesn't matter if it's my fault or not. First, Trista, and now, Steuart."

"What's happened to Steuart?"

"He's in Bellamy."

"Are you serious? Steuart went to Bellamy? How did he do it?"

"Two days ago we made a trip over. He stayed behind."

"You're telling me that you've been there too? What's it like?"

"It's pretty. It's similar to Maybell, but also different. We made a mistake trying to come home."

"It's not an exact science," Ed interjected, "Timing is everything."

Sam shook her head. "It's not. It seems that Steuart and I were out of sync when we began to transport. I ended up back home at Atchison Point."

"Where's that?"

"Home? It's a long way from here. It's on the bay. I still don't understand what happened."

"What do you know?"

"First, we tried to transport together. I ended up here. Steuart wasn't with me. I got Ed to go back with me. He and I traveled together thinking that Steuart would still be at the tree house. He wasn't. I transported home alone so that Ed could stay behind and look for Steuart. That's when I ended up at my grandmother's house. She lives more than a thousand miles away."

"You've been busy."

"This is a nightmare. My mother's going nuts. She thinks Steuart was kidnapped. She's waiting for a ransom note or something like that. She thinks I'm responsible because I was with him."

"You need to find Steuart."

"Ed found him already."

Dotsie looked at Ed, "Where is he?"

"The Minor Protection Agency. I found him, but wasn't able to bring him home."

"Harrumph," Toriah spoke, "Forgive me if I come across in an indelicate way, but Ed, I understand why you were unable to bring the young lad home."

"Why's that?" Ed asked.

"Comedians are not always diplomatic. I believe that I might be able to help."

"Thanks. I wondered how long it would be before you took charge."

"I have no desire to take charge. However, it does appear that you might benefit from an extra hand."

"Old man, we need all the help we can get."

Sam agreed, "He's right."

"Sam, why did you and Steuart go to Bellamy?" Dotsie was curious. "Tell me about it?"

"It was an accidental trip. We didn't intend to travel. We were playing."

"But you knew how to get back?"

"We figured it out, but as you can see, it wasn't a complete success. Ed has been helping me."

Ed turned towards Toriah, "I didn't give her the information." He looked at Dotsie, "It's against *the Code of the Guide.*"

Toriah nodded, "True. True."

"They found their way over and Sam found her way back. At that point, I realized that I had to step in and help."

"The code has provisions for emergencies," Toriah interjected.

Ed continued, "Steuart needs to come home. He's too young to be alone."

"Who went with you?" Toriah asked Sam.

"No one. We did it accidentally. We weren't sure about what we were doing. And now, I'm here—and Steuart's there. My mother's upset with me. She doesn't understand what's happening."

"I can imagine," Toriah said.

Sam continued, "I can't explain this to her. She'd think I made it all up. Last night I heard her tell my grandmother she wishes she'd never adopted me." Sam began to cry, "I feel completely lost. Steuart's stuck in Bellamy, Trista's not responding, and my mother hates me. This is all my fault."

"Sam," Dotsie said, "you're not responsible for what happened to your brother or Trista. You can't blame yourself. You're such a nice person."

"Nice people are the ones you don't know. You and I've just met."

Dotsie touched Sam on the arm and nodded, "Nice people are the ones who share their hearts and invite you inside. That's what you did the first day you visited me at the hospital."

"We have to go back and help Steuart," Sam looked at Ed. "I don't know how we're going to get him out of that place.

"That's where you come in," Ed turned towards Toriah.

Toriah listened.

"I can help too," Dotsie said.

Ed smiled at Dotsie and then turned to speak with Toriah. "If you're available, we'd appreciate your help. As you've said, a comedian is not always able to handle the most delicate of issues in Bellamy. I know Steuart's exact location, but I worry that we may be running out of time. He may be moved before we can get to him."

Toriah nodded, "Children adopt out quickly." He took a deep breath and let out a huge sigh. "My dear man, it would please me greatly to be of service to you and your lovely hostess Sam, as well as her young brother Steuart. However, I am currently in the employ of the lovely Miss Caples and absolutely unable to leave her at this time. While I would like very much to help you, I must decline. Please understand and accept my most sincere apology. Miss Caples is my first responsibility. I hope you understand."

Ed, Toriah and Sam looked at Dotsie. Toriah continued, "As you know, Miss Caples has extenuating circumstances of her own and has been through a difficult situation recently. Her health is not the best. Although she is in remission, she depends on me. She depends on my daily companionship. I fear that were I to leave she would be most unhappy. I am needed here."

"I have the solution," Dotsie looked at Toriah, "TT, I don't want you to leave me. I want to go too. I can help." Ed and Sam exchanged glances. "I can be helpful," Dotsie said. "I'm ready for the adventure."

"No, Dotsie, you don't need to do this," Sam said. "Traveling can be dangerous. It sounds like fun, but too many things can go wrong. You have to think about your health. I don't think this is a good time for you to go."

"There may never be a perfect time for me. Now is as good as any—I'm in remission. I feel great. Is there ever a perfect time for anything?"

"You have a serious condition," Ed looked at Dotsie. "We'd be responsible for you. Neither Sam nor I would be able to forgive ourselves if something happened to you. It's difficult enough trying to rescue Steuart."

"I'm not your problem. I'm responsible for myself. I can help."

"Dotsie," Sam asked, "what would your parents say?"

Dotsie became quiet for a few minutes, "My father's not here. He passed away before I was born. My mother is away at a medical conference this week. She'll be gone until Sunday. I'm here with Anita. I can go with you and be back in Maybell before Mother gets home. I can tell Anita that I've been invited to keep you company."

"I appreciate that you want to join us, but we can't let you take the risk," Sam looked at Ed.

"Oh, I understand. You want to take my doll away from me and you want to go off and have a big adventure while I stay here and die? Is that it?"

"No. I have to find my brother and bring him home. I also want to see if there's anything I can do to help Trista while we're in town. Steuart and I didn't plan all of this. We stumbled upon anagrammatic travel. Ed and Toriah may understand what they're doing, but I don't." Sam shook her head, "Nothing is exact. Things happen. That's why Steuart is where he is right this minute."

Dotsie rolled her eyes. Sam continued, "Things go wrong. Things go right. You don't know what's going to happen. I ended up traveling to my grandmother's house—all the way down south. I'm not happy about traveling now. If we weren't in the middle of a crisis, I'd stay home. I'm going because I have an obligation to bring my brother home. I have to rescue him. You don't have to do this. What if you go over and get sick while we're there? What if going causes you to go out of remission?"

Dotsie insisted. "Like I said, I'm responsible for myself. I feel well and I can help. I'm helpful, and I'm smart."

"You're also stubborn," Ed said softly.

Toriah folded his arms and looked sternly at Dotsie, "That is the understatement of the day. Are you up to this Miss Caples?"

"Does it matter?"

"I understand. You mean well. It's okay," Sam said.

"Thank you for understanding. We appreciate your understanding." Ed walked towards Toriah, "We'll be back with Toriah as quickly as possible."

"Who are *we*?"

"Sam, Toriah and myself."

Dotsie folded her arms and shook her head, "Absolutely not—I need to be with TT. If I don't go, he stays here with me."

"Look kid," Ed insisted, "If anything happened to you, we would never forgive ourselves. Sam would never get over it. The kid has a huge heart and even though you've only known her for a short time, you've found a place inside. Sam would never be able to handle it if anything happened to you. Do you understand?"

"I understand much more than you realize. I can take care of myself."

"Then there's no problem. You'll be fine for a short while if Toriah takes off with us."

"No! Absolutely not."

"She should go," Sam looked at Ed. "Dotsie should go."

"What?" Ed turned to Sam, "I thought you said..."

Sam looked at Ed and then turned to Dotsie. "You should go,"

Dotsie smiled.

"Traveling is an adventure. It's different from anything you've done before. I can't tell you what's going to happen. We have no way of knowing," Sam shook her head, "but I think you should come along. We need your help. I'd like for you to join us on our journey. Will you help us find Steuart?"

Dotsie hugged Sam, "You bet I will."

"We can't lose much more time. It's getting late. We can't go today. We can go early tomorrow morning. How early can you meet us at the tree house?" Sam looked at Dotsie and Toriah.

"I have breakfast at eight. I can get out of the house anytime after that and not look suspicious."

"Ed and I will wait for you and Toriah until nine. We'll all go as soon as you arrive." Sam drew a map showing Dotsie the location of the tree house. "It's not hard to find. Wear simple looking clothes. You'll want to blend in when we get to Bellamy. The temperature is similar to what we have here."

Ed looked at Sam, "We need to go now."

Dotsie smiled, "Thank you Sam."

The two girls walked downstairs together. Sam turned to Dotsie, "I'm glad you're going. I just want to know you're safe. If you change your mind, I'll understand."

"I won't change my mind."

"Thanks for helping."

Snow continued to fall at a steady pace as Sam walked towards the road with the dolls inside of her backpack.

Dotsie waved to Sam from the lobby, "Be careful going home."

Anita joined Dotsie waving good-bye, "Did you have a nice afternoon? How nice that you have a new friend."

"Yes."

Anita reached for Dotsie's hand, "Let's go inside. It's time for your medication."

NINETEEN

Sam woke early on Saturday morning. She heard Olivia and Ida in the living room. Olivia was crying, "Mother, where can he be? It's been almost three days—no notes, no calls, nothing. This is a bad sign. Why do these things have to happen?"

"Keep your faith," Ida said. "I believe Steuart will be home soon."

"Do you know something I don't know? How did Samantha Leigh end up at your house? I am so confused by all of this. Has she mentioned anything you haven't told me?"

Ida shook her head, "I don't have any answers. I do believe that Steuart's okay and I believe that he'll be home soon. I can't believe anything else."

"I want to know that my child is safe. I want my baby to come home. Where is he Mother? I've repeatedly told those two to be responsible. They never listen to me. I'm so tired. I can't sleep. I can't think. I'm fried."

"Let's keep thinking positive thoughts. We're all worried."

"*We* are not *me*. I am Steuart's Mother. I have no doubt you are concerned, however you are not me. Who is worrying about me? Does anyone ever worry about how I feel? My son is missing. Does anyone listen to me?"

"Mother, I worry about you." Sam walked in the room towards Olivia.

Olivia turned away from her daughter, "Please, don't even talk to me unless you can tell me something that will help bring my son home. I can't bear to look at you unless you can tell me where I can find Steuart James."

"Olivia!" Ida looked at her daughter with fiery eyes, "Don't you dare speak to Sam in that tone. She has done nothing wrong."

Olivia sat silently with *Right, Good, and Appropriate* in her lap. She stared blankly at Sam.

Sam turned to leave the room. "Come over here, sweetheart." Ida called out to Sam. "I need a hug." She looked at Olivia, "Where did this ugliness come from? Shame on you."

Olivia shrugged, "Mother, at this moment I don't care what you say or what you think."

"Samantha is every bit as worried about Steuart as I am and every bit as worried about him as you are. You are not alone in this and neither are you the only one suffering. This is an extremely stressful time for all of us."

"That's an understatement." Olivia said.

"A very stressful time for all of us." Ida continued, "We need to remain calm and show our love for one another."

"I'm sorry, Grandmother," Sam gave Ida another hug and looked at her mother.

Olivia looked at Sam, "You need to tell us what happened to your brother. Where is he? Who were you with? Where did you leave your brother?"

Sam felt tears on her face. She shook her head and looked at her grandmother, "I don't know."

"You're lying."

"I'm not."

"Olivia," Ida snapped, "stop that this instant."

"Grandmother, it's okay. I understand."

"No, it is not okay. Your mother's worried, but that's no excuse. Your mother loves you very much. I do too."

Sam walked into the kitchen and poured a glass of milk. Back in the living room she approached Olivia, "If there's nothing I can do here, I'd like permission to visit with my friend Dotsie. She lives in the towers. Is that okay with you?"

"Go ahead—you might as well go play. There's nothing you can do here unless you can tell me where to find your little brother."

* * *

Sam had tears in her eyes as she put on her coat. Ed was tucked into her backpack with Trista who remained motionless. Sam walked towards Ida and exchanged a hug. She walked towards her mother who motioned her to leave. "I don't need a hug now. It's okay. We can hug another time."

Sam left the house crying. Snow was heavy on the path. She decided to walk.

Ed reached up and patted Sam on the back, "Your mother doesn't understand. You're doing all you can to bring Steuart home. We have a big day ahead of us so don't allow her to get you too upset."

"I know."

"It's not an excuse, Sam, but sometimes people say things they shouldn't say. Your mother's upset, but I'm certain, in her own way, she loves you very much."

"Thank you Ed."

"Everything will be okay. We'll find Steuart today and bring him home."

"I hope so."

There was a heavy fog as the temperature was rising. The walk to the tree house was wet, slushy and slippery. Ice on the bridge and along the path made the walk difficult. Sam slipped twice. "We're the only ones out here. I hope Dotsie and Toriah are able to meet us. What if Anita won't let her leave the condo?"

"We'll understand and proceed on our own. Frankly, I was surprised that you were allowed to leave the house this morning. This weather is terrible."

"We need Toriah."

"With or without Toriah we'll work things out. I promise you. We'll find Steuart and bring him home."

Sam climbed the ladder.

"Hey," Dotsie said, "I'm happy to see you. We worried that you might not be allowed out of the house."

Sam let out a sigh of relief, "We thought the same thing about you."

"I wouldn't have missed this opportunity. What do we do now?"

"It's simple. We named the tree house. We say the name out loud and we're transported."

"That's it? That's all?"

"I told you. It's almost too simple—we say it three times. I don't know if it matters, but that's what we did."

"Coming back we have to repeat the anagram."

"Three times in unison?"

"That's how we did it."

Dotsie looked at Toriah who nodded, "It's that simple and you wouldn't tell me?"

"You know we're not allowed to tell you much. You have to learn by yourself."

Sam removed the handmade Sam-Steuart sign from her backpack, "On the count of three we need to say it together. Is everyone ready?"

"Yes."

"Wow," Dotsie smiled. "I've been wanting to do this for over a year."

"Are you serious?"

"She is," Toriah nodded. "Miss Caples has been ready and trying to work this out for a long while."

"Let's do this," Dotsie said.

"Ready?" Sam asked.

"Yes."

"Okay, one, two, three."

"Sam-Steuart. Sam-Steuart. Sam-Steuart." The wind picked up. A chill was felt in the air. Nothing seemed to change. Disappointed, Dotsie looked at Sam and Toriah, "Why didn't it work? Let's try again."

Sam and Toriah looked at Dotsie.

Dotsie looked around the tree house. "Where's Ed?"

"Down here," Ed called out.

Sam looked down and saw a 5-foot 9-inch Ed. "He's down there," she pointed out the door. "What are you doing down there?"

"Not sure."

"Whoops," Toriah looked at Sam, "I forgot something. Sam, may I borrow your sign?"

Toriah held the sign. He turned it over and quietly repeated the words three times. "Sure-as-Matt. Sure-as-Matt. Sure-as-Matt." He disappeared and then quickly reappeared, this time at a height of 6-feet and 4-inches.

Dotsie looked up, "TT, you are very tall. My goodness."

"Sometimes Miss Caples, that is true. How are you feeling?"

"I'm good. I feel wonderful."

"You'll let me know if that changes?"

"Don't worry. I feel great. I can't believe that we're finally here."

Toriah, Dotsie and Sam descended to the bottom of the tree house where Ed waited. Looking up at Toriah, he said, "No matter how many times I do this I never come back any taller than this."

"I must be the bigger man," Toriah chuckled.

Ed looked at his friend and reached to poke his ample stomach, "Even if we were the same height, you'd still be the bigger man." Toriah swatted Ed's hand away with a grumble.

Sam looked at Ed and removed Trista from her backpack. Trista didn't move. "I'd hoped traveling might bring her back."

Ed put his arm on Sam's shoulder, "I don't know what more you can do at the moment."

* * *

As in Maybell, a house stood at the front of the property. Oddly, this house looked more like Point Taken than Ceil's. Ed walked to the back door and then motioned for the group to join him. "No one's here," he whispered.

"Looks like no one has been here in a while," Sam said.

After peeking into the windows, Ed walked around to the side of the house where he found an unlocked door. He went inside and quickly returned, "I was correct. The place is deserted, but it's not empty."

The group walked inside.

"Sam, you and Ed should settle in," Toriah suggested. "I think I should go into town and make a few contacts." He cleared his throat, thrust out his chest, and straightened his shoulders.

"Good idea," Ed nodded. "Meanwhile, we need to come up with a plan."

"Agreed—I have a few ideas. Just wait until I return." Toriah looked at Dotsie and extended his hand, "Miss Caples, will you accompany me?"

"Yes," Dotsie nodded, "I want to go." She turned to Ed and Sam, "Will the two of you be okay if I go with TT?"

"Of course, we'll be fine. Miss DuBoise and I are going to see what we can figure out from this end."

Toriah raised an eyebrow. He opened the door and motioned to Dotsie. He looked at Ed and Sam, "Be careful. Please stay where you are. We all want to find young Steuart, but without having a firm plan, I believe it's best if you wait. We do not need to end up searching for the two of you."

"Don't worry, Sam and I are not going anywhere." Ed turned to Sam, "Care to do a little in-house exploration?"

* * *

Sam was surprised by how similar this house was to Point Taken. "I'm going upstairs. I want to see if there's a room like mine."

"I'll join you," Ed followed behind.

Sam found a room that was quite a bit like hers, complete with an antique bed and a dollhouse. There was even a little writing desk in one corner that was almost identical to the one she had at Ida's. There were other similarities; a room like Steuart's and another one similar to Ida's bedroom. The room that would be in the same spot as Olivia's was also in this house;

however, in this house, the room was set up for sewing, complete with equipment, tools and supplies. The sleeping porch was there too, complete with twin beds, much like Point Taken, however, the big difference was that this porch had glass windows and looked out over an icy river. Sam found a notecard on the porch. The name *Laurel Ivy Hood* was hand printed across the front—the backside of the card was blank.

"I've seen this before," she told Ed.

"What is it? Who's Laurel Ivy Hood? Do you know this person? Is she a friend of yours?"

"No," Sam shook her head. "I have no idea who she is, but I've seen the card and I know that she visited Atchison Point. She's been to my grandmother's house."

"How do you know? Did you meet her?"

"No, I told you, I don't know who she is. She's been there, but I didn't even see her—Steuart did. He had this card. He showed it to me the morning we moved to Maybell. He said Mother had a visitor the night before. Apparently, according to Steuart, Mother and the woman argued. He said that Mother made the woman leave."

"That's interesting. I wonder why the card's here."

"Steuart said that Mother was angry, but as she was leaving the house the woman dropped this card in the foyer. Mother didn't see it. Steuart picked it up because he was hoping it held a clue."

"And? Can Steuart identify the woman?"

"No, he told me that she had a scarf wrapped around her head. He also said that the lighting was awful. He didn't see much. He was disappointed that there was nothing other than a name on the card."

"Did he hear anything?"

"That was the strangest part of the meeting—what the woman said to Mother."

"I'm listening."

"The woman accused Olivia of taking something that didn't belong to her. She was asking her to return whatever it was."

"Do you have any ideas?"

"No, I don't believe it. Olivia can be difficult. Sometimes she upsets people without trying. I know that, but I do not believe that she stole anything from anyone. She's not dishonest." Sam shook her head, "It doesn't make sense."

"Sounds like a mystery to me. I'm curious about the fact that the card's here. What does this mean?"

"It lets me know that, unless there is more than one of these cards, Steuart was here. He was in this room. This must be the same card. I can't imagine that another card with the same name magically appeared here. It's hand printed. This has to be the same one."

"It looks like Stew Boy was here. That's something."

"I think he was trying to leave a clue." Sam looked around the room, "How did Steuart end up at The Minor Protection Agency? How did he get there? What can you tell me about that place? Is my brother safe?"

"I don't know very much about it, but I think he's safe. I don't think he's being mistreated if that's what you're asking. It's a government agency. They help homeless children. I believe they have a good reputation."

Sam let out a big sigh.

"It's hard not to worry, I understand."

"That's an understatement; it's impossible not to worry. I need to find my brother and go home. This is such a huge mess."

"Sam, I feel certain that Steuart's safe, however, if he's there, we may have to do a bit of work to get him out."

"What do you mean, if he's there? You told me that you saw Steuart. You said he's being held at The Minor Protection Agency. Are you telling me that you don't know?"

"Calm down, Steuart was there when I checked."

"Was there?"

"Yes."

"So, why are you worried?"

"Part of what gives the agency such a good reputation is their record for placing children quickly. It is possible that Steuart could have been adopted by now."

"*What?* I can't believe what you are saying."

"Don't worry about this."

"Don't worry?"

"Don't worry. No matter what happens today, we'll find Steuart; but it will be much easier for us if he hasn't been moved to another location."

"This is ridiculous. My brother's been missing for less than four days. How could they find a new family for him so quickly? Don't people around here care about allowing families the time to find a missing child? What will we do?"

"The agency tries to place children as quickly as possible so that the abandoned child can begin to adjust."

"My brother wasn't abandoned."

"We know that, but the agency doesn't. The good news it that adoptive families are aware that they will have to allow the child to go home if a family member shows up and makes a claim during the legal time allotment. If Steuart is moved we'll have to find him."

"How will we do that?"

"My daddy always said you can't ride an elevator before you enter the building."

"What does that mean?"

"It means we'll worry about that when, and if, it happens."

"I can't stand the idea of my brother being sent to live somewhere far away."

"No matter what happens Steuart will be treated well."

"We're talking about my brother. I don't want him to live with another family."

"I'd like to know how Steuart ended up there. Obviously," Ed pointed to the notecard, "he was here for a while."

"I hope he's okay."

"He'll be okay."

"That is not a consolation, nor is it an option. I don't even know how you can make a statement like that. You don't know that to be a fact."

"Sorry. I'm trying to help."

"If I can't go home with my brother we may have to find a new family for me. Olivia already blames me for Steuart's broken arm and now she's blaming me for his disappearance. Steuart doesn't need a new family. He has us."

Ed put his hand on Sam's shoulder, "You don't need to worry. We're lucky to have Toriah as part of our team. He always knows exactly what to do."

"What about you? Don't you always know what to do?"

"I'm good, but Toriah's better."

Sam and Ed sat side-by-side on the sofa and waited for Toriah and Dotsie to return. "I can't get over how similar this place is to my grandmother's house. It's eerie. Don't you agree?"

"No, not really."

"No? How can you say that?"

"I see this all the time."

"My grandmother's house?"

"No."

"What then?"

"Parallels, they flow in every dimension."

"I'm not in the mood for your riddles."

"I think I know what happened when you ended up at Point Taken."

"You do?"

Ed nodded, "I've seen this before. You may have been standing in a section of the tree house that was aligned with that parallel. You thought you were traveling to the tree house in Maybell, but instead, you ended up at your grandmother's on the bay."

"Are you saying that we can travel from here to my grandmother's house?"

"Possibly," Ed stood and looked out the window. "I wonder if this house has a name? Stay here for a minute."

"Where are you going?"

"Not far. Stay put. I'm walking to the front." Ed walked along the winding driveway and briefly disappeared. He came in through the side door, "It has a name. Nations Kept."

Sam ran the letters through her mind. "I don't understand. It's close, but not a match. I thought it would be a match. Grandmother's house is *Point Taken*. There's no letter *s*."

"You're not thinking Sam."

"How can you say that to me? I'm working my brain over time. Traveling is exhausting."

"How many times do I have to tell you that this is not a precise universe? Things don't always match up. Actually, more often than not, they don't."

"Maybe I'm too tired. I'm not getting it."

"If everything linked perfectly you'd have an exact mirror image of where you've come from. You might not even be aware of the changes."

"You're telling me there would be no need to travel?"

"Exactly. Why would you want to go anywhere? There would be no need for exploration because you would have all of your information and answers in one spot."

Sam took a deep breath, "Why haven't you been making jokes lately?"

"I'm not feeling humorous."

"You're so serious today. It makes me nervous."

"As a guide I take my responsibilities seriously. First, Trista was hurt and then Steuart turned up missing. Now I'm concerned about Dotsie making the trip. I hope this isn't too difficult on her."

Sam stood. She walked across the room, opened doors, looked inside of cabinets and thumbed through books as she searched for clues. "Grandmother would tell me not to look through things belonging to other people. She calls it plundering."

"Extenuating circumstances. It's okay."

"I wonder who owns this house. Where are the people who live here?" Sam opened a drawer and pulled out a stack of photos. "I wonder…."

TWENTY

Ed heard footsteps coming up the walk. "Move Sam! Duck!"

"Why are we hiding?"

"It might not be Toriah."

"I'm scared."

"Shh..." Ed put his finger to Sam's mouth as they crouched together and waited. "We'll be okay."

"Is it them?"

"Shh..." Ed repeated.

"Sorry."

"Shh..."

The front door opened. Voices entered the house. "Where did they go?" Dotsie asked.

"I instructed them not to go anywhere," Toriah huffed. "Ed is a good man and an excellent guide; however, he is not always one to follow directions. Where are they off to now?"

Ed and Sam sprang up from behind the sofa, "Ta Da!"

"Thank goodness it's you," Sam said.

"Do not do that to me!" Toriah jumped.

"What?"

"Send me to an early grave by way of a heart attack ... frighten me to death." Toriah held his hand against his chest and made a face. "I am not a young man." He calmed his breathing, "What were the two of you doing hiding behind the furniture?"

"We didn't know who you were. We needed to be cautious," Sam said.

"Good thinking," Dotsie said.

"*Good man who doesn't always follow directions?*" Ed raised an eyebrow. "Thanks for the kind words." He turned to Sam, "I retract everything nice I've said about Mr. Toroar."

Toriah shook his head, "Ed, don't get me started. This isn't the time for your antics. We have much work to do yet."

"Did you find Steuart?" Sam asked.

"As they say, I have good news and I have bad news."

"Good news," Sam said, smiling and nodding, "I'd like the good news first."

"Bad news," Ed said. "Let's get it over with."

"Yes, that's what I said. I have good and bad news. You need to choose which you prefer to hear first. It doesn't matter to me. We will cover both."

"Bad news first," Sam said. "Ed's correct. Let's get it over with."

"Give us the good news," Ed said. "We need to hear something uplifting."

"Okay," Sam looked at Ed and then at Toriah, "Let's begin with the good things."

Toriah took a deep breath, "Ed, you are correct. Steuart is exactly where you said we would find him."

"That's wonderful," Sam said. "Did you see him? Did you talk with my brother? Why didn't you bring him with you?"

Toriah stood silently.

"What's wrong?" Sam asked. She turned towards Ed. "Something's wrong. What's wrong with Steuart? Where's my brother? Tell me."

Sam looked at Toriah.

Dotsie stood quietly. She looked at Sam and then looked away.

"Did you see Steuart?" Sam asked. "Did you see my brother?"

Toriah sat down and nodded, "Yes, we saw Master Steuart."

"That's good, right?" Sam let out a sigh of relief. "That's a good thing, correct?"

Ed touched Sam's arm and looked curiously at Toriah. "Wait, Sam, he's not finished." Ed turned to Toriah, "What's the bad news?"

Toriah cleared his throat, "We were unable to speak with Steuart."

Dotsie nodded.

"Is that all?" Sam asked. "That doesn't sound so terribly bad. You know where he is and you've seen him. That's a lot. All we need to do is go get him. I thought you were going to say something awful."

Toriah cleared his throat again, "There's more."

"More?" Sam looked at Toriah and waited.

"A family is interested in Steuart. He's being taken to their home this afternoon for a trial visit—in the country."

"Is that a weekend thing?" Sam asked.

Ed shook his head and looked at Toriah, "In Bellamy a trial visit can become a permanent visit if all parties are in agreement."

"I'm not in agreement! They can't just throw my brother into a new family. It makes no sense. We have to do something now."

Ed agreed, "You're right Sam. This could become much more involved if Steuart moves from his current location."

"We can't lose any more time," Sam looked at Ed. "We need to get Steuart now. Let's go."

"My feelings exactly," Toriah interrupted. "That's why Miss Caples and I made a stop on our way back."

"For what?" Sam asked.

"We've rented a car."

"Car?" Ed asked.

"Yes."

"You drive?" Sam asked.

"When the need arises. Yes, I do. I'm a capable and experienced driver." Toriah reached into his pocket and removed his wallet. "I'm even licensed here."

"What good will it do for us to rent a car?" Sam asked. "Are we planning to follow the family that wants Steuart? How will we get him away from them?"

"No. That's not the plan. You're getting ahead of things," Toriah cleared his throat. "This is much simpler. We plan to go inside The Minor Protection Agency offices pretending to be the family coming for Steuart."

"Will that work?" Sam asked.

"I believe it will. However, we're looking at a time sensitive situation. The most important thing is that we arrive first."

"Are you sure? Do you believe this will work?"

"Absolutely, as long as we move swiftly and create enough confusion, everything should be fine. We'll have your brother home in short order." Toriah cleared his throat. "I'd be dishonest if I didn't tell you that this will be tricky."

Ed looked at Sam, "Remember the three rules."

Sam nodded.

Toriah continued, "We each have an important job. This depends on all of us doing our part and working together as a team." He pulled a folded paper from his coat.

"What's that?" Ed asked

"Important information. This folder contains the name of the family coming for Steuart. The man's name is Sal Sebby. His appointment is scheduled for three-thirty this afternoon."

"Today?" Sam asked.

Toriah nodded, "Today."

"We need to go now," Sam insisted.

Ed put his finger to his mouth in an effort to calm Sam. "Listen to Toriah. First, we need to go over the plan."

"The four of us will ride over together. Ed, we'll drop you off first. Sam, we'll drop you off after that. Ed will walk from the corner to The Minor Protection Agency. He will enter the building first and make contact with the clerk. She's a rather tall, thin woman with short red hair and black frame glasses. Her name is Prim Tate. My research tells me that she's a helpful person, but also meticulous about her work."

"By the book, obsessive?" Ed asked.

Toriah nodded, "Ed, do you remember the Metro Cup affair?"

"Only our finest hour. How could I forget? That's what you have in mind?"

"That is precisely what I have in mind. It worked beautifully last time and I see no reason that it won't work equally well for us today."

"Any special changes?"

"None."

"You've done this before?" Sam asked.

"Something similar," Ed said.

"Similar," Toriah nodded.

Ed turned to Sam, "This is a solid plan. It's simple. It should work."

"As long as we focus and work as a team." Toriah continued, "Ed will be followed by Miss Caples and myself. We will enter the building together."

"What about me?" Sam asked.

"You have an important job. It sounds simple, but timing is key. You'll walk into the office behind Miss Caples and me. I suggest that you wait about four minutes before coming inside. The situation will be chaotic, but I need you to ignore the confusion because it's a big part of the plan. Pay no attention to anything you hear. Instead, we want you to walk down this hall," Toriah produced a map showing Sam the layout of the building, "Turn to the left and continue to room number twelve. This is where you'll find your brother. You'll quickly explain to Steuart that we've come to take him home. At that point, the two of you will quickly and quietly retrace your steps and walk through the front door where you'll go straight to the car. Open the door, get inside and wait for us. We'll follow behind shortly."

"Won't the clerk say something when she sees Steuart leaving with me?"

"Dear girl, please believe me when I tell you that the clerk will not see either of you."

Ed, Toriah, Dotsie and Sam practiced the plan several times before piling into the car and leaving for The Minor Protection Agency.

Sam looked at Dotsie, "This has to work."

* * *

"I'm nervous," Sam said.

Ed put his hand on her shoulder, "You can do this. Believe in yourself."

"What if something goes wrong?" Dotsie asked.

"Everything will be fine," Toriah cautiously drove towards the office. He stopped at the corner and looked at Sam in the rearview mirror, "Are you ready young lady?"

"Ready," Sam opened the car door and stepped out onto the curb.

"We can do this," Ed looked at Sam. "Pretend this is a game. I'll see you in a few minutes kid-oh."

Sam felt her heart beating fast. She stood on the corner and took several deep breaths before walking in the direction of the office building.

Toriah stopped at the next corner. Ed exited the car, "Good luck Toriah. Good luck, Dotsie."

Ed put his hands in his pockets and began whistling as he walked towards the office building. He opened the front door, strolled inside, walked to the front counter and slapped the service bell, whistling as he waited.

A woman emerged from the back and stood behind the counter, "Good afternoon, may I help you?"

"Prim!" Ed laughed loudly.

"Yes," the woman nodded, "I'm Prim Tate. You are?"

"Prim Tate, as I live and breathe. Wow. It's so great to see you. As they say, longtime, no see. How great," Ed laughed, coughed, and then rubbed his nose with the palm of his hand before reaching out for a handshake.

The woman declined.

Ed continued, "I'm impressed." He winked and then raised and lowered his eyebrows, "Looking good baby."

"Excuse me...?"

"No need," Ed waved his hand and shook his head. His speech became rapid. "Please, don't say that you've forgotten me." He threw his hand over his heart, "I'll be destroyed. I know I should have called. Hey, we both should have done something, but I lost your number, time passed and well, life got in the way. But after that magical night there were so many things going on. Like I said, you could have made contact." Ed coughed again.

Prim looked confused, "I am afraid that..."

Ed interrupted, "No need to be afraid. I'm fine with things. There's no need to be embarrassed. It was a natural thing. There are beginnings, there are endings, and there are *in-betweening*."

The woman frowned, shook her head and tried to speak, "You must be..."

"Delighted. That's what I am. I am delighted to see you." Ed leaned in across the counter, "You don't have to say a thing. Your expression is priceless."

"Sir, are you playing some sort of game with me?"

"How could you even think that?" Ed threw his hands in the air. "With our history ... It's been a long time, but some people are extra special .... Life happens ... we move on to other things and we find happiness, but we rarely forget that magic. You're a big girl. You understand that these things happen."

"What?" Prim shook her head, "I don't understand. What are you trying to say to me?"

"That's not why I'm here. Hey, I had no idea that you worked here." Ed stopped and took a deep breath. "Sorry, I was so shocked to see you that I temporarily forgot my reason for visiting."

"And that is?"

"I got a call that my nephew's here."

"Your nephew?"

"Yeah, I'm here to pick the kid up and take him home."

"Your nephew?"

The door opened. Toriah and Dotsie walked quietly into the room and stood at the opposite end of the counter. Prim glanced at Toriah, "Sir, I'll be right with you."

"Thank you, Ma'am," Toriah nodded.

Prim turned her attention to Ed. "Sir, who are you here for?"

"Mossy Gibin, that's his name. We never know where that little guy will end up. He's a busy kid. Where've you got him? You can tell him that I'm here." Ed reached in his pocket and took out a wrapped peppermint. Prim watched as he unwrapped the candy, popped it into his mouth and bit down.

"Oh, gosh," Ed stopped. "I apologize, I only had one. I didn't think that you might want a bite." He opened his mouth, pulled the candy out and offered it to Prim."

"No, thank you. Please put your candy back in your mouth."

"I'm trying to be polite." Ed rubbed his nose again, "I don't want to pressure you, but I need to get going. Can you please get the kid so we can be on our way?"

"Sir," Prim hesitated, "There is no one here by that name. Do you know who contacted you?"

Ed became serious. The pace of his speech picked up, "Of course I know who called me. It was you." Ed glanced at Toriah and back at Prim. "What kind of joke are you trying to pull on me? I'm here to pick up the kid and take him home to my sister. She just had an operation. She's in no position to be down here, so I said *don't worry sis—you can count on your brother.* That's what a good brother's for. Am I right?" Ed nodded and leaned in towards the counter, "Of course she'll owe me for this one, but that's not such a bad thing. Where's Mossy?" Ed began drumming on the counter and winked at Prim. "We need to get out of here. I've got places to be. I have a busy night ahead."

"Sir, we do not have a child here with that name. Perhaps someone is playing a prank. I've not contacted you. I cannot be of any help."

"Can't, or won't help me? Prim? Mossy may have given you an alias. He's a sly kid, sort of like his uncle."

"Sir," Prim took a deep breath, "I am at a loss for words."

"I don't remember words being your true talent."

"What?"

"Get the kid, please. He's a busy one. I'm sure he's going nuts back there. You know what they say about nuts and trees don't you?"

"I'm certain that I don't. Sir, I cannot help you. I can't. I don't know what else to say to you. Now, please excuse me." Prim turned towards Toriah, "I'm sorry for making you wait. Sir, what can I do for you?"

Ed interrupted, "Excuse me sir, Miss Tate was helping me first."

Prim looked at Ed, "We are finished. There is nothing that I can do for you. We do not have a child here by that name." She looked at Toriah, "I'm sorry sir. How may I help you?"

Toriah glared at Ed and shook his head, "No problem. I'm Sal Sebby."

"Mr. Sebby, I didn't recognize your voice. How nice to meet you. I'm not quite finished with your paperwork. Things have been hectic. I need a few minutes to finish up and then we can send you all on your way."

"Take your time. We're a little early."

"Take your time," Ed mocked Toriah and then looked at Prim. "You'll help him and you won't help me. What's going on here?"

Prim looked at Ed, "Sir, *what's going on* is that I cannot help you. I'm asking you to leave. The child you are looking for is not here." Prim turned towards Toriah. She let out a big sigh.

Ed continued ranting, "I want my nephew! I'm calling the authorities. I'm going to report you. I demand that you produce my boy." He slapped his hand on the counter. "Where is my nephew?"

Toriah looked at Ed. "Sir, did you hear the lady? She cannot produce a child who is not on the premises. Surely you understand."

"Understand?" Ed stuck his nose in the air, "Ohhhh, hoity, toity listen to you. No, I do not understand! What have you done with little Mossy?"

"Sir, please calm down."

"This isn't about my nephew. This is because you've never forgiven me." Ed looked closely at Prim, "I get it. I understand. You're not happy with me and now you want to take it all out on sweet little Mossy."

The argument continued to escalate between Toriah, Ed and Prim. Dotsie stood quietly beside Toriah and held his hand. She pulled on his coat sleeve, "Daddy, where's Steuart?"

No one noticed Sam as she entered through the front door, walked along the hallway, turned and then found room twelve.

The clerk tried to talk with Toriah and Dotsie. Ed continued creating chaos. "This is ridiculous! I want my nephew, now! Do you understand me? Where is Mossy? I insist that you help me—this instant!"

"Sir! How many times do I need to tell you that I cannot produce a child who is not in the building?"

"If he isn't here, where is he? Where's Mossy?"

"Not with me."

Prim turned towards Toriah as she tried ignoring Ed, "Mr. Sebby, let's get a few forms signed and I'll have you and Steuart on your way." She took a deep breath.

"What's wrong here?" Ed's voice continued to grow louder. "You are willing to help this enormous, big, giant, irritating, bag o' wind, but you are refusing to help me? Discrimination! This is discrimination!"

Prim turned towards Ed. She slammed her hand on the counter and raised her voice. She pinged the bell on the counter repeatedly in an effort to get Ed's attention. She screamed, "Sir, we have no child for you! How many ways can I give you this information? Do you understand? Do I need to call the authorities?"

Ed lowered his voice, "Yeah, lady, I get it. You're still ticked off with me. You thought you were *all that,* but you weren't even a thing."

Toriah bent down and consoled Dotsie as she began to cry, "It's okay dear, we're going to pick Steuart up and be out of here as soon as we have the paperwork completed. We have to complete the proper forms. It's okay. Don't worry."

Dotsie pulled at Toriah's coat sleeve, "I want my new brother."

No one saw Sam return. She stood directly behind Ed and gently touched his hand. Ed continued his rant, "This is incredible. What kind of office are you running here? This is discrimination. I have never been treated so badly in my life. I've never seen a more poorly run office than what you have here. You should be fired. I insist that you produce my little Mossy immediately!"

Sam continued pulling on Ed's arm. Toriah and Prim continued trying to talk. Dotsie sobbed quietly.

"He's not here," Sam whispered.

"It's because he's dressed nicer than me," Ed pointed towards Toriah. "That's it. I get it. You people are completely screwed up. You're a real piece of work, Prim Tate. I am disgusted by your lack of professionalism. I can't believe I ever had feelings for you. I want my nephew, now!" Ed repeatedly pounded on the counter with his fist. "Where is Mossy?"

Sam continued pulling on Ed's arm until he whipped around and yelled, "What do you want kid?" Sam jumped back. The room became silent. Ed swallowed. He didn't move anything other than his eyes. He looked at Sam. He looked for Steuart. He jerked his head in the direction of the front door before bending down to Sam's level.

Sam whispered in Ed's ear, "Steuart isn't here."

"*Whaaatt?*"

"He's not here," she repeated loudly.

"Are you..."

Sam nodded, "sure-as-Matt."

Ed put his hands on Sam's shoulders, pivoted her towards the door and yelled, "Go!"

Prim became frantic, "Who is that child? What does she mean, Steuart isn't here?" Prim turned towards Toriah, "I'm sorry Mr. Sebby. I need to see what's going on. We'll get this figured out. I'll be back in a minute." She began walking around the counter in Sam's direction. "Young lady..."

"Where is the boy? We need to be on our way," Toriah insisted. "Is Steuart ready?" Dotsie began crying again.

Prim turned around as Sam exited. She looked at Toriah. "I'll check sir." She changed directions. "Please stay put. I'll be back in a minute." She walked down the hallway towards room twelve.

On her way to the car, Sam bumped into a man and woman who were walking into the building. Dotsie followed Sam outside. Ed and Toriah exited the building together, got into the car and drove away. Several blocks down the road, Toriah turned onto a side street and stopped.

"Where is my brother?" Sam cried. "What are we going to do now?"

"I don't know," Ed said. "We have to think of something."

"Where's my brother? I have to find Steuart."

Toriah turned in his seat, "I'm sorry Sam." He shook his head, "I thought this was going to be a simple operation. It's become more involved than we hoped. We need to regroup."

"What are we going to do?"

"We're not going to find Steuart today."

Ed agreed, "It's too late."

"We can't stop now," Dotsie said. "We need to find Steuart."

Sam pressed her face against the car window and stared at a brick wall. "This is awful. I have to find Steuart."

"We'll figure this out," Ed said. "We'll find Steuart, but we can't do anything more tonight. We'll start fresh in the morning."

"Let's get some dinner." Toriah looked at Dotsie, "Are you okay?"

"I'm fine."

Toriah looked at Sam, "We'll return to the house and think about what to do next. We'll come up with another plan."

"This is awful," Sam said. "How are we going to find Steuart now? We have no idea where to look."

Toriah stopped at a local drive-in and picked up food for dinner. "Things will be better tomorrow."

TWENTY-ONE

Sam and Dotsie walked to the dining table. Ed looked for napkins while Toriah pulled food from the bags.

"Where have you been?" Steuart walked down the stairs. A life-size Trista stood behind him.

Sam jumped from her chair and ran over to the two of them. She began crying, "Where have *I* been? Where have *you* been? What are you doing here?" She had trouble catching her breath. "I've been trying to find you for three days and suddenly, you're here." She looked at Trista, "I don't understand. I don't know what to say. I'm happy to see you, both of you. You're okay?"

"I'm fine," Steuart said.

"I'm fine too," Trista nodded.

Sam took a deep breath. She exhaled and turned from Trista to Steuart and then back again to Trista. "I'm so sorry about everything, Trista. I'm so..." Sam turned towards her brother, "I'm sorry we got separated. I've been sick with worry. What happened?"

Ed, Toriah and Dotsie listened. Sam breathed hard and shook her head, "I don't understand any of this. We tried to rescue you. We've been trying to find you. You weren't there. How did you get here?"

"I think I rescued myself."

"You certainly did," Trista said.

Sam, Ed, Toriah and Dotsie looked at Steuart. Sam hugged her brother and hugged Trista again. "Tell us everything, please."

Steuart looked at Trista, "Would you like to go first?"

"No."

"Okay," Steuart exhaled. "I'm trying to think about where I should begin."

"Just start," Ed said. "We'll piece things together."

"I've been busy." Steuart looked at his sister. "I haven't had much sleep. At first, I didn't understand what happened. One minute we were standing in the tree house together and then I was standing there alone. You disappeared the same way that Ceil did. I tried to find you."

"I was trying to find you too," Sam said softly.

"At first it was fun, but then it got scary," Steuart looked at Ed who gave him a slap on the back followed by a hug.

"You had so many things right, Stew Boy."

"What did I do wrong?"

"Sometimes you can have everything right and still not transport. It's the nature of things."

"I wished for both of you. I kept trying, but I got tired. Eventually, I came up here and looked for a warm place to take a break. The side door was unlocked and it didn't look like anyone was here. I was very cold, so I came inside."

"How long did you stay?" Sam asked.

"Not too long. I was sure you'd come back and look for me, but I didn't know what you were dealing with at home. I walked down to the tree house on and off to see if you were there, but it was getting colder with the darkness. There was a lot of snow, so I decided to stay here. It was too cold to be down there. I found a closet of quilts and blankets, got warm and even took a short nap. But then I got hungry and there was nothing to eat. I waited for you as long as I could. When I realized you might not be coming right away I decided to go back downtown." Steuart looked at his sister, "I guessed that you had traveled without me. I thought you probably got stuck at the house trying to explain everything to Mother. Is that what happened?"

"Sort of."

"What do you mean?"

"There's plenty of time for my story. I want to hear yours."

Steuart looked at Ed, "If I had known you were looking for me, I would have stayed here, but I was cold. I thought about leaving a clue for Sam. I wanted her to know that I'd been here. I looked in my valise, but the only loose card I found was..."

"Laurel Ivy Hood," Sam said.

"You found it."

"Yes," Ed nodded, "It was the first thing Sam found when we arrived."

"What happened then?" Sam asked.

"I walked to Trista's studio," Steuart looked at Trista.

"He was shocked when I came to the door. I must have just missed the two of you when you came by earlier."

"I was really shocked," Steuart said. "I was hoping to find someone who knew Trista with the idea that they might have information about traveling. I had no idea I would find Trista."

"We stayed together until I had to leave for an appointment." Trista looked at Steuart, "I suggested that he stay put and not leave the studio."

"Is that how you ended up at The Minor Protection Agency?"

Steuart nodded, "I knew Trista was okay and I knew that I needed to go home."

"I was late coming back."

"I didn't know how long she'd be gone. I was worried about getting home because I knew you were going to be in deep water with Mother. I walked downstairs to the coffee shop and I asked the wrong person for help. That's how I ended up at that place."

"Who did you ask?"

"Prim Tate."

"You're kidding me."

"No. She's a nice lady, but she didn't understand what I tried to tell her. It was apparent that she knew nothing about traveling."

"Obviously," Ed said.

Sam looked at Trista, "How did you get home? We took you to the hospital. You didn't get better."

"You had my placeholder repaired, not me."

"How can that be? This was you." Sam pulled the doll from her backpack and handed her to Trista.

Trista smiled, "Yes, I know." She looked at Ed and Toriah, "Would one of you like to explain what happened?"

Ed spoke, "I was hoping, but I didn't want to say anything in the event that I was wrong."

Sam looked at Ed, "What were you hoping for?"

"Trista experienced a blunt force trauma that was so intense it created an instant portal at the place of impact. That caused her to travel immediately from Maybell to Bellamy. At the moment of impact she switched places with her placeholder."

Trista looked at Sam, "You saved my life. Do you realize that?"

"I don't understand," Sam shook her head. "How did we do that? You transported but you were still injured."

"Did you have my doll repaired?"

"You know we did. We took her to the doll hospital."

"How many days was she there?"

"Five."

"You saved my life by taking her to the hospital and having her repaired. If the doll had stayed broken, I would probably still be on life support."

"They would have turned it off," Ed said softly.

"Can you come back with us?" Sam asked.

"No, I've done all the traveling I need to do for a while. I'm okay, but I need to take it easy."

"I'm sorry that my mother hurt you."

"It was an accident."

"*Please*," Ed blew a raspberry.

Trista gave Ed a sharp glance and looked again at Sam and Steuart. "It was an accident."

"How can you say that?" Sam asked.

"Don't waste time being angry about things you can't change. It's not worth it."

Sam nodded.

"I know you have to go home soon. Promise me that you'll visit and that you won't wait long before you do. I'm a very good hostess. You're always welcome at my house. I'll give you a painting lesson." She turned to Dotsie, "You're invited too. Do you like art?"

"Oh, yes." Dotsie smiled, "That sounds like fun."

Trista reached down and hugged the children. She shook hands with Toriah and then reached to hug Ed, "Take care of our kids."

Ed smiled. He kissed Trista on the cheek. "I'm thankful that you're okay."

"You're record stands."

Ed took a deep breath, "I hate to break up this reunion but we need to start back. People are looking for you two and Dotsie's mother will be looking for her soon." He looked at Trista, "You know how it goes, once travel begins it continues on and on."

"I know."

"We'll see you again soon."

"I have to go. My family's waiting for me." Trista turned to Sam before leaving, "Will you please see my doll safely home, and return her to Dr. Klesel?"

Sam nodded.

Trista hugged Sam and said good-bye. "I love you, Sam."

* * *

"I'm still confused." Sam looked at Steuart. "How did you get away from Prim Tate?"

"I walked out."

"You're kidding."

"No," Steuart shrugged. "She was busy. I watched for my opportunity and I walked out. Then I went back to Trista's. We came here together so that she could help me transport. You arrived as we were about to walk down to the tree house."

Ed looked at Toriah, "I've taught them well."

"I have a feeling these kids have always done well on their own."

Sam looked at Ed, "I still don't understand how everything worked out with Trista."

"What are the main things I've taught you?" Ed looked at Sam and Steuart.

"Know your audience," Sam said.

"Timing is everything," Steuart said.

Dotsie smiled and interrupted, "And, it's not an exact science."

"Correct. And in this instance the timing was perfect. If it hadn't been, Trista wouldn't have traveled. If you hadn't taken her to the shop, she wouldn't have been repaired. You're timing was right."

"I wish she could travel with us."

"A small price to pay when you consider what could have happened. She's home and she has an opportunity to continue her life."

Toriah cleared his throat, "She's fortunate."

"I know," Sam said. "I'm still angry with my mother. Trista said it was an accident, but I believe she was trying to smooth things over and help me feel better about what happened. I don't understand Olivia. She's so busy living by her book that she misses the most important things."

"Books are not bad things," Toriah said.

"I know, but she reads things the way she wants them to be and then justifies her point by picking one or two phrases. Even though she didn't know what she was doing, she was still hurting someone."

Ed shook his head, "Sam, you can't change people."

"I've got an idea," Sam said. "Let's find Mother's doll and mail it to the pirates. I think it would serve her right."

Steuart smiled, "Turtle soup?"

"Exactly—I don't want to go home. I don't want to explain this to Mother."

Ed nodded, "Some things can't be avoided."

* * *

Toriah and Dotsie disappeared into the kitchen for several minutes and returned with freshly brewed tea. Dotsie poured. Toriah proposed a toast, "To a job well done."

"Here, here! Well done," Ed said. "Steuart, here's to you. It's good to have you back."

Sam hugged her brother, "Cheers to you, Steuart. You came close to having a new family."

"Don't say that."

"You're the one who always said you wanted another mother."

"Don't tease me, Sam."

Sam walked to the desk and picked up Steuart's note, "You might want to put this back in your valise."

"I do," Steuart nodded and studied the note. "I wish I understood this."

"Laurel Ivy Hood?"

"Yeah. Why was she arguing with mother? What did she want returned? Who is she?"

"Hey," Ed addressed the group, "I hate to break up the party, but people are looking for us. Stew Boy, it's time we all go home."

Toriah and Dotsie exchanged glances. Toriah cleared his throat and then spoke, "Miss Caples has something she'd like to say."

"I'm not going back."

"What?" Sam shouted as Ed raised an eyebrow at Toriah.

"I'm staying here."

"You can't do that," Sam insisted.

"Yes, I can."

"No, you can't. You have to go home."

Toriah spoke to Dotsie, "I think you need to explain."

Dotsie looked at Sam, Steuart and Ed. "I've not been honest with you."

"What do you mean?" Sam asked.

"If I had told you the truth, you wouldn't have let me come."

"Miss Caples is correct."

Sam looked at Toriah.

"This was her decision, Sam. She's been planning this for a long while."

"I don't understand. What do you mean, *planning*? Dotsie didn't even know how to travel before today. This is crazy. Dotsie, you can't stay here. You have to come home with us."

Ed and Steuart stood quietly. Toriah shrugged his shoulders.

"What did you lie about?"

"I'm not in remission."

Sam put her hand up to her mouth.

"It's okay because I'm not sick here."

"What?"

"A long time ago, when I was in the hospital ... before you visited me ... I heard the doctors and my mother talking about my illness. It wasn't good. I'm well here."

Toriah nodded, "That's correct. Miss Caples is much better here. Traveling was a risk, but it's a risk she was willing to take. Please know that this took great courage. I'm extremely proud of her."

"How can you be sick there and well here?" Sam asked. "You're not making sense."

Dotsie looked at Toriah, "Will you explain?"

Steuart interrupted, "I think I understand. Sam, it's the same with my arm."

Toriah spoke again. "Things are similar but different in each place—rearranged. Miss Caples no longer has the illness that she had in Maybell. However, that does not mean that she will never have another illness. It only means that whatever she gets may not be as serious."

Ed looked at Toriah, "You realize this is completely against the code?"

"I do."

"There may be consequences."

"I know."

"Are you prepared?"

"Always."

"So, why did you come?" Sam asked Dotsie.

Dotsie reached for Sam's hand, "I was running out of time."

Sam cried, "You can't do this."

"I have a future here. My days in Maybell were coming to an end."

"No." Sam looked at Ed.

"Apparently, there's no such thing as a brain tumor in Bellamy."

Dotsie reached for Sam, "You're my friend. I'm always going to be your friend. You and Steuart are travelers. You can visit with me anytime. You can visit with me when you come to see Trista."

Ed folded his arms, "What about your mother?"

"That's..." Toriah paused and glanced at Ed, "been taken care of."

Ed stared at Toriah, "You didn't?"

Toriah nodded. Ed shook his head.

"Who's going to take care of you?" Sam asked.

"TT's adopting me."

Ed glanced at Toriah.

"I'm retiring. I'm staying here with Miss Caples."

Ed extended his hand, "Toriah, you may be the biggest bag of wind I've ever encountered, but you're also the best."

"I could say the same for you," Toriah put his arm around Ed and gave him a hug.

Ed stepped back, looked at Dotsie, and nodded, "You'll be fine." He turned towards the children, "We need to get going."

* * *

"What do you say? Are we ready? Let's get things right this time. On the count of three we'll say it together."

There was a chill in the air. The wind picked up outside. Together, they stood in the darkness.

COMING SOON
The Wayward Gifted
Grey's Case

Keep in touch with The Wayward Gifted
http://www.TheWaywardGifted.blogspot.com
Like us on Facebook
https://www.facebook.com/TheWaywardGifted
Email The Wayward Gifted
MiloNerak@Gmail.com

Made in the USA
Lexington, KY
27 June 2013